The Retribution

The Retribution

Shankar N Kashyap

MyBooks Publication

First Published in September 2017

by

my Books
Think | Create | Publish

MyBooks Publication
publish@my-books.in

ISBN: 978-93-86474-26-1
eISBN: 978-93-86474-27-8

eBook & Cover Design
DigiConv Technologies

Dedicated to all those book lovers out there.

"I would like to thank Brooke Powley for her excellent editing and proof reading of the book. Her input in various stages of the book was invaluable. I would also like to thank Shahid Khan for a fantastic cover. My thanks to Moolchand Chauhan for his valuable help. My gratitude to everyone at the MyBooks Publication for all their help in getting *The Retribution* out onto book stands!"

ABOUT THE AUTHOR

Shankar Kashyap is an orthopaedic surgeon originally from Bangalore, India practicing now in the United Kingdom. He has had extensive experience in publishing scientific papers in peer-reviewed journals over the last 25 years. His first book, "A Kangaroo Court: A Triumph of mediocrity" was published in 2011.

Over the years he has been interested in ancient history of India and has undertaken extensive research into the subject. The aim is to take readers through the third millennium BCE in India using archaeological and literary evidence available along with characters and events from the enormous Vedic corpus. There has been a resurgence of historical fiction novels, particularly the success of Christian Jacq with Ramses series. There has been very little written about the great Indus Valley Civilisation in the popular press and most of what is written has been aimed at serious historians and archaeologists. Many have always wondered what the life was like during the period of that great civilisation. The Harappa Series consists of six books, each dealing with different aspects of Indian pre-history in a fictional form. The first three books of the series – Lure of Soma, Fall of Shuruppak and Dasharajna: The Battle of Ten Kings have been published so far.

This is his first foray into crime fiction. True events of an unfortunate murder spurred him to write this. Coming from a medical background, the psychological aspects of the case intrigued him and he has brought out the conflict of faith, beliefs and emotions in this book.

DISCLAIMER

The following account is purely fictional. All the characters, places, places of worship and organisations are fictional and imaginary. Any resemblance to any individual living or dead is purely coincidental. Any resemblance to any place or religious institution or organisation is also not intentional and purely coincidental.

Shankar N Kashyap

CONTENTS

LENNY

A bright full moon was struggling to light up the alley through scattered dark clouds. The man walking down the alley could hear his own footsteps. He realized that it was quiet, eerily quiet. A bit too quiet perhaps for his liking. He had been down this alley several times before, but today there was something different. Everything was still. There was not even a breeze. A sudden chill went through him and he shivered, pulling his jacket collar up and his hat down over his ears. He hadn't noticed it being cold when he left home earlier. In fact, he had felt hot and sweaty and had a splitting headache. He bent his head down and shoved his hands inside his jacket pocket as he hurried along.

There was sound of someone else's footsteps. Or was it the echo of his own? He stopped and the other footsteps stopped too. It must be his imagination, he thought, and carried on. But soon the footsteps started and they definitely not his own. They were quicker and appeared to be getting nearer. He stopped again and looked back. There was nothing in the alley apart from dark shadows in the doorways where the dim streetlights couldn't penetrate. It was the silence that appeared to bother him more than anything. He peered carefully into the dark doorways along the alley. Still nothing. Not a soul in sight. Not that he expected to see anyone at this time of the night in that alley.

It was pitch black after Belgrave road, which was lit up like a Christmas tree by the shopkeepers for their festival of lights. This was why he chose the place. As did others, who wanted what he was looking for. Just the thought made him hot and sweaty again. He took off his jacket and cap. His hands were shaking, and nearly dropped the cap on the ground. The October chill would not cool him down. In fact it was a freezing cold breeze, which was blowing through the alleyway like through a tunnel. He better find him soon. The pain was getting worse. This had happened before when he had run out of money. He had tried to kill himself when he could not get his fix for nearly five days. It is nearly that stage now. He had lost his job as a delivery man and there was no money. This was not the first job he had been fired from. He was desperate for money. He was nearly caught trying to rob the corner store the week before. His hands shook so much that he could not get the knife out of his pocket in time. The shopkeeper was laughing as he stumbled out of the shop that night empty handed.

He was woken out of the reverie by a crash and a bang and the screech of a cat as the dustbin it had jumped on had fallen. The lid made a racket as it rolled for a good minute before stopping with a clatter. He was startled by the noise and nearly jumped out of his skin. He was being unnecessarily nervous, he thought. But the cat started to run towards him and it got bigger as it ran. It was frightening.

"You stay away from me. You hear. Shoosh. Get away you silly cat." He shouted.

The cat stopped in front of him and just stood there with it's tail up. Almost crouching for a jump, its fur standing up in defiance. It was jet black with a streak of white across the throat. The cat bared his claws and hissed as it stopped in front of him. It was enormous. Nearly as big as himself. It's green eyes shot blood out of the corners and the nostrils threw out flames as it hissed. He wanted to scream, but no voice came out of his throat. He wanted to run, but his feet were stuck to the ground. He lifted his hands to brace himself as the cat jumped on him. Next thing he knew, he was on the floor on his back trying to wriggle out of the way of the huge cat's claws. He started to flail his arms around to protect himself.

"Get away from me!" He screamed. "Somebody help me. I am being killed by a monster!"

But no sound came from his mouth and no one came to help. He soon got tired of fighting the now enormous cat and closed his eyes and stayed still. He managed to cover his face with his hands and curled up into a ball.

'This is it' he thought, *'this is how I'm going to die.'*

He was not sure how long he was lying there on the floor of the dirty alleyway. Soon the quietness was back again and he found himself alone. He looked around to see if the cat was still there. There was no sign of a cat anywhere. In fact the alley was still completely deserted with not a soul in sight. There was something lying on the ground not far from him. It appeared to wriggle. 'My god! Not again. Not another monster!' He thought. He could not make out what it was. At least it was moving away from him.

'That is good,' he said to himself 'it is running away from me.'

He tried to sit up and look closely at this thing. He suddenly realised that it was his jacket, lying on the ground where he had thrown it.

'I better get it before it runs away.' He thought 'That *is the only jacket I have.'*

He crawled towards the jacket and tried to pick it up. But kept slipping away from him. After the third attempt, he grabbed hold of the jacket and held it firmly. There was a distant sound of an ambulance siren as he stood up and brushed off the dirt from his shirt. He could barely stand up and was nearly back on the ground again. He braced himself against a fence as he stood up. It was freezing cold again and he put his jacket back on.

'Where is my cap?' he said to himself as he felt his head.

He looked around to see where he had fallen. It was pitch black and he could barely see anything. He better get the cap or he would be in trouble. That was a present from his new girlfriend. He would not hear the end of it if he went back without the cap. He had to concentrate hard to finally see the bright yellow woollen cap lying on the ground where he had found the jacket. He leant forwards to pick it up and toppled over. Although it took an enormous amount of effort it seemed to pull himself up again. This time he was clutching his cap in his left hand as he pulled himself up holding on to the fence. He again brushed off the dirt from the alley floor and pulled his cap down around his ears. That is when he saw the cat again. It was rustling in the fallen bin apparently oblivious to his presence.

'I'll teach you to scare me to death.' He muttered under his breath. 'It would be so easy to trap the cat inside the bin and kill it.'

'Go for it.' Someone said. He quickly turned around to see who said that.

There was no one.

'I am hearing things now.'

'Don't dawdle. Go for it. Kill the cat.' The voice said again.

"Who is that?"

No reply.

The bin was within his reach and the cat was too busy poking at something inside it to notice him. He slowly leaned forward and put his hand on the bin. The cat kept scratching at something inside the bin. He put his other hand on the bin and still no movement from the cat. He heaved the bin over with one almighty push and trapped the cat underneath the bin. The cat screeched loud enough to wake the neighbourhood and started to scratch on the bin from inside. Lenny found himself struggling to keep the bin down as the cat heaved against it from inside. It kept screeching and he could feel the bin rolling from side to side. He felt himself weaken and was about to let go when the voice said again.

'Don't let go. You have always been a loser. It's only a cat.'

He shouted,

"Who the hell are you?"

But no sound came from his dry throat. He looked around to see who was talking to him. The alleyway was still deserted with not a soul in sight. Soon the bin stopped moving and there was no noise from inside the bin.

'It must be dead.' He thought.

"Are you sure?" the voice was back again.

"It's gone quiet. I can't hear anything and it's not moving either. So it must be dead." He said.

"How do you know? It could be still alive."

"You think so?"

"Or it could be dead too." The voice said. "Is it possible that it could be both alive and dead?"

"What the hell are you talking about?" Lenny shouted.

"Look at yourself." The voice replied. "Are you alive or dead?"

Lenny was confused. He felt silly talking to thin air. His head was splitting and he felt sick.

"I'm alive. I'm feeling sick. I'll die if I don't get my fix soon. Where is that Bro?"

"You could be both alive and dead."

"No, no, no ……" Lenny screamed. "I'm alive I am telling you. I am alive. You stupid or what?"

"You'll only find out when you come out." The voice sounded distant now. "Just like the cat in the bin. You don't know if it is alive or dead or both. You are trapped by Bro. You could be dead or alive or both until you come out of his control. You are under his control now ……"

The voice trailed off.

"Where are you? I'll kill you if I see you. You bastard. Come out."

He was flailing his arms about and hitting thin air. The sound of screeching tyres was so close that he jumped. He looked around but saw no one. The bin was still lying on its side where it had fallen and there was no sign of the cat. He looked down at his hands, his knife was out in his left hand and he was shaking. His head was splitting now and he started to retch. He nearly dropped his knife. That won't do. Sharon had insisted he carry the knife all the times. "You don't know what kind of creeps you would meet," she had said. Can't afford to lose it. He closed the knife and shoved it back into his trousers. He closed his eyes and rubbed his forehead. Every time he closed his eyes, he could see a burst of colours with a bright orange ball of fire in the middle.

'What a nightmare. I better find Bro soon."

The rumble of a distant police siren sounded soothing for some reason. There was a wry smile on his face as he continued on. The sound was something 'normal' and seem to settle him down. He was back to himself and started to think about where he was going. That brought a smile to his face. He looked forward to these visits. They seem to give him strength and take him back to his youth. He increased his pace.

There it was again. The sound of footsteps. But this time it was coming from the opposite direction. Someone was walking towards him. He lifted his head and peered ahead. Nothing. The alley was still deserted and completely empty. He stopped again squinting his eyes to see ahead. Nothing. There was nothing.

'Where the hell is he? He had promised to be here.' Lenny thought.

That is when he saw the silver BMW parked round the corner from where he was, its nose just sticking out into the alleyway. He recognised the car immediately despite the darkness. He should, as he had been in that car countless number of times before. He quickened his pace with relief. Suddenly, he could hear the engine spring to life and the headlights came on, lighting up the alley.

'He is going away! He can't do that. Not without me. I had told him I would come. Why is he going away?'

"No!" He screamed. "Don't go. Please wait!"

He wanted to run, but his feet would not listen to him. He realised that the car was not moving. He dragged himself one step at a time with a huge effort towards the car. He sighed a relief when the engine stopped and the headlights went out as he neared the car. The man got out of the car. He was well dressed as usual. Natty, with jeans, bright pink shirt and a leather jacket with an ever present brown cap pulled low down on his face. He noticed the man's shiny new black shoes as he stepped out of the car. He shut the door of the car and stood there looking in the direction of the alley, not moving. Bro, as he liked to be called, was a 'cool dresser' and always impressed everyone around him with his smile and mannerisms. He was also his supplier.

"Hello Lenny. I thought you were not coming." Bro said.

Lenny had reached the car by now and leaned against the car to stop himself falling down again.

"Why... why wouldn't I? I am... I'm here aren't I?" Lenny replied testily. "I.. I thought you were driving off! Now, where is the stuff? I need it now. Give it. Give it to me now."

He almost screamed. His lips were shivering and his hands shook as he took them out for the "stuff".

"I don't have it here. You know better than that." Bro replied with a smile on his face. That smile again. The smile which had drawn Lenny to him in the first place. "What do you take me for? Do you want the cops to catch me with the stuff on me? It's at the house."

Lenny got agitated. "Why didn't you tell me before?" he screamed. "I could have come to the house straight"

"You look filthy." Bro said. "What happened to you? Have you been in a fight? I have told you before not to get into any fights. Next time they catch you, they will put you away for life."

"No. No, I have not been in a bloody fight." Lenny screamed. "I was attacked by this giant cat monster."

Lenny's face was almost touching Bro's nose as he screamed. He was clutching at his hands to stop them from shaking and now, the headache was intense. *'Why is that street light so bright?'* he thought, *'It's hurting my eyes'* He covered his eyes with hands but it made no difference.

"I am just checking. You know I would not want you to get into any trouble." Bro replied in a soothing voice, "Come, let's go to the house and get you fixed up."

Lenny smiled.

"I knew you would fix me up. You are good to me, Bro. I don't know what I would do without you." He was drooling as he staggered towards the passenger door of the silver BMW. "You know I would do anything for you, Bro. I would kill for you. Or.... or, I would die for you."

Suddenly four men stepped out of the shadows.

"Is there a problem here?" the tall guy in the black hoodie said. Bro was startled and turned around to see who it was and recognised the man. Bro immediately relaxed. The guy was wearing black jeans and a jacket with the hoodie covering his head. He had not seen them arrive in the alley before. *'I am slipping here'* Bro thought. *'They could have been cops.'*

"Oh. It's you, Prem! No, there is no trouble." Bro appeared a bit peeved at this turn of events. And in a whisper to the new guy in the hoodie, "This is one of my wards and I am trying to help him."

Prem walked up to Bro and looked at Lenny closely. Lenny was getting increasingly agitated by this time. He appeared to be visibly in pain.

"Come on Bro, we go to the house now." He mumbled this time as he struggled to open the passenger door of the BMW. "You are wasting time."

His voice was getting increasingly garbled.

"Come on Bro, we will take you to the house." Prem said taking Bro by the elbow leading him towards the other side of the alleyway. "I don't think you are safe with him on your own in his state. He could do anything to you." He whispered.

"It is Ok Prem. I can handle him." Bro protested. But by that time he was already half way down the alley way towards the road and the second guy hemmed him in. Prem was a burly weight lifter type of guy and when he held someone by hand, he did not move. The second one was leading Lenny along holding on to his other arm. The third guy, short and squat, looked around and followed them in silence. They led the two men towards a six seater black Ford car parked in the darkness at the end of the alleyway.

Lenny had not seen the car just a few minutes ago when he entered the alley. The fourth guy, a lean tall chap, had his head bent down and did not get into the car as they drove away. The drive to the house on Harrison road was in silence. Lenny was mumbling and seem to be getting incoherent by the minute. There was drool at the corner of his mouth and his head lolled to one side on to the shoulder of the short, squat guy sitting next to. All three were young Asian men, Bro had seen them several times before at the temple. He seemed to know them quite well.

Their car stopped as they entered Harrison road and Prem got out to speak to a couple of guys standing in the corner. There was a quite a bit of agitated whispering going on between them before they got back into the car.

"They will bring your car over to the house." Prem said. "Give them your keys."

Bro was getting a bit uneasy and fidgety now. But there was nothing he could do. He handed over the keys of his car over to one of the young men in the corner.

They stopped at the end of a terrace of houses and the short squat guy got out and briskly walked away. He could move fast for a fat guy. He stopped at the corner, looked around and disappeared out of sight. Bro was struggling trying to keep Lenny from falling over on the back seat. They knew the house and did not need any directions from Bro. It was a nondescript house towards the end of a row of terrace houses, very similar to thousands of houses dotted around the city of Leicester. Harrison road belonged to the enclave around the hub of Belgrave road shopping precinct. Well known for its Indian shops and eateries, the enclave was a sort of a ghetto for all Asians.

At this time of the night, there was no one in sight as the car cruised down the road to stop in front of the house. Bro got down as soon as the car stopped and opened the front door with his keys. Prem got out of the driver's side and was standing next to him before he could get the keys out of his jacket. He could move very fast for a big guy. The other two got out quickly and helped Lenny out of the car. He appeared to be in a daze by this time and staggered as he struggled out of the car. The three men bundled Lenny and almost carried him into the house.

The cold October air seem to wake Lenny up a little and straightened himself up.

"Good, we are at the bloody house finally." He mumbled rather incoherently. "Give me the bloody stuff. You promised."

His eyes could not focus. He tried to clutch at Bro's jacket. He was looking at no one in particular when he said that. Finally he collapsed on the dirty green sofa in the sitting room. It was all a bit too much for him by then. He could still see that great black monstrous cat every time he closed his eyes. The three men looked at each other and Prem nodded his head ever so slightly. The third guy was going around drawing the curtains to cover the windows. It was unnerving to see him move his short fat bulk around so quietly. Bro was too busy racking his head as to how to get out the situation. Prem saw his predicament and smiled.

"Don't worry Bro. We know what he wants. Give it to him. Otherwise he will keep going like this and wake up the neighbours."

It was nearly two in the morning by that time. Bro looked at Prem for a long time and visibly relaxed.

"I have to help the poor man." He turned to Lenny and said, "Wait here. I will get it for you."

He went upstairs to one of the bedrooms. The three could hear Bro moving around upstairs, pulling draws, closing doors and a lock being opened and shut. Sound of steps coming down the stairs hurt his head. He returned after a couple of minutes with a little brown paper packet. Lenny was suddenly awake at the sound of the packet being unwrapped. He appeared to know what happened next as he stood up, walked into the dining room and sat at the dining table. The two were busy at the dining table for a few minutes and they could see a puff of smoke coming from the dining room. The tinkling sound of glass breaking was loud in the stillness of the night. The three men just stood there not saying a word. Prem wrinkled his nose at the stinking smell coming out of the dining room. Bro led Lenny back into the sitting room and sat him on the big green sofa. He was a lot quieter now and his eyes had a glazed look on them.-

Lenny looked at the three men and said,

"Who are they? What are they doing here?"

"They are friends, Lenny." Bro said, "Nothing for you to worry about. You just chill and relax. You are with me now, you are safe. Everything will be fine."

Lenny was not so sure, but he could not be bothered to argue.

"If you say so, Bro."

He curled up on the sofa and was fast asleep before anyone could say anything. He could not remember how long slept for. He was woken up by a loud thudding sound. The two men were speaking in Hindi amongst themselves and Lenny could not understand them. The drugs were kicking in now and he was losing focus. He had to concentrate to hear what they were saying. There was a lot of gesticulating and whispering. They seemed to be arguing among themselves. He still could not understand what was going on. He thought *'something is not right here. Why is Bro on the floor? Why have I got a knife in my hand?'*

His mind started to wander and he felt himself floating in the air. He was at peace with himself. He sighed deeply and closed his eyes. Everything became black. Bro was right, this was the special stuff. He was so happy. He was at one with the world. He felt powerful and knew he could do anything he wanted. He was in a colourful world of his own. There were no fears and no demons where he was right then. That nasty cat he saw in the morning dare not come here. He would slaughter him if he does. And there was no one to tell him that he was dead or alive. He was alive. He never felt as full of life as he did right then. He never knew there were so many colours before. His breathing became shallow and he was soon snoring away happily on the settee.

He was woken again by another loud noise. This time, it was a door being slammed shut. The room was dark and filled with smoke. He couldn't see properly and the room was spinning. *'Wow, someone stop the room from spinning please,'* he thought. He tried to stand up and fell down promptly on the floor. His legs were like jelly. He laid down there for while trying to focus his eyes. 'Why is my legs not moving? Wow, this junk Bro gave me is strong stuff.' He squinted his eyes to see what was going on. *'Is the house on fire?'* he thought. *'Oh my God, yes, the house is on fire. I better get out.'* The harder he tried more difficult it was for him to move his legs. He couldn't remember how long he laid there on the floor. He must have dozed off again. The smell of burning plastic woke him this time. He opened his eyes and tried to sit up on the floor. He could finally start to see what was going on.

There was no one in the room. Panic started to set in and Lenny managed to stand up and stagger towards the door. There was something blocking it. It was the single sofa, which was belching out smoke. The smoke irritated his eyes and they started to water. *'Which idiot blocked the door with the sofa?'* he thought. *'Oh my god. It is really on fire! I better get out of here!'* He tried to shift the sofa, but could not budge it. There was someone leaning against the wall near the window.

"You better get up. The place is on fire." When the figure did not move, he said, "Didn't you hear me? Come on let's get out of here!"

No movement. He leaned forward to take a closer look. He was shocked at what he saw. The guy on the floor had his eyes wide open and staring at him. It was unblinking. There was froth at the mouth and thick syrupy liquid at the corner of his mouth had trickled down to his neck. He just turned and ran to the dining room and the back door. He staggered out of the back door into the alley. It was still dark and it had started to drizzle.

It did not seem to affect him as he staggered through the alleyway out towards Harrison road. He realised he still had the knife in his right hand as he reached Belgrave Road. He looked down at the knife under the street light. The blade was covered in thick dark stuff, sticky and slimy. The bright lights did not hurt his eyes as much as before. He threw the knife into the rubbish bin that was placed at the side of a restaurant and looked around to see if anyone had seen him. He stared at his hands, which were sticky and wet. He wiped them on his trousers and looked around to see if anyone saw him. There was not a soul in sight. He took a deep breath and started to walk as fast as he could towards the Mowmacre hill. The sound of a dust bin lorry trundling down the road was reassuring somehow.

MOMBASA

He was big and very dark. His hands were huge as he took Dev's hand and led him to the back of his room. He had a very soft and gentle voice for such a big man.

"Come on son. Don't be afraid. You have been a very good boy, haven't you?"

He said as he led the little boy to a small door behind the desk. Dev was apprehensive as he thought the door was not big enough to let the big man through.

"Yes, Brother Francis," he said.

"Come inside, I have something exciting to show you."

Dev's eyes lit up. He came from a poor priestly family and with money being scarce he never got anything exciting. There was a small enclave of Hindus in outskirts of Mombasa Island who had chipped in and converted an old church hall into a temple. Most of them were shopkeepers and businessmen who depended on the goodwill of the Gods in the temple for their salvation. His father, Ramcharan, was the priest of the temple and he wanted Dev and his two brothers to do well and become professionals—adults - like doctors or engineers. Nearly half the family income went on the school fees. But, Dev's father wanted them to have a *"convent education"* and he had enrolled them into the local Jesuit school, much to the mortification of his family back in Gujarat, India. Dev remembered the first day his father had made him stand in front foot well of the scooter with Kishen , his elder brother riding at the back as they were taken to the *"convent school"* in bright blue and white uniforms with a dark blue tie. The faded blue Lambretta scooter was his father's pride and joy. The battered old scooter was a gift to him from one of the devotees of the temple. It would break down almost every week and spend time in Suleiman's garage round the corner. Suleiman was another immigrant from Pakistan who made a living looking after all the expat's vehicles. He would tell Ramcharan 'there is still a lot left in her.' He spent so much time tinkering with the scooter that his mother, Meera Ben would complain, *"You are married to that scooter and not me."*

His neighbours were openly jealous of Ramcharan getting admissions for his boys at the local Jesuit school. *"They will have the children converted in no time."* Dev's grandmother back in Gujarat had grumbled when she had found out.

Dev followed Brother Francis into the little room at the back of his office, which was also the bedroom and kitchen. Brother Mombasa went to the cupboard and took a lollipop out of a box and held it out to little Dev. The room was quite dark with just a small window set high up on the wall. Dev could only see the white teeth in the Kenyan's face and the lollypop in his hand. He hesitated a moment before putting his hand out to grab it.

"Go on, take it. There is more if you want." Brother said as Dev took the lollipop into his hand. Brother held Dev's hand and led him round to his bed at the corner and sat down.

"Thank you." Dev said in his small squeaky voice.

"Come and sit with me." Brother said. "I can get you lots of sweeties if you want."

Dev was still not sure as he climbed on to the bed and sat at the edge of the bed. His feet could not quite reach the floor and he dangled his legs out as he stared at the lollipop. Brother slid across and put his enormous arms around Dev's shoulder.

"You can come here as often as you wish, you know son and help yourself to sweeties." Brother continued with the same grin on his face. Dev was busy unwrapping the lollipop as Brother Francis lifted Dev and sat him on his lap.

"This is more comfortable, isn't it?" Brother said. Dev was too busy with the lollipop to bother. "It is very hot today. I will take my smock off, I think."

He sat Dev back on the bed and stood up to take the white smock off. He only had boxer shorts and a vest underneath as he sat down again on the bed.

"Come and sit on my lap." Brother said looking closely at Dev. "I have something to show you."

As Dev sidled over, Brother picked him up and sat him on his lap. Dev was too busy sucking at his lollipop to realise what was happening as Brother took Dev's right hand and put it on his huge lap. Dev thought it was strange to feel something very hard and took his hand off in surprise. As Brother tried to take his hand again, there was a noise outside. Someone was knocking on the door of his office.

"Who is that?" he put Dev down quickly and put his smock back on. " I am coming. Please wait."

There was no panic in his voice and no urgency in his movements as he led Dev out of his bedroom and to the door.

"You take care now, son." Brother said to Dev as he opened the door. "You come back after school tomorrow and I will help you with your maths."

That was the start of a Dev's regular trips to Brother Francis's office to *'get help for Maths.'* Dev's father was thrilled to see that Brother Francis was giving Dev extra help. *'There is no stopping Dev now. He will be a big engineer when he grows up'* were his words to Dev's mother. He used to show off Dev to the community as the 'brainy one in the family' much to the anguish of the other little boys in the congregation.

"Brother Francis is giving Dev extra tuition for free because he is so bright," he would tell them.

All those middle aged women visiting the temple used to come and pinch his cheeks and say, *"Oooh! He is a sweetie and brainy at the same time!!"*

Dev and his 'extra tuition with Brother Francis' was big news in the dull lives of all those housewives.

Dev soon realised that he was not the only one getting 'special lessons' from Brother Francis. His friend Peter Ngyo was getting the same sort of attention. Dev would feel jealous whenever he saw Peter walking to the back office. He had a special friendship with Peter. They had been friends for a couple of years-and the two of them would spend a lot of time together. They played cricket at the back of Peter's house as they had both been told that they were not good enough to play for the local team. They would go down to the beach in Peter's father's car whenever they could to watch the big ships going in and out of Kilindini harbour. Dev enjoyed the car drive as much as the beach itself. He would sit at the back his face glued to the window watching the city go by. The street on the way to the beach had many Indian shops displaying colourful dresses and clothing for all kind. In the evenings the loudspeakers would be blaring out Hindi songs from the latest blockbuster in Bombay. The battered old Morris Minor, a left over from the colonial days, was the pride and joy of Peter's father. The two boys would spend half a day on weekends cleaning the car with soap and water. Peter's grandfather would watch them clean the car and would give them some old bees wax at the end to get a polish. Dev prided himself at getting the best shine from the chrome bumpers of the car where he could see his own reflection.

Their treat would be the ride to the beach. His father could not afford a car with his meagre salary at the temple. They would play for hours on the white sands of the beach collecting shells and building castles. They would strip naked and dive into the warm waters of the beach and swim until tired. Both of them enjoyed drying each other out after a dip in the sea.

Soon the trips to Brother Francis' room at the back of school became regular and they would often go together. Dev was not sure whether he liked it or not to start with. But once Peter started to go with him, he began to enjoy the trips and would look forward to them. He did not understand exactly what was happening at first. Brother Francis would take Dev's clothes off him – 'it's too hot to be wearing anything now.' He would take his clothes off too. Brother would strip himself first and strip the little boy slowly taking his time. He would lead Dev to do things, which was strange in the beginning. Dev's apprehension soon gave way to curiosity replaced by amusement and finally began to enjoy the visits. He always came out of the room with some present or other. Mostly chocolates or biscuits, "brought all the way from England" as Brother Francis would say. "You don't need to tell your parents what we do here. It will be our little secret." He would wink and touch his big sweaty nose. Sometimes, it would be a set of colouring pencils or books. He could not understand was why the other kids were jealous of him. He would stand next to Brother Francis holding his hand, chest stuck out proudly during morning prayers at the school.

Some of the older kids would bully him and there were more than one occasion when he was beaten up in the schoolyard. Ramcharan had come into school to meet the Headmaster to complain. The culprits were never found and no one was punished to the utter dismay of Dev's parents. He would go to Brother Francis's room and cry himself to sleep on his lap.

It was not until a year later when the scandal broke out. There were police in Dev's house asking lots of questions to him and his brothers. His father was mortified when he was told by the police that Brother Francis had been arrested for sexual abuse of school children. There was even talk of the school closing down completely. The rumour factory swung into overdrive and it became increasingly difficult for Dev's family to live in Mombasa anymore. People were pointing fingers at Dev wherever he went. Ramcharan tried to keep himself busy at the temple. There were taunts within the temple too. He had to put up with accusations from a section of the local Hindu community.

'You should not have put him in that Jesuit school' they said, 'We told you something like this would happen' 'You can't be a priest in the temple, it is not holy' or 'the boy needs to be cleansed.'

Dev's mother could hear whispers and sniggers as she walked to the grocers in Wellington road. She could not understand what was happening and was bewildered at the comments made some people at the grocer shop she frequented. Sexual abuse to children was an unheard of concept to Meera Ben, coming from an extremely sheltered Gujarati upbringing.

"We will have to leave Mombasa. We will go back to India." Dev's father said to his wife, Meera Ben.

"What will you do there? Will you get a job in a temple again in India after this scandal?" Dev's mother was constantly crying ever since the police had come to his house. "I told you not to put him in that school of heathens. God Krishna will not forgive us. We will rot in hell for this sacrilege."

"We have no money to go anywhere else. Sharma ji has already said that the community leaders will be asking for me to leave during the next meeting." Dev's father said. "And that is only next week."

"You can ask your uncle in England to help."

"I have not spoken to him in years. How can I ask him for help now?"

Meera Ben started to cry again. She had the end of her red pallu in her mouth, which was soaking wet by then. Dev and his brothers were hiding behind the door, too afraid to say anything. Dev did not understand what the problem was. He had come to enjoy his visits to the Brother's office every evening after school. He used to get lots of sweeties and gifts almost every time. Brother Francis had bought him new clothes and shiny black shoes to wear to school. He was nearly as smart as those boys of rich merchant family of Sharmaji. He had gone around showing everyone the big colouring book in the school. It was his birthday present from Brother Francis.

"Ok. Ok. Please don't cry any more. I will call him from the post office first thing tomorrow morning."

It took Ramcharan a few days before he could get hold of the uncle. The uncle was surprised to hear from Dev's father after so many years. It turned out that he was not happy with his local temple in Leicester and he wanted to bring someone from Gujarat to start another temple.

"Let me speak to my friends in the Gujarati association here in Leicester and see what I can do."

Time passed with no word from his uncle in Leicester. Ramcharan tried to get hold of his uncle again a few times with no luck. He would spend hours sitting in the post office after 'booking a call' to England waiting to be connected. Finally, one rainy day his call was connected as he was trying to dry himself inside the post office. The torn umbrella did not keep much rain off his clothes as he walked two miles from the old house to the post office. The battered old Lambretta scooter had finally conked out despite Suleiman's efforts and it had been languishing in his garage now for months. The connection was bad and Ramcharan could not hear everything his uncle said over the phone. The uncle was arranging a sponsorship for Ramcharan and family to come over to England.

"You bring the family over here and we will fix something for you." It did not fill Ramcharan with a lot of confidence, but he was running out of options and money.

"What about a temple?" Ramcharan had asked hesitatingly.

"That will take some time. But I have seen a place in Leicester where you can run a grocer shop till we sort out a temple for you."

Ramcharan had thanked him profusely just as the connection was lost. 'A grocer shop is something better than nothing,' he thought. A letter arrived a couple of weeks later but no sign of a sponsorship from the uncle for a British visa for the family.

Ramcharan was getting increasingly despondent by the day. He could see his family on the streets. The temple committee would throw the family out of the house any day now, he thought.

Dev was sorry to leave his school and his friends. He never saw Brother Francis again after the day when the police had come home. His elder brother, Kishen took him to the school for a few days afterwards. But the continuous taunting and interminable fights made school intolerable. Going home with a bruise here and there became a normality almost. When he came home with a torn shirt one day, Meera Ben was distraught.

"I knew this would happen. I told you not to put him into that Christian school. You did not listen to me. No one listens to me." She complained to Ramcharan with tears in her eyes as she sewed the shirt back. One day he was called to the Headmaster's office where he found his father waiting for him.

Father Phillip, the Headmaster smiled at him as he was ushered into the office.

"Come on son. See who is here to see you?"

Dev could not understand what his father was doing at the school. He was too scared to say anything and stood there twiddling his hands with head bent down on his chest.

"Dev, father Phillip says that you are getting into fights with other boys. Is that true?"

Dev lifted his head up to stare at the father Phillip first and then turned to look at his father.

"It is they who start the fight, father. They call me names. They make fun of me all the time." He paused for a minute and looked down as he continued. "They beat up my friend Peter Ngyo."

"You should come to me son." Father Phillip said. "Next time anyone picks on you, I want you to come straight to me."

This went on for a few months. There were two more visits to the school by his father. Then one day he was told he does not have to go to school anymore. His mother was crying and there were a lot of arguments in the house. Dev was confused and angry. He found his father had stopped going to temple. There was a new priest in the temple who had come from India. A young man, recently married with a young bride. Just like Ramcharan all those years ago. There were arguments in the house all the time and it always seem to end up with his mother crying and father storming out of the house. The promised sponsorship letter came through the post just as Ramcharan was losing hope of ever going to England. He had written to his family and a couple of friends back in India with no response. From a 'rising star' as he left the shore on the ship at Bombay all those years ago, he had become a pariah all of a sudden.

It took Ramcharan several months to get the air tickets, passports and make the shipping arrangements. They packed their meagre belongings and bought air tickets with the money given by the community leaders as a leaving present. They were happy to see the back of the family. The rich merchant, Sharmaji gave him an envelope full of money one day and said,

"What happened is not your fault Ramcharan. You have been a good priest all these years and you have done an excellent service to our family and the community. God will protect you."

The envelope had a sizeable amount of money. Ramcharan cried at the sight of it and tried to bend down and touch Sharmaji's feet. He had never seen so much money in his life before.

"No, no. You mustn't. That would be a sacrilege. I hope this will help you till you set up in your new life wherever you are going."

Dev had watched the burly African men load their wooden boxes and gunny sacks on to the truck which would take the boxes to the ship on the way to Southampton in England. Ramcharan took Dev to the Kilindini harbour to see the loading of the boxes. Peter's dad was a carpenter and had made some boxes from discarded railway sleepers they had managed to salvage from the sides of the old Mombasa to Nairobi railway line. All of their worldly goods were in those roughhewn wooden crates which looked pitiful amongst the huge containers.

The day of departure from Mombasa came, a bit too soon for Dev. He had come to think of it as his home. It was Dev's first flight and he was excited and at the same time, very sad to leave the place he had come to call home. A battered taxi took them to the Moi International airport on a rainy Monday morning. His mother, Meera Ben had flustered the night before the journey trying to make sure she did not miss anything to pack. Ramcharan looked at the three battered old suitcases and a cardboard box on the floor as they were waiting for the taxi. Two of them were the cases he had brought with him from India over fifteen years ago. The day when he boarded the ship at Bombay docks with his young bride was as if it was only yesterday. He was a "most eligible bachelor" with a good job as a priest in Mombasa come to Bombay looking for a bride. Tears rolled down his cheeks as he turned to no one in particular and said,

"Not much to show for nearly fifteen years of hard work in this blessed country."

Meera Ben held both Dev and the little Vijai close to her as she replied.

"This is not the time to lose hope. You have been so strong for us all this time."

Dev's elder brother, Kishen, almost fifteen now, went to Ramcharan and touched his shoulder. He was nearly as tall as his father.

"I am sure we will be fine in England father. You said so yourself."

He had just started secondary school, but was more mature than most boys of his age. Dev's friend Peter Ngyo and his father the carpenter had come home to say goodbye. Ngyo gave a brand new note book to Dev as a going away present and said,

"I want you to write down everything you see and do in England. I want to read it when I come to England when I grow up."

Dev looked down at the book Peter had given him. It was a bright red hard bound school note book and the pages were fully lined. It was the notebook he had always wanted from the school book shop, but the one that Ramcharan could not afford. They had hugged each other and cried. Dev could see his friend waving his hands through the back of the taxi until it turned the corner of the street.

As they reached the airport, the two boys became excited and were chatting away. Mother just looked out of the window at the passing scene of old Mombasa with its rickety trucks filled with vegetables bound to the Mombasa market going in the opposite direction. Taita Bantu women carrying huge baskets filled with plastic utensils to the local market with children tagging behind. Pavement hawkers selling everything from t-shirts to mud pots to tribal jewellery seem to go on mile after mile. The scene of the sunrise over the sea as the taxi chugged along the old Fort Jesus enthralled Dev as he sat looking out of the back window until it turned into bustling road going through the city. As they neared Chaani, the airport traffic was busy and noisy. Once they crossed the bridge over Tudor creek the huge towers of oil refinery came into view. Ramcharan had hopes of making his sons engineers so that they could get good jobs at the oil refinery. Now they were forced to leave the country, Ramcharan had come to regard as his adopted country and where he had visions of making his family's future. His father was quiet most of the journey as he himself was unsure of what he would face in a strange country with very little money. He was not sure how long the "going away gift", the local community had collected and Sharmaji's generous help would last. His uncle had reassured him with.

"It will be fine. It will be hard in the beginning, but you can make a good living out of the grocery store till we get a temple established."

Ramcharan felt a bit humiliated at the thought of running a grocery store after being a respected priest for so many years, but it was beyond his control. The family landed at Heathrow on a cold November morning. Uncle had come to meet them with his white van. The first thing Dev noticed was how cold it was. It was dark even at midday and the freezing cold rain made him shiver as he was taken into the white van. It rained all the way to Uncle's house in Leicester.

Dev hated it the minute he got out of the van. It was still raining and dark. And then the silence. There was deafening silence everywhere. All the houses looked exactly the same and there were no people. *"Where are all the people?"* Dev wondered. There was no hustle and bustle of Mombasa. It was depressingly quiet. *'What happened to all the colours? There are only two colours here,'* he thought *'only grey and black.'* He wanted to go back to Kenya and his warm home in Mombasa.

He was put into a school where there were a lot of Asian boys and girls. They teased him about his clothes and his funny accent. He became morose and sultry. He blamed his father for bringing him to this wet and cold country where everyone spoke and behaved differently. He often thought about his little house in Mombasa and the field behind the house where he would play cricket with his friends. One of the devotees in the temple had made him a wooden bat which was one of his prized possession and it had spent many hours in the field with it with his friend Peter Ngyo. Brother Francis had bought him a new tennis ball to play with the bat. He was still bitter about leaving the bat back in Mombasa.

"The box is full. We can't afford to take another box in the ship." His father had said. "I will get you a new bat when we get to England."

That never happened. It was always too cold and wet to play cricket in Leicester anyway, he thought. Father was not earning enough money to buy him a bat. The first year in England passed by painfully slowly for Dev. He would sit at the window of their little terrace house, watching the traffic go by in a constant drizzle. The silence seemed to stun him after the hustle and bustle of Mombasa. He went into a shell with no friends either at school or home. He missed going to the beaches, the hot scorched white sands. He missed those trips to the Fort Jesus where he was allowed to buy snacks from stalls around the old fort.

His father watched Dev transform from an ebullient kid to a morose brat. He started to get into fights again. Ramcharan managed to set up a grocery shop with the help of his generous uncle on Harrison road not too far from Belgrave Road, where most of the Indian shops thrived. The money he had brought from Mombasa did not last long despite help from his uncle. The money from the shop was just enough to feed the family with three growing children and keep a roof over their heads. Ramcharan would call up his uncle whenever he got an opportunity to remind him of the temple that was promised. There were difficult days and the family coped with the help of the generous uncle now and again.

LEICESTER

"This is an awful country. You made a mistake bringing us here." Meera ben complained within a few days of arrival at their little rented house. "It rains all the time and there are no people here. Where are all the people?"

"It feels that way coming from a very busy place. We have been given warm clothes by Uncle and it is not that cold inside the house," Ramcharan replied. "We are going to see the community Church hall on Wrexton Street tomorrow and, God willing, we should be able to get the hall. It has a great potential to be turned into a nice little temple for Lord Krishna. He will protect us."

Unfortunately it was not quite as easy as he thought it would be. Ramcharan had not counted on the bureaucratic quagmire he had to go through before they could even think of buying the Church hall. It was not like Mombasa where word of mouth helped move the bureaucratic machinery. Nearly a year passed before the Uncle could get planning permission and had collected enough money to pay for the hall.

Meera Ben was going from bad to worse. She hated the place. "This is place is too cold and wet. It is always dark too. Very unhealthy. Children will fall ill," She would complain.

"It feels cold coming from a warm country like Kenya. You will get used to it. The children are strong and they will not notice the difference, Ramcharan would reassure her.

But Dev had noticed the difference. *'This place is cold, dark and wet all the time. I want to go back to Mombasa. There are no fields to play here and where is the beach?'* He thought. Dev missed his friend Peter Ngyo. He did not enjoy the school particularly. He did not make many friends until he got into high school. He would stay indoors sitting next to the window watching the traffic go by and thinking about his days in Mombasa. He had taken the little note book his friend had given him the day after he arrived in Leicester to write in it as promised. But he could not think of what to write because there was nothing happening here.' He spoke to his brother Kishen about it.

"What do you think I should write in this notebook?"

"Well, you have travelled thousands of miles from Mombasa on a plane. Not many boys of your age would have done that. Why don't you start writing about our flight?" Kishen had replied.

He had started to write slowly at first, not exactly sure what to write and what to leave out. It soon became a habit. He would sit on his bed last thing at night and write everything that happened to him on that day. Some days there would be nothing on the page apart from *"very cold again and wet."* Soon the book was almost full. He would read what he had written the year before on the same date. It was now well worn and corners were turned up and somewhat discoloured. He did not want anyone to see the note book so he hid it under his bed. He would check every day as soon as he came back home to see if anyone had touched it. When the edges of the notebook started to tear, he bought a plastic sleeve and tied a ribbon around it.

Dev's father took him to the local school to enrol him in the summer. That was the first time he saw some boys of his own age. He found the school exciting and scary at first. He would come straight home from school unlike his classmates who went to play in the field afterwards. Dev became increasingly withdrawn and glum His mother's constant complaining only depressed him further. He could not bear to see her so unhappy. She had never managed to pick up much English while in Mombasa as her life revolved around her family and the people who came to the temple. Even the grocer near her house spoke Gujarati.

It was a couple of years before they found an old derelict Church hall on Wrexton Street, which was not too far from Belgrave Road. The Uncle had gathered a group of local

Gujarati businessmen to pool together some money and bought the Church hall.

Dev remembers a lot of excitement in the house and there was discussion of what deities should be installed in the temple. There was an almost daily run of strange people appearing that Dev had never seen before, who came to discuss the planning and decoration of the temple. The Uncle was obviously a community leader of some sort and there were a lot of "volunteers" to help convert the Church hall into the temple.

The day that God Krishna's idol was installed in the temple saw his mother wore her wedding *saree* and Dev was running around the temple. Ramcharan had bought him a new *Kurta* for the occasion. He seemed happiest while in the temple. That seemed to be a turning point for Dev. He was home. But after the first day, there were hardly any devotees coming into the temple apart from weekends when there was a *Havan* and free lunch from a chosen devotee.

Daily collection from the temple was meagre. If it were not for the grocery shop still running well, they would have starved. Soon they were moved into a house next to the temple, paid for by Uncle and his friends. Ramcharan noticed that Dev had started to spend more and more of his time in the temple. He would not go out to play like he did in Mombasa. None of his school friends came home with him either.

"There are no people here. They all speak a strange language. I don't understand any of them," Dev told his father.

"Give it time. They speak English with an accent. You will soon get used to it. There is a large Gujarati community here and most of them are from Africa. Either from Kenya, Tanzania or Uganda." Ramcharan would reply. "Our temple is still new. Soon we will have a lot of devotees."

He was right. Soon the word spread that there was a temple with a Gujarati priest and the first festival of stick dance (*Gharba)* was well attended. People started to come to the temple and it became a meeting place for the trading Gujarati merchant community of Leicester. They would ask Ramcharan for advice on matters of faith and religion. He was asked to perform several marriages. Dev took part in all the temple activities and appeared to thrive in it. Meera Ben was much happier now that she had made several friends. She had a privileged position as the wife of the priest and the elderly women folk looked up to her and even asked her advice about family issues. She made it a point to be at the temple every evening and all day during Sunday when the special *Havan* took place.

The little grocer shop on Harrison road was ticking along providing a small income and the temple had started to thrive with a large Gujarati community as its back bone. Kishen had started to spend some evenings in the shop while father went to the temple. Dev would help out some days in the shop during his school holidays, but he would rather spend the time at the temple. Ramcharan finally decided to make both his sons into priests. But there was no priest school in England. Dev and his brother were packed off to their grandparent's house in Gujarat in India, and enrolled into a Priest's school. Little Vijai was born while Dev was studying in India, much to the disappointment of both the boys. They wanted to come back to England to see the baby. But the Grandfather was a strict disciplinarian and would have none of it.

India was another experience all together. He had difficulty understanding the children when they spoke and particularly the grandfather. He got used to them very quickly however and found that he was quite comfortable conversing in Gujarati. He really enjoyed the Priest school and took to it like duck to water. He was a high flyer in his class and graduated with no difficulty. He would go to his Grandparents house for the holidays. The two years at priest school passed swiftly, maybe too swiftly for Dev. He did not forget to take Peter Ngyo's note book and wrote diligently a couple of sentences everyday while he was in India. Graduation saw him pack his bags again back to England.

By the time Dev returned, the Krishna Mandir had become a leading temple in Leicester, quite close to the Indian enclave of Belgrave arcade on Wrexton street. The Krishna Mandir was not the biggest temple in Leicester, but it attracted enough clientele to be successful. Dev relished working in his father's temple as his assistant to start with and soon became quite close to a lot of regular visitors to the temple. He would be in the temple almost every day after school. Quite often one would see him sitting in the corner of the temple doing his homework. He had filled Peter Ngyo's notebook a while ago and he was filling up any empty spaces he could find. He used to write to Peter regularly and get a reply at least once a month. Lately the letters had become more infrequent. Peter Ngyo had gone on to become a vicar and Dev was invited to his ordination. Dev was very disappointed when he was told by his father that they could not afford an air ticket to Mombasa to attend the ceremony.

As he grew up past teenage years, Dev brought a young crowd into the temple. He was particularly liked by the younger generation as he spoke fluent English like a local and knew the language as it were of the young people. He had lost his African accent by now and it was hard to make out that he was of Indian descent over the phone. Dev became a "people's person" and was always appeared to be surrounded youngsters of his own age and younger ones too. He left school with quite good grades and went to Leicester University to get a degree in Sociology. When he got a job as a Social Worker at Leicester city council, his mother had done a big ceremony in the temple and would go around telling everyone that her "Dev has got a government job." For her, getting a "government job" was a pinnacle of achievement.

His interest in the temple work increased and he would work on the scriptures whenever he got the chance. He had come out of the shell he had cocooned himself during his school years in Leicester and enjoyed making new friends and going out. He started doing the *Aarti* every now and then with the help of his elder brother Kishen, particularly when there was a young crowd in the temple. This made a difference to the youngsters attending the temple for the first time. Most of the young Hindus identified well with him as he was seen as one of them. Dev would try and explain the rituals and meaning of the hymns in English to the devotees, which was immensely popular with the younger crowd. There were a few eyebrows raised when he started to mingle with the crowd in the middle of the rituals as Kishen continued at the altar.

"Hinduism is not a religion, it's a way of life, a way of thinking, a way of disciplining oneself, physically, spiritually and emotionally." He would say to the youngsters, who were mostly his own age. "The word religion has been attached because there isn't any equivalent word to the Hindu Dharma in the Oxford dictionary, so the nearest thing to dharma in English is religion. It is a way of life. It is a faith. It embraces you if you embrace it."

He was passionate about his religion and wanted the younger Asians to grasp the meaning and the essence of the Sanatan Dharma or eternal faith, as he would call it. He mixed with the young generation of Leicester quite freely and did the same things as everyone else did. He did not agree with some of the practices within the temple. He would try to stop the segregation of women in the temple during temple rituals. He encouraged them to sit together with families along with men. He also detested the way the widows were treated within the temple and also in the wider community.

"A woman needs to be helped and nurtured when she loses her partner. This ostracising of widows destroys their lives and it must stop." He would say. "It is not their fault that their husband's died. That is nature and God's will. There is no need to punish them this way."

It did not go down very well with many of elders in the community. There were minor rumblings and arguments behind closed doors. This only made him more determined and vociferous. He dreamed big and 'wanted to be somebody one day.' His younger brother little Vijai, looked up to him and followed him everywhere while in the temple. It was not unusual for Dev to go 'out on the town' after the day's work at the temple and *Aarti* at night.

Dev had made a lot of friends while studying at college. He had joined the National Association of Hindu Priests as well as the Hindu Federation. He was very active in both the organizations and he soon found he was climbing the ladder in both the organizations. It meant a fair amount of travel, not only in the UK but also abroad. He was being noticed by the local councillors as well as the local Member of Parliament, Fred Homuz. He became quite close to Fred Homuz and would often meet him socially. They would speak to him with any issues concerning the Hindu community in the city.

He was very vocal on social issues and he was quoted by media regularly on some controversial issues. When the news of a club in London for Asian homosexuals and lesbians was being named after Kali, he objected vehemently.

"I have nothing against gays and lesbians but people are trampling all over the image of the Goddess." He was quoted by the local newspaper. "They are people like you and me. But they should not offend any religion or community." He went to the local councillors and the local Member of Parliament and managed to stop the name. He was in the forefront of the protest marches both in Leicester as well as in London.

Dev would go out of his way to help others in need. An episode where he bought food for a bunch of homeless refugees in the middle of Leicester hit the headlines in local newspapers and TV. He was on his way to the temple after work when he saw a bunch of eastern European refugees huddled together in the cold trying to keep warm with a fire on a rubbish heap. He stopped the car and reversed to take a closer look. They were mostly women and children in ragged clothes. When he stopped the car, he could see the look of desperation and fear in their eyes. He got out of the car on an impulse to speak to them. They started to pull back at his approach holding onto their children tightly trying to protect them.

"Don't be afraid. I just want to help if I can." He said. "Who are you people?"

None of them could speak proper English. One of them said, "Romania. Hungry." She went on to say something in Romanian which Dev could not understand. She put her right hand out palm upwards still holding onto her baby tightly.

"I don't understand what you said. You wait here and I'll try and get you some hot food." Dev was gesticulating to the group hoping they would understand. He got back into the car, still signalling them to wait there and sped off towards the little take away near the temple. He bought several bags of food, got one of the boys from the take away to help him carry and returned to the group who were still struggling in front of the fire. The two of them distributed the food to a grateful bunch of women and children on the pavement.

"I will try and speak to someone in the council and see if we can find some accommodation for you."

They did not understand what he said. But they just nodded with broad smiles on their faces. They were so happy to get some hot food. They probably had not eaten any hot food for days. The take away owner spread the word to the local rag and the news hit the headlines the next day.

"I see you have made the local newspapers," his workmates at the council said. Dev smiled and explained what had happened.

"I felt really sorry for them. They were mostly women and children in rags. It did not look like they had anything to eat for days."

"Unfortunately there are a lot of such immigrants from the eastern European countries and many of them are scattered around Leicester. Our council can't cope with the numbers coming into the city." His colleague, George Crawford had said.

"But we have to do something for them." Dev said. "I felt horrible when I saw all those women and children huddled on the footpath."

"We could meet the manager and bring it up at the next meeting." George said. "You would be lucky to get anything done. Our system is so much bogged down in bureaucracy that by the time any money is released they would all be dead and gone!"

"But we can't just leave them like that." Dev insisted. "There are women and children there."

George sighed deeply and said, "I know what you are saying. But you know how tight it is with the council. I would be surprised if the manager agrees to spend any money."

"Be that as it may. I am going to give it a damn good try."

"We can certainly try. I am just warning you so that you won't be disappointed."

The two of them tried to speak to their manager regarding the plight of the refugees who were clogging up the footpaths of Leicester with no luck.

"Thank you for bringing their plight to my attention, Dev." The manager had said. "You are right, we can't leave them to starve like that. I'll tell you what. You do a report and a feasibility study and bring me the recommendations and I'll see what can be done."

No amount of cajoling from Dev and Stuart helped. The manager wanted everything done according to the rules and wanted everything written down on paper.

"It is going to take time to get all this done. Are we going to leave them to starve in the meantime?" Dev was losing his temper.

"There are several charities who deal with this kind of problem. I am sure they will look after them in the meantime." The manager had insisted.

Dev decided to do something about it himself. He would drive around the areas where the refugees appeared to concentrate and try to help. He would spend his own money to buy rice and groceries and cook for them. He became a familiar face around the Belgrave area. The homeless and the refugees looked up to him. The news was picked up by a local rag and he became known as a sort of a 'saviour' for the refugees.

He wrote diligently in the notebook from his friend Peter Ngyo. He had figured out a way of adding pages to it and now it was nearly twice the size it started off with. He would write profusely on the days he was angry or stressed. The day his request for help with the refugees was refused he was scribbling patiently until after midnight. He had a neat handwriting and he was very proud of it. He still hid the notebook under his bed and checked the place every time he came into his room. The plastic sleeve he covered the notebook was stained in sweat and now looked more brown than white. He would often go to the beginning of the book to reminisce about old days and it would bring tears to his eyes.

STUART DAVENPORT

Ramcharan felt that Dev should have a job to fall back on if the temple was not successful enough to support all of them. So Dev had joined Leicester Social Services department as a Social Worker and he appeared to be thriving on it. He had progressed swiftly become the Manager and was in charge of Social Services for helping people with learning difficulties. That is where he met Stuart Davenport who He was also a Social worker at the time, but with big ideas. The two of them were part of a team looking after people with learning disabilities in their ward. Stuart was also a self-styled businessman and landlord. They would go out for a drink on a Thursday night and talk about their dreams.

"Have you seen the state of that care home on Loughborough road?" Stuart said to Dev one day.

"Terrible!! Not very good at all. Last time I went there was nearly a year ago and I did a report about the bad conditions. Nothing seems to have been done about it. It broke my heart to see the state residents are made to live in."

"You are right." Stuart agreed. "I did a report as well. Spoke to the Manager at the office. She says there is no funding to increase the staffing at the centre."

"I just don't understand how though. The number of staff in the centre in Spinney Hill is exactly the same and their residents seem to do well."

"I tell you, you should be the manager and things will change." Stuart had laughed out loud.

"I have finished all my exams now and even got the Diploma. Next time there is a vacancy, I am going for it." Dev had said with a passion.

"Best of luck to you. I hope you get it."

"It is time these places are run by professionals who know their job. Not just by any business with cash to throw." Dev said with some feeling. He had worked hard with his books and attended courses to get his diploma and certificates and felt that his expertise would make a difference.

"You know I do have a couple of houses down near Loughborough. They are now rented out to the college kids. We could easily convert them into the care home."

"That would need a lot of money!" Dev replied. "Where are we going to find that kind of money?"

"Leave that to me. I will arrange the cash, if you would go into partnership with me. I can't do it on my own."

"Give me some time to think about it and let me speak to my father too."

"That is fine. But don't take too long about it. We know the ropes and we can make it big in time if we work hard."

Well, that is how it started. Stuart had taken Dev to see the houses he had near Loughborough. He was impressed with what he saw and said yes as soon as he saw them. The two of them worked hard day and night with builders and got the place turned into a care home for people with learning disabilities. Dev had spoken to the Manager at Leicester Social Services and the application for approval passed through without much hassle. Dev never asked Stuart where the money came from. But they were able to expand with two more Care homes, one more in Leicester and one in Milton Keynes. Money started to pour in. Dev soon developed a flamboyant lifestyle. He bought a silver BMW, which became his pride and joy. He spent money on flashy clothes and shoes.

His mind often wandered to Mombasa and his childhood. He could still remember the time when he had only one pair of shoes to go to school in. He would walk everywhere else bare foot. Apart from the customary school uniform, his clothes were mainly hand me downs from his elder brother, Kishen.

Now that he was 'rolling in money,' he was going to make the best of it. He still had not forgotten his friend Peter Ngyo, who was a Priest in Mombasa now and from his letters was doing very well indeed. He still wrote in the 'little notebook' – which had become quite a big notebook now. He did not write as often as he did during his school days. But he would find time at least once a week to note down what happened. He would ask Peter Ngyo to come over to England in every letter. He would tell Peter about the little note book and the entries in the notebook in every letter.

Dev met a young and extremely attractive law student, Sheena in the temple. It had started as an acquaintance and soon grew into a close friendship as she started to help out regularly in the temple. While his friendship and feelings for Sheena was getting stronger, he felt that there was something missing. He would feel attracted to some of the young boys who came into the temple – lot younger than himself. He noticed one particular young boy who used to come to the temple regularly and sit in the corner throughout the evening and leave quietly before the *aarti* finished. He was intrigued and felt a bit sad too as he was always alone. One evening, he got his younger brother Vijai to do the *Aarti* and went over to talk to the young lad. The boy saw Dev coming towards him and quickly got up and started to walk towards the door.

"Wait please." Dev signalled to him quietly and hurried over to come between the young lad and the main door. The boy bent his head down and pushed his hands deeper into his jacket pocket. He would not look at Dev even when he put his hands on the shoulder.

"Wait until the *Aarti* is over and take *Prasad*."

He shrugged off Dev's hands off his shoulder and stepped back.

"I don't want any *Prasad*." The voice was a squeak and barely audible. "Let me go please."

"It looks like you are not happy. There is something bothering you, isn't it? Why don't you tell me?"

The lad wouldn't speak. He kept his head down and started to shuffle his feet nervously.

"We can go into the office room inside if you want. Don't be afraid. You can talk to me about anything."

Dev opened the door and walked into the corridor without looking back - not sure if the lad would follow him or not. He waited for a couple of minutes and went into his office down the corridor when the boy did not come through the door. He heard the footsteps as he sat down at the desk. His heart was pounding hard and the images of his days in Brother Francis's office came flooding back to him. A warm sensation appeared to flood through him as the steps came nearer. He was waiting expectantly when there was a soft knock on the door.

"Come in." said Dev. "It is open."

The young lad walked into the office room and stood in front of the desk still looking down at his feet.

"Sit down please. What is your name?" Dev could scarcely recognise his own voice. It trembled and he had to clear his throat a couple of times.

"Sanju." Came a hesitant reply.

"It is nice to meet you Sanju. I don't think I have seen your parents in the temple."

"They don't go to temples."

"I see. It is nice that you come to temple." Dev said softly. "I am glad you like coming to temple. You can meet lot of people here and get lots of friends."

"I don't have any friends. No one likes me."

"I am sure you are wrong. You seem to be such a nice boy. I am sure lots of people like you." Dev was much calmer by now and his heart had stopped pounding in his chest. He was feeling much more comfortable now that he was giving advice and help.

"No one talks to me. They think I'm weird."

"Why do they say that? I find that so sad." Dev replied standing up and coming round the desk.

The story started slowly and soon picked up speed. It was like an avalanche once started. He had realised that he was gay soon after he got into his teens. He was too scared to discuss it with anyone. His family had noticed that he had become morose and withdrawn and his school mates openly started to make fun of him. Out of desperation to seek some support and help, he told his mother. Unfortunately it did not have the effect he had hoped for. Instead of help and support, there was a lot of derision and incredulity from his parents. Ever since he told his parents about his sexuality, he had been ostracized from all social contacts. He was sixteen years of age and his parents would take him everywhere. He was not allowed to go on his own even to ~~the~~ school. His father, though an atheist himself, had decided that going to the temple would be the best for his son and would drop him at the temple every evening and pick him up outside the temple every night.

Dev felt stirrings in him as he heard the story. Stirrings he had not felt for a number of years. Stirrings he had felt all those years ago in Brother Francis' office in Mombasa. He felt strangely attracted to the young kid. His heart started to race again and he felt his palms go moist.

'*This is wrong. I'm a priest and Godly man. I must not have such feelings.*' He said to himself. 'But Brother Francis was a priest too.' A voice seem to say inside his head. 'Servant of God,' he had heard him say about himself. He had to force himself not to touch the young Sanju and hug him and kiss him. He wanted to hold him in his arms and sooth away his pain. '*Think of Sheena. This will go away. This is not right.*' He walked over to the window to avoid looking at the young boy. His legs felt like lead and felt as if it took forever to reach the window. He looked out of the window at passing traffic to take his mind of the young boy sitting in his office.

'He is so vulnerable right now. So easy to take advantage of.' Dev thought.

He dared not turn around for fear of losing control of his raging emotions. He clenched his fist and thought about Sheena. He could hear Sanju talking away in the background with his head bent, completely oblivious of the reactions of Dev. Sanju had a traumatic childhood, not too dissimilar to his own. He was taken away from his childhood home in a village outside Mumbai at the age of six and stuck in an alien environment of a wet and cold northeast of Scotland. They had moved to Leicester only a year ago – 'to get away from those demons in Sanju's mind' as his father would say - and it had not changed young Sanju's situation. He still felt alienated in a society he did not understand and coming into his teenage years had made him aware of his own sexuality. That the other school children found his behaviour strange only made situation worse, especially when they started to call him names such as 'faggot' and 'queer'.

The demon in Dev had been woken and he was fighting his own battle now. He tried to count the number of cars passing the window to take his mind off the young lad. He tried to recite the difficult vedic chants to himself. He could hear the drums of lord Shiva play inside his head as the Sanskrit chants went on in his mind to try and drown the emotions that were raging inside him. The drums got faster and louder to try and drown the voice of Sanju and bury his emotions. He could not remember how long he stood there in front of the window until there was a gentle tap on his shoulder. Dev turned around to see Sanju standing closely behind him. Dev had to fight hard not to put his arms around the young lad and hold him tight.

"It is a good thing we had chat like this. Doesn't it make you feel better now? You can come in anytime you want and have a chat with me." His throat was completely dry and his voice croaked. "Here, I'll give you my phone number. Call me whenever you want to talk about anything. Don't hesitate now."

Sanju lifted his head up for the first time during the entire episode and looked at Dev. He had deep black eyes and Dev felt himself magnetised by his look. Dev felt himself drowning in the dark pool of his eyes. He averted young Sanju's eyes when he could not stand it any longer.

"Thank you for listening. No one else does."

Dev scribbled his number on a piece of paper and handed it over to Sanju. There was a feeling of an electric sensation rushing up his hands to his throat when his fingers touched Sanju's.

"You are welcome Sanju." Dev could not recognise his own voice. "Come in any time you feel like you need to talk. I am always here for you."

Dev walked the young lad out of the temple just as the last of the devotees were leaving. Vijai had finished the *Aarti* earlier than usual and getting the temple ready to close. Dev walked outside with Sanju in the hope of catching his father coming to pick him up. Sanju did not look back as he walked towards the corner of the street where a dark car was parked in darkness with its engine running. Dev waited on the kerb till Sanju got into the car and drove away. He sighed deeply and walked back into the temple. His mind was in a raging turmoil as entered the temple and he did not see Vijai trying to come out and nearly knocked him over.

"Wow. Easy, Dev. Where are you going? The temple is secure. Come, let's go home."

Dev let Vijai drive the car home as his mind was too pre-occupied to concentrate on the road.

Stuart found Dev very quiet the next afternoon at lunch time as they sat together on the bench outside the council hall. Several attempts at conversation by Stuart brought out monosyllabic responses from Dev. Then suddenly Dev asked,

"Do you believe in fate Stuart?"

Stuart was taken aback with this question as he had not received any response to his soliloquy about football so far.

"Why do you ask?" Stuart asked. "What brought this on?"

"I met this young lad at the temple last night." He paused for a minute before continuing, "I think it was fate that brought him to the temple."

"You get lots of kids coming into your temple, Dev. What is so special about this one?"

"I don't know, Stuart. But I noticed him and took him inside and even counselled him. I have never done that in the past."

He then went on to explain what happened leaving out his own response at meeting him. Stuart listened attentively and said at the end.

"You do have a way with people in trouble. I know what to do." Stuart was enthusing. "Why don't you take up counselling? I know several organisations struggling to find counsellors. I will speak to the guys running the Gay helpline. You can then help many more that way."

Dev was thoughtful for a moment before answering. 'Would that be a good idea for me? Where would that take me? I am not sure if I am cut out for that sort of thing regularly, Stuart."

"Why don't you give it a try and see how it goes. You can always drop out if it doesn't suit you."

Dev took a while to answer and finally said with a shrug of his shoulders, "OK. I will speak to them."

To cut a long story short, Dev was on the Gay Helpline switchboard twice a week talking to many youngsters who were unsure of their sexuality or in trouble because of it. He soon found out about the Gay clubs such as Quebec night club, a dazzling silver and steel bar-cum-night club with a predominantly gay clientele in the heart of Leicester's city centre. Against a backdrop of the latest remixes of Kylie, Spiller and Steps, the handful of Asian men and women willing to be 'out' in public dance flamboyantly under the mirrored balls and flashing strobe lights. He persuaded Stuart to come with him to the Quebec one night after *Aarti* and found himself enthralled and rejuvenated by the experience. He became a regular at the club and developed lots of friends.

It was a few weeks into this new found interest when he met Lenny Mithcell. He was walking back to his car in a poorly lit open car park, when he found this thin young lad being beaten up by a couple of hoods. He walked across to them and shouted,

"Hey. What are you doing to him? Leave him alone or I will call the police."

The two guys stopped and turned around.

"Mind your own business mister."

"I'll give you what for if you don't." The second guy hissed.

Dev took out his brand new mobile and held it out.

"I am calling the police now." And he started to dial. The two took to their heels and ran out of the car park before he could finish dialling. Dev walked across to the man now lying on the floor bleeding profusely from a cut on his cheek and lower lip. He helped him up and said,

"You are bleeding badly. Where also are you hurt?"

"Thanks for your help Bro." blood splattered out of his mouth as he spoke. "I don't think I'm hurt anywhere else. Thank god, you came in the nick of time. Otherwise I would been a goner."

"Come I will take you to the hospital. You need that seen to."

"Thanks Bro. You don't need to do anything now. I'm OK. I can get to the hospital myself."

"Don't be silly - you can barely stand up. I think you might have a concussion. Come let me take you to the hospital." Dev insisted and walked across to where he had parked his car.

“Thanks again, Bro.” He had said as Dev started the car. “By the way, I’m Lenny Mithcell. What do I call you?”

“I am Dev. It is nice to meet you. Why were they beating you up?”

Lenny looked furtively at Dev and took his time to answer.

“Dunno. Never seen them before.”

Dev was not convinced.

“OK. I think you should report this to the police once you have been seen at the hospital.”

“No. No police.” Was the quick reply.

Dev dropped him off at the front of Royal Infirmary gates. Lenny had insisted that he would go inside himself. He thanked Dev again profusely as he got out of the car and walked into accident and emergency department.

Dev thought no more of it until he saw Lenny again at the car park a few days later waiting for him as he got out of the Quebec. He had Stuart with him as he walked towards the car. Lenny had come out of the shadows and gave the two of them a bit of a fright.

“Hi Bro. It’s me, Lenny”

Dev had recovered quickly and replied.

“Oh. Hello Lenny. How are you? Hope you got sorted out at the hospital?”

“Yes. Thanks to you.” He stood there shuffling his feet, not moving from Dev’s path.

“Is there anything else I can do for you? Have you been waiting for me here?”

“Yes. I have been waiting for you. I did not thank you properly for saving me that day.”

“Don’t worry. It was nothing. Anyone would have done the same thing.”

“No. You don’t understand. They were going to kill me if

you had not shown up that day."

"Well, that is Ok. Don't worry about it. It was the least I could do. I hope you have told the police about them."

"Anyway, I want to give you this. Just to say thanks, you see."

Lenny shoved a packet into Dev's hands and turned and walked off before either of them could say anything. He disappeared into darkness. Dev opened the brown paper packet to see what it was. It had a brown plastic bottle with what seemed like a white paste inside. The bottle was sealed and there was no writing on it. He took a sniff at the opened bottle. Strong sweetish smell was slightly overpowering and at the same time exciting.

"Looks like he has given me something they gave him at the hospital!" Dev exclaimed. Stuart leaned over and took the packet from his hands and looked closely.

"Let me see."

He took the packet and took it to the single lamp that was in the corner of the car park.

"I can't see properly in this light. Let's get into the car." Stuart said. "Why would he give you his medicine? I can guess what this might be."

They sat in the car and Dev switched the lights on to take a closer look. As soon as the lights came on, Stuart smiled. He took the bottle to his nose and sniffed.

"I thought as much." He said with a wide grin on his face. "They are poppers."

"What are poppers?" Dev was a bit confused. Stuart laughed at this.

"He obviously thinks you are gay seeing you coming out of Quebec. Lot of Gays use it regularly to get their kicks and other things."

"What other things?"

“You will soon find out inside the club if you flash it around enough.” Was Stuart’s cryptic reply. Dev had let go of it at the time. It did not take him long to find out what the “poppers” were once inside the club. He felt very apprehensive at first, but soon forgot about it.

Dev had not said anything about his own urges and stirrings that he had felt with Sanju to Stuart so far. Stuart still thought Dev was helping all these Gay Asian men who were frequenting the club as a social service.

“Do you think I should give it to someone at the club?”

“It is up to you. I am not sure how useful it is for straight men. You don’t even have a girlfriend yet.” Stuart replied. “Anyway, what are you doing with that guy? He looks like trouble. He is not an Asian gay. Don’t tell me you are helping all gays now!”

Dev went on to explain the fracas in the car park of the club and how he had helped Lenny.

“You better be careful with that guy. He looks like a ‘rent boy’ to me.” Stuart’s voice was serious.

“What do you mean?”

“These kind of people are usually run by gangsters. You don’t want to be mixed up with them.”

“No, Stuart. I have only met him a couple of times.” Dev said. “Anyway, what is a ‘rent boy?”

Stuart laughed and explained what a ‘rent boy’ was. “Young men who offer their services to other men for a fee.” Stuart was laughing now. “And they are usually run by unscrupulous characters, just like the prostitutes.”

Stuart did not know about Sheena at that time. His father was still ‘arranging’ the liaison with her family and there was nothing definite yet. His friendship with Sanju was growing daily. He was now coming into the temple every night and they were spending a lot of time together. His urges had become stronger and he almost was ready to give in. He knew Sanju wanted it too. He had asked the boy to come to the care home office where he was also a part time Manager. Since taking over the running of the care home, Dev and Stuart took turns to work as a 'Manager' of the place. It was felt better to do that rather than appoint an outsider to run the place.

The meetings started tentatively at first and became regular as time went by. Dev soon found that he was attracting several good looking boys at the Quebec and this did not go unnoticed by other punters. He would make it a point to move in groups of young men, mostly white young men. He would splash his money on the young kids who stuck to him like a magnet most of the time within the club. He was supposedly in the club to help Asian gay men as part of his job as an "Asian Gay Helpline" worker. But he would often ignore most of the Asian gay men in the club.

Jealousy set in and there were a few verbal skirmishes now and then. He turned down approaches by some of the boys and developed a reputation of being 'off handed' and 'arrogant.' Stuart was not entirely surprised at the revelation that Dev was bisexual. He was not amused by his promiscuity though and he tried to warn him against it.

When he found out that Dev was frequenting the Central Motors, as the toilets under the Belgrave flyover was called, he was deeply concerned. At first Dev denied going to the Central motors.

"You better watch out Dev. You are getting into an unknown territory." Stuart had said after one particularly ruthless verbal exchange with some men at the bar one night. "Drug dealers and pushers frequent that joint and you can easily get into serious trouble. I won't be around to protect you all the time."

Stuarts prediction came true late one night, but not from the clientele of the club. Dev got out of the club late one night and noticed that the single light that used to light up the car was not working. The place was completely dark and he could barely see the cars. He was struggling to locate his car, trying to squint in the darkness when he thought he heard something. He stopped and listened carefully for a minute. There was nothing. Deathly quiet apart from a distant siren of an ambulance. 'It must have been the breeze,' he thought and walked towards where he thought he had parked his car. There it was again. Shuffling sort of sound and he thought he heard someone clearing his throat. He stopped again to listen. Again there was nothing. He was getting a bit worried now. His heart beating faster, he called out.

"Hello. Is there anyone there?"

There was again absolute stillness. He noticed that the breeze had stopped and there was no sound whatsoever. He wished he had Stuart with him. Stuart's visits had become less and less frequent lately. Dev had his own circle of 'friends' from the club who he would spend his nights with. Stuart himself was not comfortable with Dev's 'friends'. He understood Dev's needs, but felt uncomfortable the way he was fulfilling them.

There was no response. He thought he could see his car at the far corner of the car park and started to walk quickly towards it. He started to walk faster towards the car and was almost near his car. As he passed a parked van, a hooded figure came out of the darkness in front of him and at the same time he was hit on his back with something very hard. He immediately fell to the ground in severe pain. The figure in front kicked him on his head and started to scream abuse at him.

"You filthy bastard! You ruined the sanctity of my marriage. You ruined our lives."

Dev could not understand what he was screaming about. There were two other men who also started to kick him. Dev tried to protect his face by curling himself and covering his face with his arms. It was no use the attack was relentless. As was the verbal abuse. He tried to see who was attacking him, but it was too dark. They had chosen the darkest corner of the car park to attack him.

"You knew you were a queer and yet you did my wedding. My life is ruined. The whole world knows you are queer. You should not be allowed to do anything sacred." He could make out that there were at least three of them and all of them were wearing hoodies. The Indian accent of the one who was shouting was unmistakable. The same voice was shouting while the others kept kicking him in silence and guy with the hockey stick was beating him up. Dev heard a crack of the wood breaking as one of the hits missed him and hit the ground hard. After that it was just kicking all over him. He could do nothing but tried to lessen the blows by curling himself like a baby. He thought that 'this is it. I am going to die' as the incessant kicking went on for what seemed to be forever. The last thing he remembers was a dirty boot coming at his face with some speed.

He woke up the next morning in a hospital bed at the Royal Infirmary with a drip on his forearm and oxygen mask on his face. He opened his eyes and as a reflex tried to get up only to drop back on to bed wincing with pain.

"Look who is awake now," said the pretty little nurse who had turned up on hearing his grunts of pain. His chest felt like it was going to burst every time he took a breath.

He smiled weakly at the nurse and tried to speak. The nurse took the oxygen mask off his face so he could speak clearly.

"I don't think you should be moving around too much now." She said. "I will get the sister to come and talk to you."

She came back with a stern looking, rather portly sister in a dark blue uniform.

"Mr Sharma. How are you feeling? I am Sister Florence."

"It is nice to meet you sister." Dev replied and winced with pain as soon as he said it. "Why does it hurt so much to breathe?"

"You have been well beaten up, I'm afraid. It looks like you have broken ribs. I will get the doctor to come and explain to you." Sister Florence said. "You have been written up for some strong painkillers. I will get the nurse to give you some now. You have some relatives waiting outside. Do you want to see them now?"

'Oh my God. What will father say?' was Dev's first thought.

"Yes please sister."

"You can have two visitors at a time and try to rest. I will get a couple of them to come inside after I have given the painkilling injection."

She sauntered off to get the injection.

Ramcharan and Kishen walked in after he had the injection. There were tears in his father's eyes as soon as he saw Dev. He just sat next to the bed, tears rolling down his face and stroking Dev's hand. He didn't say much. Kishen did most of the talking. Dev was not really in a mood for any long winded explanations. He told them he did not know who the assailants were or why he was attacked.

"It must be a racist attack." Kishen said. "I think you should stick to giving advice over the phone rather than going to these clubs at night. It is not safe."

"You may be right *Bhaiya*." He was not going to tell his brother or anyone else what the assailants were saying when he was being beaten up. They stayed with him for half an hour and left promising to bring mother back the next day despite his protestations not to bring her into the hospital.

It was another hour later when a doctor came around with his folder in his hands and a stethoscope slung over his neck.

"Mr Sharma, I am Dr Kumar." An Indian boy, not much older than his younger brother Vijai, spoke with a strong south Indian accent that he could not place. "You were brought in by ambulance last night. Can you tell me what happened?"

Dev smiled weakly and winced with every breath as he spoke.

"I don't really know doctor. I walked out into the dark car park and I was set upon by some men. I could not see much."

The doctor looked at him and scribbled something in the notes. "Do you know what they hit you with?"

"I can't remember much Doctor. Sorry."

"That is OK. You have broken three ribs in the right side of your chest. You were lucky that there was no internal damage. You also have had a concussion. The CT scan did not show any internal damage in the head." He was scribbling in the notes as he spoke fast. "You have been very lucky to get away with only external injuries apart from the broken ribs. It does not need any active treatment apart from rest and painkillers. If you are still stable by tomorrow, we will get you up walking and you might even be able to go home tomorrow."

Dev grasped only part what was being said. The pain in his chest and head was so immense and he was getting drowsy. He must have passed out at that stage as when he opened his eyes again, it was dark with very few lights around and all the patients around him were fast asleep. It still hurt like hell when he moved. He tried to stay still and go back to sleep.

The police came later the following day. It was a Detective inspector Mick Mills who had come to see him. A dapper young man, a man of the streets by his accent and dialogue, did not mince his words.

"They have done you in good and proper, haven't they? Who attacked you, mate?"

Dev was slightly taken aback by the question. "I don't know. It was too dark to see anything."

"They must have worked you over for a while looking at the state of you. I am sure you must have had a chance to look at who is beating you up?"

"No. Not really. I was trying to cover up my face to protect myself."

"It doesn't look like you have done a good job, have you?" He laughed. Then immediately, "I'm sorry that was uncalled for. My sympathies. I can understand how it must have happened.

Unfortunately we don't have any leads to go on. Even the guy who reported seeing you on the floor of the car park to the club bouncer has scarpered without leaving any names. No one seems to have seen you being attacked. It was lucky someone did come when they did, otherwise it could have been a lot worse." Mick said.

He kept asking the same questions from different angle for a long time. The answer was always the same "I don't know." The guy sitting next to Mick, who was furiously scribbling something in a notebook as they spoke and never said a word throughout the interview.

In the end, Mick stood up and said,

"Well. I might as well be off then. I will let you know if we turn up anything. Bill Wardle here who has been scribbling while we talked will bring the statement back for you to have a look tomorrow and if you agree, sign it for us, will you?" He started to walk away without waiting for a reply and suddenly turned back and gave Dev a card. "This is the phone number you can get me on if you remember anything. Any little thing at all."

Mick Mills opened the door of the ward on his way out and turned around to speak to him again,

"One word of advice. The Quebec is not a place to be on your own that late at night."

The two of them had left leaving Dev exhausted. He fell asleep, only to be woken up by Sheena standing next to him. It was already the evening visiting hours. He was quite shocked to see her there. He tried to sit up and collapsed back onto bed wincing with pain. She immediately leaned forward and touched his hands.

"Don's strain yourself please."

"I am sorry. How did you know I was here?"

"You have made the headlines in the local newspapers last night." She replied.

"I think it was partly my own fault." Dev said.

"You trying to help other people will get you killed one of these days. The papers say that you were at this club helping young Asian Gay boys?"

Dev didn't know what to say. He was torn between the strong feelings he had for her and the waves of urges he felt when he was in the presence of young boys. Not necessarily Asian. He found conversation difficult initially, but soon started to ease off as Sheena kept chattering away completely oblivious to his reticence. He soon forgot the pain and the injuries and the Quebec and even Sanju. She sat with him chatting away for nearly an hour and he felt lonely as soon as she said good bye.

He was torn between the deep love he felt for her and his desire for the young boys. He would have to give up "poppers" too if he married Sheena, he thought. 'Would it be worth it? How would I get my buzz otherwise?'

Dev was in the hospital for two more days before being released home. It took him a few months to recover from the fractured ribs. His face was bruised with two large black eyes which nearly closed his eyes for several weeks. The black eye lasted a couple of weeks and it was nearly three months before the bruises on the face disappeared. It was painful to eat as his jaw hurt every time he tried to chew anything. Breathing was painful and he had an agonising pain whenever he coughed. He did not get out of the house for over a month and was nursed by his elderly mother who fussed around him almost constantly.

Stuart came to visit him in the hospital the day after he was attacked and said he will let the Council know and arranged for a sick note from his doctor to be sent to the Council. Stuart looked down at a battered Dev and smiled a sardonic smile as if to say *'I told you so.'*

"I know, you warned me before." Dev said with a weak smile, which looked more like a grimace. "But they were not the mafia you keep telling me about. They were Asian men who kept swearing at me for being what I am."

"You were lucky this time then. Once the mafia get involved, you can be in real trouble." Stuart still looked concerned. "At the rate you are going, it won't be long before they do. You should seriously think of giving it up. Stick to telephone advice from now on. You have enough on your plate with the temple and the work at the Social services."

Dev promised Stuart that he would think about it. He did not go to the temple for a couple of months. It would have been too hard to explain the black eye and bruises on his face to all the devotees.

THE SUITS

Sean shook his head for the tenth time. The headaches would not go away. He had been popping pills all morning like smarties and they didn't seem to be touching him. The night before was a blur. He was as sober as a judge when he entered the pub around ten the night before. He had been sitting at the bar nursing a whisky when this girl had accosted him. She was good looking in a sort of brash earthy girl sort of way. Her dark haired and an olive skinned face had seen the world. Mediterranean, maybe Italian or Greek descent, he thought.

"Hi sweetheart. Mind if I sit here?" There was no accent to place her properly.

"It's a free country." He had shrugged

"I have seen you here before. Can I buy you a drink?"

He had looked up at this offer. No girl had ever offered to buy him a drink. He was not what you would call a young handsome hunk. Far from it. He was middle aged, nearing 40 and wearing a dishevelled shirt, with rumpled jeans and scuffed shoes. Unshaven stubble gave him an unkempt look, but a rugged one. The dark jacket he was wearing had seen better days. He was not an attractive proposition at the best of times. He always appeared to have blood shot eyes even when he was sober.

"Excuse me?" He replied.

"It looks like you could use a drink." She replied with a smile not reaching her eyes. "You have been sat with that empty glass for the last twenty minutes."

He looked at his glass. True enough. It was empty. Just like his life, he thought. He will be forty this year and what does he have to show for it? A career as a detective inspector not going anywhere, a string of failed relationships and a mortgage he can't keep up with. An accidental fling with crack had turned into an expensive habit which he couldn't shake off and was now threatening to cost his job.

"You are right. It is OK. I will get another. Can I get you drink?"

He replied signalling the barman.

"I will have a lime and lager please. Thank you."

She looked quite attractive when she smiled. One drink led to another and finally they had both staggered back to his flat well after midnight. Back at the flat she had produced a little beauty in the form of a brown paper packet - which was the best he had tasted. They had gone at each other like wild cats and he had slumped at the end exhausted into a drug and alcohol induced stupor.

The telephone must have been ringing for a while when he eventually woke up. He fell out of bed trying to find the phone and hit his knee against the table. When he eventually found the phone, it was his chief, Philip Stoker. He wanted him in his office within the hour. Sean did not think he could cope with another grilling by the Detective Superintendent. He was a sour puss if there ever was one. The girl from last night was nowhere to be seen in the morning. He quickly checked to make sure his wallet was still in his jacket pocket and was quite surprised to find that it was still there.

"Is that you Sean? Where the hell have you been? It is nearly lunch time now." Philip had yelled at him on the phone. Exaggerating as usual. It was only eleven in the morning. "I can't see your report on the drug heist from last week. Where is it? Don't tell me you have not done it?"

He was like an express train once he started. He wouldn't give a guy chance to respond.

"Yes, Philip. I have already done it. It's with me. I will bring it over straight away."

Both of them knew he was lying. The last drug heist was five days ago and they had caught two of the members of the gang with a decent haul of crack. They turned out to be small fry and there was no sign of the leaders of the gang. They had known about the gang operating in Leicester around several clubs and even some schools now for a while. The police were struggling to find anything constructive so far. This was the first arrest they have had for months and it was not big either. The cache was in loose brown sachets ready for distribution. It was too tempting not to slip a couple of sachets in his trousers. He had just hoped that the few in his trousers will not be noticed in the count. Rest of the team was too busy restraining the gang who had put up a good fight. While they were being bundled into the vans, Sean and his assistant Bill were "tidying up" in the kitchen of the house where they had found the stash behind the fridge. Sean had to take the stuff down to the lab for the forensic guys to finish off the examination. Well, that was five days ago and he was still trying to figure out a way of hiding the fact that he had spent ten minutes on his own after everyone had left the house.

There was no time to shave now, he thought. It did not take him long to put on a "fresh" pair of shorts and wash the sleep off his face. The bundle of papers he had worked on the day before were still inside the top shelf of the bedside cabinet where he had shoved them previous night. He quickly grabbed the sheaf of papers and dashed out of the apartment. He was in Philip's office in less than half an hour. He did not want him to get any more irritated than he already was by being late. He had to wait outside the door for a while as Philip was busy with the Internal Audit guys. That is not good news, Sean thought. There were sniggers from the girls at the desks typing away reports when they saw a dishevelled Sean walk in.

The two dark suited guys walked out of the door as he walked into Philip's office. They looked at him and nodded their heads without so much of an eye contact. *'No wonder they are always so shifty'* thought Sean. *'Buggers go around digging dirt on everyone. I don't know how they sleep at night. Bastards!'*

"You took your bloody time, Sean." Philip was still in a foul mood. "The Internals are sitting on my neck. They think there is something fishy about the drug heist last week, which hit the headlines. I am not too impressed either."

"I have everything here chief. It was a straight forward hit. We got the tip off from our usual guy." Sean said throwing the sheaf of papers on Philip's desk. "We got all of the guys in the house. I don't know what they are griping about. You can never please the buggers."

"And that is another thing. You have become a tad too friendly with this informant of yours." Philip looked up staring at Sean's eyes. "That has got a few tongues wagging. Is there something you want to tell me Sean?"

"No chief. There is nothing, I tell you." He loosened his collar and a bead of sweat started to appear on his forehead. "It is just rumours. Some people just don't like me, that's all."

"How come no one has seen this guy or girl then?"

"He is too shy chief. You know how it is." Sean was getting more uncomfortable. "You must have come across these kind of guys during your time in the field?"

That was a dig at Philip and he knew it. It was big chip on a few people's shoulders as Philip had not come up the ranks. He was a college boy who had made it big without ever being on the streets. He tried to use swear words in almost every sentence as if to say he was one of the boys. And it did not sound right coming from his mouth. An Oxford white shirt and dark blue tie, looking immaculate as ever in a dark suit – well it did not somehow go with swear words. Philip stared at him as if to say *'Watch it, you are on thin ice here.'*

"That is beside the point." Philip continued. "But the internals want him or her identified and recorded. Otherwise the supplies will stop."

He was talking about the doses of crack and sometimes junk too, Sean was using as a bait to get information from his contact. There was suspicion that not all of the supply reached the contact.

"Don't do that. I am so close to getting at the big fish, the supplier himself." Sean said with some alarm. "Just give me a few more days Philip. I don't want to scare him off after all this hard work."

"End of the week, Sean. That is it. No more time." Philip went back to the sheaf of papers Sean had thrown on the desk as a sign of dismissal. "And then the internals will throw the book at you. Now get out, I have work to do."

Sean went back to his desk deep in thought. He tried to make some phone calls from his desk to trace the guy with no luck. He knew the contact would not pick up the phone if he did not recognise the number. *'I better get outside and use my mobile to get him,'* he thought. As he was walking out of the office, he could hear the sniggers and snide remarks.

"Had enough of the office, Sean." "Been working hard, Sean." "Don't work too hard Sean."

"Love you too, stuff the lot of you." He had shouted as he slammed the office door. A roar of laughter was not really muffled by the door as he walked down the long corridor towards the stairs. He needed the fresh air outside to clear his head a bit before speaking to the contact. The contact he knew only as Johnny was about to spill the beans about the big drug dealer who was supplying the Leicester market if he played his cards right. He had indicated a big drop off soon and the main guy was expected to be with the consignment. It would be the biggest catch of his career and probably the biggest catch of the department if he could pull it off. He did not want it to be jeopardised by the loony internal bastards. Not when he was so close to the bust. He went to the back of the building where the smokers hid. Johnny answered after the third call.

"What do you want?" The voice was gruff on the phone. "I told you not to call me."

"Take it easy Johnny." Sean tried to sound light. "You have not called me for weeks."

"That was a nasty stunt you pulled last week." Johnny sounded annoyed. "You didn't tell me the coppers would beat up my mates? One of them has bruises all over."

"Part of the trade that Johnny. You know the game. You knew that might happen." Sean tried not to sound too contrived. "But we have a couple of young guys who are bit over enthusiastic. It won't happen again, I promise you."

"It is not going to happen again, because you are not going to get anymore shit out of me, no more."

"Come on Johnny. Don't be like that. Where will you get the premium cuts if you don't? I get you the best there is."

"I can do without your premium bloody cuts." Johnny was nearly shouting on the phone. "You are going to get me killed."

It took all of Sean's persuasive powers to calm him down.

"Look I have two shots of the specials with me right now. I will let you have it for old time sake."

"Why would you do that?" Johnny sounded suspicious. "You are not going to get no more info from me. I don't want to be killed."

"Nothing is going to happen, I promise you." Sean insisted. "Come and get the specials tonight. You won't regret it."

It took a lot of persuasion to get Johnny to meet him that night. Sean was not sure if someone was following him as he left the apartment. Heavy clouds with a drizzle made it darker than usual and the visibility was poor. It suited Sean just right. He thought he saw the same set of car lights behind him a few times. By the time he reached The Swan, his favourite pub since moving into Leicester, he was certain that he was being followed. He stopped the car in the pub car park and switched the engine off. He sat there for a few minutes ostensibly looking for something on the floor of the car. The drizzle had turned into a steady rain and it was difficult to see.

After a few minutes a black car drove into the car park and parked at the far end of it. Two guys in dark suits got out and entered the pub. Sean could just make out a third guy sitting in the back seat only because of the cigarette he was smoking inside the car. Guys in dark suits are not the normal clientele in that pub. He started to sweat under the collar. Who were these guys? Internals? Or a rival gang? He has to ditch them somehow or Johnny would flip and that would be the end of his chance and the end of any chance of promotion.

He got out of the car, pulled the collar of his jacket around his neck and sauntered into the pub. It was quite dark inside and was already quite full. Dark oak panelling stained darker by countless years of smokers and dull lighting with musty coloured glass shades did very little to brighten the place. That suited the clientele as well as the landlord. No one looked at him as he entered the pub. He went straight to the bar and sat on the stool. He knew the landlady quite well as he was one of the regulars.

"What will you have sweetheart? I had not seen you here for a while." She came around to him with a smile on her face.

"You know how it is Daisy. Work keeps me busy." He said adjusting himself on the bar stool. "Can I have a pint of bitter please?"

"Don't tell me you started to go to that dump, Duck and Deer?" Daisy said as she pulled the pint.

"No Daisy. That is not my style."

He had been frequenting the pub since he moved into Leicester from Belfast all those years ago. It was the closest he could find to an Irish pub, which was the only thing he missed from leaving Belfast. He was seconded from Ulster constabulary to help bust a drug gang, which was operating out of Belfast and had spread its operations to several cities including Leicester. He was told that it would be for six months. That was nearly twelve years ago and he never went back to Belfast. He liked the quieter pace of Leicester with no bombs going off at regular intervals. He had got on extremely well with Philip Warraker, his liaison officer at Leicester. Philip was impressed with the way Sean dealt with the issues and had recommended the transfer to his unit.

As she got busy with another client, he picked up the pint and looked in the huge expanse of glass on the wall, which formed the back of the bar with bottles of assortment of drinks. He could see almost the entire pub in that glass. It was like watching through a frosted glass with poor lighting. The two suits were sitting near the window by the side of the door. They did not appear to be interested in him by the looks of it. Daisy wiped a non-existent spot on the bar top and placed a bowl of nuts in front of him and said,

"Don't turn around. Do you know those suits sitting near the window?"

"Why do you ask?"

"They have been around a couple of times asking about you."

"What did they want to know?" Sean started to feel hot under the collar again.

"When was the last time you were here? Who did you meet and such like." Daisy replied without looking at him as she pulled a pint for another customer. "Who are they? I didn't tell them nothing. They look creepy, especially the short weedy one."

"I have no idea who they are Daisy. But I would rather not talk to them right now." His Irish accent became more pronounced when he was stressed. He was beginning to look uncomfortable. *'It must be the Internal bastards,'* he thought. "Is there a back door I can get out of?"

"Finish your drink. I will go unlock the back door. It is down the corridor on the left side after the men's." She said picking up the pint and wiping the bar with cloth. "Don't leave till you see me coming back."

She moved to the other end of the bar and gave the drink to a giggling blonde who obviously already had one too many. She turned to the other bartender and said,

"Be back in a sec. Just going to the ladies."

Sean kept staring at the reflection of the two guys in the glass. One of them had turned around to look in Sean's direction. The second guy said something to him and there appeared to be a hushed discussion with heads bent. Sean noticed Daisy coming back into the bar in the corner of his eyes. He gulped his drink down and casually stood up and wandered towards door leading to the toilets. The two suits stopped their talk and but did not turn around. He could still see them through the stained mirror on the back wall. Sean went out of the side door and quickly walked past the men's into the dark corridor. He could not hear any footsteps following him. The back door was open as Daisy had said. Luckily it did not make any noise as he walked out. He found himself in the alleyway leading to the main street away from the car park. He started to walk towards the road and looked on either side as he reached the corner. There was not soul in sight as he walked towards the derelict warehouse where he was supposed to meet Johnny.

He kept looking over his shoulder as he deliberately took the long way round to the warehouse. He was sweating under the jacket despite being wet and cold by the time he reached the warehouse. Nobody followed him as he entered the warehouse compound through a broken gate. It was pitch black, but he knew his way around quite well by now. He walked round to the back of the warehouse where he knew the door was missing. As he entered the warehouse he could not see or hear anything. He stood there at the door for a couple of minutes to get his bearings before moving inside. He knew whoever was inside could see his silhouette in the door from the light outside. He walked towards the far right corner where the old glass fronted office was. Johnny would be there if he was going to come. He went inside the office peering in to see if he could make out anything. Nothing. He waited for what he thought was an hour. '*The bugger is not coming.*' He swore under his breath and turned around to leave, when he heard a match strike.

"Are you leaving Sean?"

Sean recognised Johnny's voice and turned around. He could see Johnny lighting a cigarette in the corner.

"You gave me a fright Johnny. What are you playing at?" Sean sounded annoyed. "I have been standing here for an hour."

"No, you haven't. I saw you coming in." Johnny replied. "I just wanted to make sure you were not being followed. Now, where is the stuff you promised?"

He took the little packet Sean gave and felt for the contents.

"It better be the specials!"

"It is the best there is Johnny. I am taking a huge risk bringing it to you. The Internal bastards are after my skin and if they catch me with it, it is curtains for me."

"That is your headache mister. Not mine." And he walked towards the door. Sean put his hand out to stop him and said,

"Come on Johnny. Don't leave me empty handed. I have been good to you, haven't I? I got you the best, straight from the stores."

Johnny slipped a piece of paper into Sean's hands saying, "This is the last time you will see me. Don't call me again."

"Don't give me that nonsense Johnny. You know I can pull you in and let the boys work on you.

Sean could see Johnny's stained teeth in the darkness as he smiled.

"You wouldn't do that, would you Sean. You are in this as much as I am. You know it would be curtains for you too if you did that. I am not a fool Sean. You know that."

"You will get your reward once we catch the gang leaders."

Johnny laughed out loud before answering.

"Best of luck with that Sean. It needs bigger guns than your pitiful police force. You have no idea what you are dealing with here."

"We will see about that when time comes. Anyway, what is this you have given me?"

"It is a phone number and if you play your cards right, he might take you to the guy running the operation here."

"What do you mean? Is this racket run from outside?"

"You will find out from the guy if he wants to talk to you." Johnny could not hide his irritation. "I can't do any better than that. He might talk to you or he might break your neck."

Before Sean could reply he was walking out of the office. Sean could hear his muffled footsteps down the empty warehouse and briefly see his silhouette as he walked out through the missing door.

Sean lit a cigarette and finished his smoke before walking out of the warehouse. When he reached the pub car park, the three suits were near his car peering into it and one of them was on his mobile speaking to someone. He stood behind the wall of the car park and watched to see what they would do. The guys were shining a torch inside the car and one of them even tried the door to see if it was locked. The conversations was obviously not going very well as the only thing he was saying was,

"I am sorry boss. It won't happen again" Repeatedly. He switched the phone off as soon as he saw Sean walk into the car park. He nudged the other guy who had his nose to the car window.

"Can I help you guys?" Sean said as he walked up to the car. "What are you doing with my car?"

The three of them stood up straight and tried to look officious. Sean recognised two of them from the morning, coming out of Philip's office. The thin weedy guy came forward and said,

"You Sean O'Connor?"

"Who wants to know?"

"I am Matt Henderson of Internal Audit." He replied flashing his badge in his wallet. "This is Andrew Kirby and Ed Miller. We would like to have a word with you."

"What about? And what are you doing with my car?" Sean sounded irritated.

"We just want to talk to you about a few things." Matt replied. "Can we go someplace quiet?"

"Why? Can I see some ID first?"

The three of them fished out their ID badges from their pockets and flashed them in front of Sean. A cursory glance showed them to be from the Internal Audit of Leicester police.

"Have you been following me? Does Philip know what you guys are up to?"

"We have been worried about some of your reports and recent strikes. We just want to clarify a few things."

"Like what? I have nothing to hide. If you have read the reports, you will know there is nothing wrong in them." Sean was really annoyed now.

"I think it is better if we sit down someplace and you answer some simple questions."

"You can come around to the office tomorrow and we can have a chat in front of Philip then." Sean said opening his car. "Now, if you will excuse me, I have had a busy day. I want to go home."

He slammed the door shut before they could say anything and gunned the car. Luckily for him the clapped out car started at the first turn of the key. There was nothing the three suits could do as they saw Sean drive out of the car park with his heart pounding. Sean could see them staring at the back of his car in his mirror. He had to fight an impulse to press on the accelerator. He was sweating profusely by the time he turned the corner and into the slip road up on to the dual carriageway. He could not relax until he was couple of miles down the dual carriageway and was sure no one was following him. He parked his car outside his flats and took the piece of paper that Johnny had given him. He could make out a mobile number with no name. He pulled out his mobile and called the number. It was picked up at the first ring.

"Yeah."

A gruff voice said. Too short to make out an accent.

"Johnny gave me your number. I am Sean O'Connor. Can we meet up somewhere?"

"No. You can't meet me."

"I can be very useful to you and I can be very discrete,"

There was laughter at the other end.

"No, you can't. Don't kid yourself. The guys you are looking for eat kids like you for breakfast."

It had been a long time since anyone had called him a kid. Definitely not English, Sean thought. It is the way he said 'kid.' Maybe one of the European, either French or Italian. It had a soft end to the K.

"That would be my problem, wouldn't it?" Sean replied not to be outdone. "Are you going to help me or not? Johnny said you would."

"Jonny should learn to keep his mouth shut if he knows what is good for him."

Sean did not reply for a minute.

"Are you still there?" The guy asked.

"Yeah, I am still here."

"Well if you want to get killed, go to the warehouse no 17 at the Silver link industrial estate around ten at night day the after tomorrow. Wait for a truck with Spanish plates to turn up." There was a click on line and went dead. Sean looked at his phone and wondered if this was a genuine tip off or a trap. He got out of the car and walked inside the dinghy flat. It was dark despite all the light being switched on – a legacy of going out with a girl who was into gothic designs and colours for a few months. He called Philip Stoker and let him know about the info about the next supplies drop from Belfast.

It did not go very well. The guys were expecting them and it was lucky that the police got away with just injuries and not deaths. The police force under the control of Philip Stoker did not stand a chance. What stuck Sean was the kind of firepower they had. There was no match to the semi-automatic guns the police had.

It was a fiasco for everyone to forget. As expected Sean got the blame for leading the police force into a trap. There was increasing pressure on Philip to repatriate Sean back to Ulster Constabulary and the start of troubles for Sean.

SEAN

Sean had made an effort to make himself look presentable. A clean shave to get rid of the week old stubble and a clean shirt did make a difference to his appearance somewhat. He had spent the night before going over the previous strikes and his reports with a fine toothcomb. The habit of keeping copies of all his reports at home had paid off. He would spend hours filing private copies of his reports and logging them in his computer at home. This had caused a fair amount of friction in his social life and was responsible for the breakdown of at least one of the relationships he had been in.

"You are married to your work. You don't need a home. You don't care what happens to me. I don't know why I even bother with you."

Lucy had screamed at him when she found him again buried under papers in front of his laptop. She had spent most of the evening dolling herself up to go out. They had been together for over a year now. It was all hunky dory to start with and Sean had taken her out regularly to wine and dine. They had done the usual run of the shows and clubs. He would make an effort to dress himself up and even joined Ballroom dancing classes. Sex was magical and both would enjoy each other after a night out dancing regularly.

But when a new case came on with good leads, he immersed himself in work again and the evenings out became once a week at best. He was too tired at night and sex became a routine for him. Lucy would do her best to entice him by dressing up. But he would be too busy with his papers to be interested.

"That is not true." Sean had said closing the laptop and pushing the papers away from him. "You know I love you and I would do anything for you."

There was no conviction in his eyes as he smiled.

"You don't love anyone. I have gone to a lot of effort to dress up for you and you have not even looked at me once." She said with one hand on her hip.

"That is not true. You look beautiful babe. Is that a new dress?" He said standing up. "Come here, I will show you how much you mean to me."

He tried to put his arms around her and kiss her. She pushed him away and turned towards the window.

"That is all you want nowadays. Just sex." There was bitterness in her voice. "Every night is the same. Wham bam thank you ma'am. That too, when it pleases you."

"You are exaggerating Lucy babe." Sean started to panic as he found the pattern repeating. He did not want to lose her like his other girlfriends. "Just give me two minutes and I will be ready."

They had gone out and he had made a real effort to please her. He tried to spend more time with her to rekindle the romance. But it was no use. As the cases progressed he found that he was coming home late and spending a lot of time in front of his laptop at home too. Lucy tried her best to make the relationship work. She pleaded with him, shouted at him and threatened to leave him. He would change back to the old Sean for a few days and even that became less frequent. Finally, like the previous girlfriends, she too had stormed out of the apartment. She was his last girlfriend and he had thought he had found his life partner. After that, his life had become work mixed with numerous one-night stands, drink, smoke and over the past year, Crack.

Now, the whole thing appeared to be falling apart around his ears. He had never thought that he would ever be in a situation to be investigated by the internals. He knew he was bloody good at his work and it was only time before he would be made a Detective Chief Inspector.

Until recently, everyone respected him and his work. Philip would call him for the hardest cases as he knew Sean would get results. There were several in the force who wanted to pull him down. He had not let his habit of using drugs affect his work. Some of the new guys in the department did not like his style of work. Sean would not share his informants with anyone. And he had numerous contacts, not just in Leicester but in several other cities including London.

'I am sure Brennan and Joyce put the internals up to this.' He thought to himself as he gathered his papers and notes. *'I will show the buggers. I have nothing to hide.'*

The girls in the office glanced at him as he walked past them to Philip's office and there were whispers he could not hear as he opened the door. The three suits from the night before were already in the office as he entered. The thin weedy guy who had called himself Matt Henderson, was sitting in front of Philip's desk. The other two guys were standing against the wall with folded hands with expressionless faces. Philip looked up as he stood at the open door.

"Come in Sean." Philip said with an uneasy expression on his face. "I believe you have met Matt and his colleagues."

"Yes, I have Philip, and very nice people too." Sean said with an undisguised sarcasm.

"I must say that what you did was highly irregular, Mr Henderson. I am not used to my officers being accosted in car parks without my knowledge." Philip said looking at Matt. "How dare you go and question my officers without my permission?"

The weedy guy smiled and said,

"I am sorry about last night, Philip. But, can I point out I don't need your permission to question anyone. We were just doing our job."

"You never said anything about questioning Sean without me being present yesterday." Philip sounded annoyed. "I told you that any interviews you want to do have to be here in my office. The guy you are questioning is one of my most senior officers and is well respected in the force. You had no right to treat him like a crook. I will not stand for it."

Sean was quite surprised and a little touched by that. He had not realised that Philip held such a high opinion of him.

"We are just doing our jobs you know Philip. Just like you." Matt replied. "If you had a clean department, none of us would be here to start with." There was a snigger in his voice and a look of triumph.

"Don't give me that crap. I run as clean a department as any in the force. I've got a good mind to speak to the commissioner about all of this nonsense."

"Why don't you do that then Philip? You will see it's come from the top." Matt was daring Philip to do something, which both knew was not going to happen. Turning to Sean, he continued, "It's in your own interests to cooperate Sean. If you think you haven't done anything wrong, there's nothing for you to worry about."

"I haven't done anything wrong. You have all my reports with you." Sean replied.

"Let's get started then. Sooner we start sooner we can finish."

"Come on Sean, let's get this over with. I don't think you have anything to worry about. It's all a storm in a tea cup. We will go to the conference room. It's already set up." Philip said getting out of his chair. Everyone trooped out to the big conference room at the back corner of the police station. Sean could feel everyone's eyes boring into him as he walked past through the office. He heard a couple say, "Good luck, Sean" and "Give them hell, Sean." Sean just nodded his acknowledgement in response with a wry smile on his face. He was not sure where this was heading yet.

There was a large table at one end of the room with three chairs and one chair to the left of it and another across it. The three suits sat at the top of the table with Philip on one side and Sean sitting across the table. It looked more like a hearing rather than an interview. Their brief cases were full of sheaves of papers, which they took out and Sean could recognize some of his reports. Matt arranged them neatly in front of him and the other two were busy with their own papers. Sean could not see what papers they had in front of them.

Questioning began in earnest once Matt was satisfied he had everything in place and a writing pad and pencil. The other two guys also had their own writing pads. Kirby, the short squat one sat nibbling at his pencil almost throughout the interview. Matt went through Sean's reports one by one. He would pick a section in a report and ask Sean about it and all the three would write furiously for a minute before something else next. Matt gave Sean a few pages at the start.

"These are copies of some of the reports we will be going through." Matt said. "Can you just check them and confirm that they are your reports please?"

Sean glanced through the sheets of paper in front of him. They appeared to be random sheets from his reports, some of them going back to the 90's. He could recognize his work quite easily.

"They look like my reports. But it will take me some time to go through them to make sure they are all mine."

"Take my word for it. They are all your reports." Matt replied.

"If you say so." A hint of sarcasm in Sean's voice did not go unnoticed.

"Let me take you to this report on as drug heist you lead on Mowmacre area."

Sean rustled through the papers to find the papers Matt was talking about. He remembered the heist very well.

It was the first time Sean had met his contact, Johnny. It was not one of the big ones. They had found a few packets of crack at a tenement block south of the canal. He had a tip off about guys doling out the drugs near a school. He had gone on his own at first to check it out. He had parked his car around the corner of the school in a supermarket car park. He walked slowly towards the school when he noticed a group of kids on pushbikes hanging around the corner of the street just outside a newsagent's. Nothing unusual about that at lunchtime of school. A stocky guy in an anorak caught his attention. 'It's middle of July. Too hot to be wearing an anorak!' He walked towards the group unhurriedly with head bent down. The kids saw him coming and took off in the opposite direction. The stocky guy walked into the shop. Sean had followed him into the shop and bought a packet of cigarettes. As he was paying for the cigarettes, that stocky guy had walked out of the shop. Sean did not wait for the change and had shot out of the shop only to see him get into a battered old Mini and drive off. Sean had run back to the car with a hope of catching up. It was too late. By the time he could get his car going, the Mini was nowhere to be seen.

"Shit! I have lost him." He cursed to himself and started to cruise around the block a couple of times. Just when he was about to give up, he caught a glimpse of the red Mini parked in the alleyway behind the school facing away from him. He stopped his car and reversed into the driveway of a nearby house. He got out of the car and left the door open to walk across to the alleyway. He kept to the shadows of the huge Plane trees that lined the street and got behind the tree at the corner. He could see the Mini clearly from where he stood. There was no one in the car. It looked as if it was deserted. He waited for what seemed to be a long time. There was no activity. The street was completely deserted apart from him and the red Mini. He walked across to the car to take a closer look. It was a ten year old car, with large dents on the side and back. It was beginning to rust at the edges and wheel arch was nearly falling down. The

shadow of the huge Plane tree made it difficult to see inside the car. He peered through the window only to see the passenger seat littered with empty soda cans, crisp packets and a dirt rag. There was an old canvas duffel bag on the back seat, which had seen better days. The zip was obviously broken and contents spilling out. He was trying to squint to see the contents when there was a tap on his shoulder.

"What are you doing with my car?"

Sean pulled up slowly and turned around to see the stocky man growling at him. He looked unkempt with a dark blue anorak, thread bare at the edges and stains over the front. Sean could see his nicotine stained hands tremble as he spoke.

"Is this your car?"

"Yeah, it's mine. What of it? Who wants to know?"

Sean took his badge out and stuck in front of his face.

"I just want to ask a few questions."

"Why? I haven't done nuthing wrong."

"I didn't say you had." Sean smiled "What were you doing with the kids from the school?"

"I tell you. I done nuthing wrong."

He was getting a bit belligerent now.

"Well. Suit yourself." Sean said, still with a smile on his face. "You can either have a friendly chat with me here or we can all go down to the station and you can talk to the gaffer."

"You can't make me go anywhere."

"Want to bet on that my friend?"

"I was talking to the kids. Nuthing wrong in that, is there?"

"I didn't say there was. What were you talking about?"

"This and that. Nuthing that would interest you."

"Try me. I am interested in everything." Sean said. The smile had disappeared off his face now.

"I got a kid in the same school."

"No. You don't." The rasp in Sean's voice made him jump. "Let's start again. What are you called?"

"Johnny Marsden."

"That wasn't too difficult, was it Johnny?" Sean said, still with a rasp. "Now, Johnny. We both know what you were doing there in front of the shop. We both know if I search you now, what we will find, don't we?"

He started to shuffle his feet and the surly expression on his face deepened.

"What do you mean?"

"Stop playing with me Johnny. You know exactly what I mean."

"I'm not playing with you. I done nothing wrong." The surly voice was barely audible.

"Speak up Johnny. I can't hear you." Sean softened his voice and continued with his hand on Johnny's shoulder. "Now, look. We can be useful to each other. You play ball with me and I see that you are all right. Come on. Let's go for a drive to the canal. We can have a quiet chat in my car."

Johnny looked at him without speaking for a long time.

"Come on Johnny. I haven't got all day." His hands pushed on Johnny's shoulder gently. He started to walk reluctantly in the direction Sean's car. They had driven to the woods near the canal and parked in an isolated spot. Neither of them had said a word while driving for a few minutes. Johnny had started without more persuasion and told Sean everything. It turned out he was only a pusher to a guy he had never seen before. The transactions always took place in a barber shop on Mowmacre hill. He claimed he had never seen the guy. For someone who was reticent to say even his name, Johnny was full of information once inside Sean's car. He stopped talking once they reached the canal.

“That is much better now Johnny. You know you can rot in jail for years for what you are doing?” Sean said as he switched the engine off. “I don’t want to send you to prison. You help me catch this boss man and I’ll make sure no one will touch you.”

“I don’t know how I can. I have never seen the guy. The first time I met him was at the Central Motors and didn’t see him properly as it was dark.”

“Don’t give me that shit, Johnny. I know you can find out who he is if you want to.” Sean retorted. “I bet you already know who he is.”

“I really don’t know. Why would I lie to you?” His voice was a shrill by now. Sean could see that he was sweating under the anorak.

“If I find out if you are Johnny, you’ll be in trouble. I’ll throw you in the nick before you can say Mama.”

“You sure, you can keep me out of trouble if I help you?”

“You bet your ass, I can.”

Johnny didn’t say anything for a minute and turned to Sean. “I’ll try to find out. But I don’t want you sniffing around. He will kill me if he finds out. I heard he bumped off the last pusher for speaking to his girlfriend about it.”

“It will be a lot worse if I find out you are lying to me Johnny. Death would be a welcome option for you if you cross me.”

The message hit home. The fear on Johnny’s face was palpable. Sweat pouring down his forehead and cheeks now. Sean could see his hands shaking. He gave Johnny his mobile number where he could get hold of with any info and he had literally ran out of the car at the end. Johnny had given him an address in Mowmacre hill where the drug squad had managed to arrest a couple of guys with a small stash of crack. The relationship with Johnny had blossomed over the months and Sean was getting decent information for him, which had led to a couple of arrests. But always small fry, never the leaders.

"You have been looking at that paper for a long time, Sean." Sean could hear the voice of Matt Henderson. "What is the matter? Can't you remember the case?"

Sean was jerked back to reality with Matt's gruff voice.

"Yes, I certainly do. I was tipped off by my contact which led to the arrest of two of the drug pushers and a stash of Crack."

"Who is this contact Sean?"

"I am sorry, I can't tell you. It is a personal arrangement. We will lose him if anyone else makes contact or if he even suspects that I have told you about him."

"I don't need to remind you that this Police business and you have to tell us about your contacts and where you get your information from." The thin weedy Matt said.

"No, I don't." Sean was getting irate now. "You are trying to tell me my job. I am good at what I do. Very good, I am telling you. I have had more arrests in one year than many Inspectors do over five."

The two guys looked at each other and there was an imperceptible signal. Kirby picked up another folder and opened a page marked with a yellow tab.

"Let's have a look at this case Sean." His voice belied his size. It was a thin squeaky voice for such a large man. "You were the arresting officer in this case too. You are right about the number of arrests. You grabbed five guys in this job. Can you look at this and see if I am correct?"

Sean leafed through the pages and nodded his head. It was yet another drug heist. He recognised his handwriting, but could not recognise the case. Then he looked at the bottom of the file. The case was back in 1991. It must have been one of his first cases as he was promoted to an Inspector in 1990. He was really flying at the time, always involved in more than one case and his arrest rate was the talk of the department and obviously not everyone liked the limelight he was hogging.

"This is my handwriting alright and it looks like my report."

"We thought so too as you have signed the report." The sarcasm was undisguised. "I am a little troubled by the amount of crack you confiscated in that heist. You have arrested five people in one house and got very little dope to show for it. I would have thought it would have been a big operation if five people were there?"

"It was so long ago. I can't really remember much about it." Then turning to Philip, he continued. "Chief, it is unfair to throw this at my face. This is at least ten years ago. I have done many more in the meantime. How can they expect me to remember it?"

"That is right, Sean." Philip replied and turned to the three suits. "You did not tell me you were going to chase up old cases and ask questions. Sean is right. He does not have to answer any questions to you without the union rep being present."

Sean was a bit surprised at the support he was getting from his boss. Maybe he had been wrong about him all along, he thought. Matt stood up and the other two stood up like automatons and closed their briefcases in perfect unison."

"Well if that is the way you want to play it. It is up to you. We were trying to be friendly and get this done and dusted informally. If you want to take the formal route, you are welcome. I will get the backroom girls to send you a summons."

The three of them had literally stormed out of the office without another word.

"Thanks Chief." Sean said looking some what relieved. "Why are they picking on me?

"I don't know Sean. Are you being straight? You are not hiding anything from me here, are you?"

"No, Philip." Sean replied and pushing some of the papers Matt had left behind on the desk towards Philip, "have a look yourself. There is nothing here."

Philip picked up the papers and glanced at it. It was a routine report of Sean checking the school area for drug pushers and dealers in Mowmacre hill. It was a rather dull routine report about a minor heist. Sean had followed that up with visits to the school on a number of occasions without any luck. They had ignored the follow up reports saying he had not found any sign of any dealers after several visits to the school. This was before Philip was transferred to Leicester.

"I am not really sure what they were getting at in this case." Philip said looking puzzled, still glancing at the pages. "Anyway they will have to produce all the papers of any cases they want to discuss if they want to take it further and make it official. You better speak to the Police Union rep. You let me know if you need any help."

"Thanks chief. I really appreciate your help."

"I don't like my best guy to be crucified by some numbskull pen pushers." Philip said with a smile as they walked out of the conference room back to their offices.

It was not until a few months later a plain brown envelope dropped through Sean's front door rubberstamped from London. He immediately knew what it was before even opening it. His hands shook as he opened the envelope. It was a bland letter informing about the coming hearing with the Internal Audit department. It said the papers would be delivered by hand to him and he is "strongly advised to seek the help of the Police Federation." Sean sat down and read it a couple of more times. It was a single page letter and still took him a while to digest the contents. He had taken the day off claiming sickness and sate down to contact the Police Union guys and arranging appointments.

It was the worst two years of Sean's life. He was dragged through the mill with claims of misappropriation of drugs and mishandling of suspects to name a few of the accusations. The number and strengths of the cases helped him immensely as did references from Philip Stoker and from chiefs of Police from neighbouring police forces he had liaised with in the past.

The Police union had hired a barrister from London to fight his case. He was on "restricted duties" while the case went on. He had to put up with jibes from some of the fellow workers and when the news was published in the local rag, he almost gave up the fight. The utter humiliation he felt made him consider ending his life on more than one occasion. It was his ex-girlfriend Lucy who pulled him through his troubled years until he started to get deeper and regular with his crack and drink habit. She came with him to London for all the hearings during the first year. This did give him a moral boost. There were occasions when he would get irrational and behave badly. When he started to get repeatedly abusive, she stopped accompanying him. He was left with lonely trips to London. A combination of stress, drugs and alcohol took their toll on him. He came close to crashing his car on the M1 motorway a couple of times and he was forced to use the train.

The panel did not find him guilty of misappropriation of drugs or misuse of the suspects, but they concluded that his methods were unorthodox and he had to undergo counselling as well as more training. That left him with spending some time up in Newcastle with their training centre for three months. It was utterly humiliating to take lessons from officers ten years younger than him with less than half his experience and knowledge. He had to bite his tongue and take it on his chin. His biggest regret was losing Lucy again from his life. He was quite sure she would not come back to him the way he had treated her.

He came back to find that he was moved to homicide, which was a much smaller unit. He was pleasantly surprised to see that Philip Stoker was leading the Homicide team too. The fact that he had supported Sean during his trial might have had something to do with the transfer out of Drug squad. Everyone had heard of Sean's trial and most of them thought it won't be long before Sean was kicked out of the force altogether.

SHEENA

It took Dev many months to recover from his injuries. His father had decided that it was better to get him 'married and settled soon.'

"I think one ~~of~~ way of stopping Dev going away at night is to get him married." His elder brother Kishen had said one day soon after the attack on Dev, which had been covered on all the local dailies.

"With his name in the news, it will be hard to find a good bride for him." Ramcharan said with deep sigh. "The police have not been of any use. No one has been caught and Dev can't remember much about the attack."

"He used to be friendly with a girl at the temple. I think he likes her." Kishen replied. "I know he likes her. She is a trainee solicitor and comes from a very good family."

"Have you spoken to him about it?"

"Yes, I have and he is very keen on her." Kishen replied. "I know the family quite well. I can arrange for us to go and see them at home if you want?"

Dev had walked in as they were still discussing the matter.

"I can hear my name being mentioned." Dev said with a smile. "What have I done now?"

"We were indeed talking about you Dev." Kishen said. "I was just telling father about Sheena, the solicitor."

Dev blushed momentarily and did not say anything.

"Kishen was saying that we should meet their family." Ramcharan said. "What do you think son?"

Dev's mind went back to the day he had met Sheena for the first time. Meeting Sheena, was the highlight of Dev's life couple of years ago. She had come to the temple with her mom for one of the big functions during Diwali. She was enthusiastic and came into one of the back rooms to help with the work along with several of the volunteers. The two of them had hit it off from the beginning. Dev could remember the day he met her vividly. He was carrying a box full of fruits and sweets rather precariously balanced on both his arms across the temple hall. He could see one of the sweet boxes starting to slide off the top. He looked desperately around to see if anyone was around to help. Having seen no one, he was about to drop the whole thing on the floor in an attempt to stop the box of sticky sweets falling off when a hand appeared out of nowhere and steadied the box. He turned to see the most beautiful girl he had seen in his life standing next to him holding the box of sweets in one hand and his left elbow in the other supporting the basket. He noticed how stunning she was in a bright red Ghagra-choli with golden tassels. Her smell nearly overpowered him. He smiled weakly and said,

"Thank you. I didn't want drop the sweets on the floor. It's very sticky."

"I know," She said with a disarming smile. "You are welcome. It would have been messy if it had fallen on the floor."

"I would have had to spend the next couple of hours cleaning it. I am the priest, cleaner, secretary, and general dog's body in this temple!"

Both of them had laughed at this. They got along like a house on fire after that and she became a regular visitor to the temple. Dev would look forward to the Friday evenings he knew she would come from the uni. He would forget Sanju and Quebec when he was with her. His visits to the Quebec became all too infrequent. Stuart had commented on that with,

"You have become henpecked already! You are not even married yet!!"

Both had laughed out loudly and Dev said nothing. Stuart had his doubts about Dev being bisexual and his developing relationship with Sheena. He wanted to ask him if he had told Anajana about Sanju. He kept it to himself and did not say anything. 'Maybe this Sheena might be a good thing for Dev', he had thought.

Soon Dev started to meet Sheena outside the temple for cups of coffee and walks in the park. It didn't go unnoticed by his elder brother Kishen.

"You do like that girl Sheena very much, don't you?"

"Yes, *Bhaiya*. I do." Dev had blushed.

"She comes from a very good family. Do you want me to speak to father about her?"

"I have only met her a few times. I do like her a lot though." Dev had replied. "But I would rather wait until I get the manager's job at the council."

Dev married Sheena the following year. Dev had found a lot of happiness during those years. He would take her out whenever he could and Sheena would come into the temple at the end of her work to help out. She would take part in all the festivals and was next to Dev at all times. People noticed and Dev would swell with pride whenever he overheard commitments such as,

"Such a beautiful couple", "made for each other" and "marriage made in heaven."

They were an ideal couple, seen everywhere together. She would help Dev out in the temple during the busy weekends and soon became part of the temple scene. The only fly in the ointment was his mother's gripe that they did not have any children after two years of marriage. Stuart had noticed that he had completely stopped going to the Quebec and he was quite sure there had been no visits to the care home at lunch time or visits to the Central Motors or the Abbey Park either.

Sheena was a breath of fresh air for Dev. He found himself falling in love with her all over again after the marriage. She was a strong willed woman with a clear mind of her own. She was also a woman of the world. They would discuss his involvement with the gay community and his work with the Gay helpline openly. Discussion about sexual preferences was not a taboo. She was ambiguous when it came to supporting the gay community, which she thought Dev was doing. He never brought up the subject of his own sexuality during those discussions. If she knew about him being Bisexual, she kept it to herself. His visits to the gay clubs, was ostensibly part of his job as a counsellor and she supported him wholeheartedly.

"I never knew that homosexuality was so common among Asians."

Sheena had said one day when there were several phone calls to Dev.

"Asians are same as everyone else. There are the same proportion of gays among Asians as any other race." Dev had smiled nervously.

"I don't think I have ever met a gay Asian person."

Dev laughed and tried to change the subject. "I assure you there are many in Leicester itself. It won't be long before you meet one in the temple. I am sure you must have met some gay people at your office?"

"Yes, I have. But they were mostly young whites."

He was still working as a Residential care officer. The promised vacancy of a Manager's pots was yet to come. The job wasn't much. It was part time working two days a week. He was looking after residential facilities for the disabled population of Leicester. It augmented his meagre income from the temple. He had finally taken over the Care Home on Albert road in partnership with Stuart. It was bringing in a good regular income. His father had by and large retired from the temple leaving the day to running to the three brothers. The grocery shop had been sold a long time ago as they could not spend time in the shop. His younger brother Vijai had just started to work full time in the temple too recently. It meant dividing the income three ways. Dev had moved out to a small terraced house near the union canal, not too far from the temple.

Dev was very content with his life until Sheena commented one day,

"It's time we had a baby. Don't you think?"

It scared him first to think of himself as a father but soon he started to feel a pang whenever he saw a baby being christened in the temple. They tried everything. Followed all sorts of advice from well-wishers, magazines and looked up on the internet too. But there was no sign of any pregnancy.

"We should see the doctor and see if there's anything wrong with either of us." Sheena had said one day. Dev wasn't so sure. He didn't want go down that route.

'What if they find I was impotent?' or 'what if they find I have an illness?'

It had taken a lot of persuasion to get Dev to see the doctor and get a referral to a fertility clinic. He had gone with her to the clinic. The doctor had said that they would have to run some tests on both of them. Dev didn't look forward to the visits to the infertility clinic. It made him feel inadequate and sometimes angry.

Kishen and his wife had moved out of the little house next to the temple with the birth of their second child. When they returned from the house warming ceremony, Sheena whispered to Dev,

"I think we should find a place of our own."

Dev looked at her and smiled.

"You are right. We can rent a house to start with and look for a house later. But this is not the right time to bring it up. Mother would be even more upset than what she is now."

Dev had found a small two bedroom house on Melton road, not too far from the temple to rent. They had moved much to the disappointment of his mother. Ramcharan was more pragmatic.

"I think it is only right that the children find their own feet." He had told Meera Ben. "It is not as if he is going away to a different city or a different country. Remember we left our families and country too when we got married?"

The Care home had picked up significantly with help from his and Stuart's contacts in the council and they were looking for a second Care Home in Milton Keynes to take over. The money was rolling in and Dev did not hesitate in flashing his earnings with new clothes, expensive watch, shoes and bought a brand new silver BMW. He had seen a house on Harrison Road, quite close to the temple, which was in need of a lot of work. The owners had finally put it up for sale after years of neglect. It was much bigger than the little two bedroom rental house they lived at present and it was much closer to the temple.

"This would be a great family home to bring up children." Dev had enthused. Sheena was not too sure when she first saw the derelict state of the house. But when Dev painted a picture of what a beautiful home it could turn into, finally Sheena had agreed and they had celebrated the day when the contracts were exchanged. Both of them would sit on the park bench near the temple and make plans for the future in the new house when it would be ready to move in. It was taking much longer than he had planned and at six months it was still far from being complete much to the chagrin of Dev and unhappiness of Sheena.

Sheena had finished her training and was offered a lucrative job in Leeds. Dev was not sure if it would be good idea for her to go away to Leeds. Especially, as they were still trying to have a baby.

"Are there no good jobs in Leicester?"

"There are very good firms here in Leicester." Sheena had replied. "But there are no openings at present. This is a God send opportunity. People would give anything to get a job with this firm. It is a big firm and the prospects for career progression are excellent."

Dev looked a bit glum as he replied, "Well, if that is what you want to do, I am not going to stop you."

"Please don't be like that. Leeds is not that far?" Sheena said throwing her arms around his neck. "I'll be coming home every Friday night and won't have to go back till Monday morning."

Both of them had driven down to Leeds to look for rental flats and he had helped her pack and do the shopping for the new flat. He had wept the day he had driven her over to leave her at Leeds. He felt utterly lonely on the way back from her new flat and felt completely lost. When he reached Leicester late that night, he drove straight to the Quebec. The car park was in darkness as he parked the car. He sat there for a few minutes without getting out of the car. His mind was in a turmoil. He missed Sheena terribly. There was a huge void in his mind and his heart felt heavy. He kept staring straight ahead at the lights of the club and some people coming in and out of the club without actually registering anything. Finally he got out of the car and pulled his collar up against the biting cold and shoved his hands deep into jacket pocket. He felt something in the left pocket and took it out to see what it was. It was the paper packet Lenny had given him a long time ago. He opened the packet to see a brown plastic bottle with a seal, drop on to the palm of his hand. He had sudden urge to try them. He had seen some men use it at the Quebec before. He went back into the car and switched the ceiling light on. He took the bottle and rolled around with his fingers.

'Should I or should I not?' He slowly unwrapped the seal from the neck of the bottle and opened the cap. There was a sticky liquid inside, more like a paste. A thin smoke came out of the bottle as soon as he opened it with a strong pungent sweet smell. He brought the mouth of the bottle to his nose and smelled it and then in an urge took a deep breath. Something exploded in his head and he could see colourful exploding stars in front of him. His legs were weak and felt himself sliding off the car seat and he dropped the bottle on the floor. He tried to bend down to pick up the bottle when there was another rush of blood to his head. He felt warm, very warm and light headed. It made him somehow happy. It took him to a place where he always wanted to be. The place was peaceful and colourful, loud and quiet, bright and soft. He felt himself floating in the air. He sat there and switched the roof light off inside the car and closed his eyes. He had not felt like this for a long time. He felt as if he could see with his eyes shut. There was an absolutely beautiful figure in dark blue dancing on the bonnet of his car. Bright orange flame formed a backdrop as the figure stooped forward to stare at him through the windscreen. He was not expecting what happened next. The once beautiful face turned into a vicious snarling monster with fire dancing out of its lips with a loud hissing noise. The face blasted through the windscreen and he could feel the fire on his face and made him open his eyes. There was nothing in front of him apart from pitch darkness outside the windscreen as before. He was sweating profusely and his legs still felt very weak. He leant forward and touched the windscreen; it was still intact.

He sat in the car for a long time before daring to get up and out of the car. He thought he might fall down if he stood up. He stood leaning against the car for a minute before daring to step away from the car and walk towards the club. Despite the nightmarish images, he somehow felt good and on top of the world. He met all the old friends and danced away till early hours of the morning. He had used the poppers again and shared it with a beautiful young man while inside the club and thought they were the best thing he had ever tried. The sky was getting light when he finally made it back home.

His trips to the Quebec and the Abbey Park became more regular after that. He would go there after closing the temple two or three times during the week and dance away with poppers till early hours of morning. He missed Sanju. He had looked for him and sent messages with no luck. He would keep looking at the door of the temple every evening hoping Sanju would show up. Once he was engaged to be married to Sheena, their meetings had been few and far between. They had completely stopped once he was married.

Dev felt a void in his life. He missed having Sheena at home and he missed meeting Sanju at the Care Home. Quebec was like an oasis for him at the end of every day. The days he was not needed at the temple were the worst. Coming back to an empty home filled him with a dread. He started visiting 'Central Motors' near Belgrave and Abbey Park to pick up young boys. Stuart knew when he had been out the night before. Dev would drink gallons of coffee throughout the day and pop tablets every couple of hours.

"You are slowly killing yourself, Dev." He said one day when he looked terrible and kept popping paracetamols like smarties and drinking strong coffee out of a flask. "You are burning your candle at both ends. It won't be long before you burn out."

"No. I'm not. I'm fine."

"No. You are not." Stuart would say. "You are popping pills like anything and spending all night at the club drowning yourself in poppers. That can't be doing you any good. I know you visit Central Motors and Abbey Park too. Do you realise you can pick up diseases as well there? That place is full of druggies."

There would be an argument ending in both of them eating lunch in silence. Dev would stop going to the Quebec for a few days. Finally Stuart had given up trying to tell him. Dev became secretive after that and he would not tell Stuart everything as he used to before. He did not tell him about his meeting with Lenny at the place. He had bumped into Lenny late one night at the Central Motors. He was about to enter into the place when Lenny had come out of thick shadows under the flyover.

"Hi Bro. Fancy seeing you here."

Dev was taken aback for a moment before recovering.

"Yes… It's Lenny isn't it?"

"Yeah, it's me alright.

Both of them stood there, not sure what to say next. Finally, Lenny said under his breath.

"I got some junk on me if you want some."

First he didn't understand what he meant. He stared at him for a long time. Lenny repeated his question. He still wouldn't answer. Lenny said with a hint of irritation,

"Do you want it or not?"

Dev had been visiting the Central Motors and the Quebec long enough now to quickly realise what he was selling. It was Heroin.

"Sure. How much do you have?"

"I got two lots. I can give you one. The other one is for a regular customer."

Dev nodded his head and took some cash out of his pocket. The exchange took place before Dev realised what he was doing. He took the brown paper packet which was in his hands and looked at it strangely.

"You used it before, ain't you?" Lenny whispered.

"Yes, of course." And then quickly, "in fact no. Never tried the stuff before."

Lenny looked around furtively and whispered.

"Come to the canal side near Mowmacre hill tonight after midnight. I'll show you."

Before Dev could say thank you, Lenny had disappeared into the night. He tucked the brown paper packet deep in his trousers and walked back to his car. He was rather apprehensive about meeting Lenny that night near the canal. He knew it was not the safest place for anyone during the day, let alone night.

He had reached the canal well before midnight. He had sat in the car with engine and lights switched off in the darkest part of the street he could find. He couldn't see the canal itself from where he had parked with large trees obscuring the view. There was no one at that time of the night on the canal side. An old man passed him walking the dog and took no notice of him. Dev thought it strange to be walking a dog at this time of the night. He kept looking at the watch. Midnight came and went, but there was no sign of Lenny. He waited for another half an hour and decided Lenny was not going to turn up. He was about to switch the engine on when he spotted some movement among the trees along the side of the canal. He quietly wound down the window of the car to take a closer look. Yes, there was certainly someone on the canal bank standing against a tree not moving.

As he watched the figure lit a match and took it close to his face to light a cigarette. There he was. It was Lenny standing there lighting a cigarette. He got out of the car and walked over to the canal bank. He climbed over the short fence to reach the bank and called out softly,

"Lenny. Is that you?"

The figure turned around and stubbed the cigarette out.

"I thought you weren't cumin. What took you so long?" A tinge of irritation in his voice.

"I got here a long time ago and waiting for you in the car." Dev replied.

"OK. Now you are here. Let's get going. Have you got the junk with you?"

Dev reached into his trousers and pulled out the brown paper packet.

Lenny sat down on the grass bank and signalled Dev to do the same. He took out a plastic carrier bag from his jacket and brought out a syringe, needle, candle and steel desert spoon.

There was a thick rubber band in the bag too. He turned to Dev and said,

"Where do you want to take it? Which arm?"

Dev hesitated for a moment and said,

"Why don't I watch how you do it for yourself this time and I can learn for next time?"

"It's yours. You paid for it remember?"

"I know. Think of it as training." Dev laughed a hollow laugh.

"You sure? You don't want to try it?"

"I am quite sure. I want to see you do it first time."

"Suit yourself. It's your money."

He tied the rubber band around his left forearm and clenched his fist. He then poured a white powder on to the spoon and asked Dev to hold the spoon while he lit the candle. He held the candle under the spoon till the powder started to melt into a brownish liquid. He drew the liquid into the syringe and mounted the needle onto the syringe. As Dev watched fascinated, he held the syringe between his teeth, tapped his forearm to get one of the veins prominent. He then expertly slid the needle into the vein in one smooth motion. He had obviously done this many time. He pushed the syringe piston to empty the brown liquid into the vein and pulled out the rubber band and the needle out at the same time. It was all done in a flash. He folded his elbow and put everything back into the plastic bag again before turning to Dev.

"You don't know what you are missing Bro. This is good stuff. I got it straight from the gaffer." He lay down on the grassy bank and closed his eyes.

Dev was not sure what to do next. As there was no sign of Lenny opening his eyes, he was about to stand up and go when Lenny laughed out loud.

"It's funny. Ain't it. You pay the money and I'm having the fun." Dev stopped midway and said.

"That is fine Lenny. You have fun. I'll see you around then."

"Yeah, see you around. You must meet the gaffer. He is a great bloke. He looks after me."

Lenny closed his eyes again and his breathing became shallow and sweat beads appeared on his forehead. His face contorted and became grotesque for a moment before smiling a devilish grin. As Dev watched, he started to snore, a deep sonorous snore and drool started to drip out of the corner of his mouth. Dev left him lying on the canal bank and walked slowly back to the car deep in thought.

THE GAFFER

Lenny did not show up for a couple of months after that brief encounter and Dev had almost forgotten about him until one night, when he materialised out of the darkness in the car park of the Quebec.

"Hi Bro. You keeping alright?" he had said without actually looking at Dev. "I've been waiting here for hours for you."

"Hello Lenny. How are you? I didn't know you were waiting outside. What can I do for you?"

"My gaffer wants to meet you."

"Who is this gaffer? Why does he want to meet me?"

Lenny looked uncomfortable and looked down at his shoes, shuffling his feet.

"I dunno. He wouldn't say. I can take you to him now, if you want." He said with some hesitation.

"I am not sure I want to meet this man, Lenny. I am not really interested." Dev replied.

"Please Bro. You'll be doing me a favour. I'm in a bit of a bother. If you speak to him, it'll get me out."

Lenny looked up. His eyes were bloodshot as if he had been crying. There were bruises on his face and a black eye.

"My god. Looks like you have been beaten up again! What happened to you?"

"It's nothing Bro. I can look after myself. But it'll help if you come and meet my gaffer. He just wants to talk."

Dev hesitated for a while and after a bit more of cajoling from Lenny, he agreed to go with Lenny to meet his "gaffer."

They drove towards the outskirts of Leicester to a tenement block, not too far from the National Space Centre. Lenny asked him to park the car outside and they walked in to a derelict basketball court at the back. It did not look like it had been used for playing basketball for a long time. There was broken furniture, a shopping trolley, buggy and even a couple of broken bicycles lying on the ground. As they walked in, a cat ran out past Dev, making him jump. There were a bunch of kids, not older than ten or twelve smoking and drinking cheap cider behind the bushes who legged it as they walked in.

Lenny appeared to know where he was going. He walked through the courtyard to the back and through a break in the fence into an unkempt field which was overgrown with gorse bushes and tall grass. There was a derelict shed few feet away from the back of the court. Lenny walked straight into the shed and knocked on the metal door. Nothing happened for a minute. Dev was getting increasingly agitated ~~by~~ now.

"I don't think there is anyone inside. Let's go back, Lenny. This place gives me the creeps."

Lenny turned around looking anxious. "No Bro. He is inside. He told me he would be here. He asked me to get you. I promise, it'll be fine."

He was about to knock on the door when it opened with a creak which sounded unnaturally loud in the silence of the night. A stocky man with a dirty brown duffel coat stood at the door, his bald head shining in the dim light of the shed.

"You took your time, Lenny. You know better than to keep me waiting." He said in a gruff voice. "Have you brought him with you?"

"Yeah boss. He is here. I told you he will come."

The guy stood at the door for a minute looking past Lenny at Dev who was becoming increasingly worried.

"OK. Bring him in. But keep him where I can see him."

He walked back into the shed and seemed to disappear into the shadows. Lenny turned around to Dev.

"Come on Bro. It's OK."

Dev walked into the dark room which was lit by a single bulb. It was sparsely furnished with a single desk and a chair in a corner and the window was covered in what appeared to be a dirty sheet, which must be to keep any prying eyes out. The stocky guy was nowhere to be seen. He looked around to see where he could have gone. He knew that guy must be still inside as he could feel his presence and there did not appear to be any other way out.

"Sit down at the desk where I can see you." The gruff voice came from the darkest corner of the room. Dev squinted his eyes to see the man, with no luck. It was too dark to even make out his figure.

"It is nice to meet you. Lenny here says you wanted to speak to me. You see ...."

"I'll do the talking. I'll tell you when you can." The gruff voice said. "I know you go to the Quebec, the Abbey Park and also the Central Motors regularly."

Dev did not say anything. He sat on the rickety chair with his arms folded looking at the corner where he thought the guy must be standing.

"There are a lot of customers for good quality junk in those places. Lenny has not been very good with his customers lately and he is falling behind on his payments. I am looking for someone else who can deliver the goods to my customers."

Dev's mouth went dry. This guy was asking him to be a drug peddler. He suddenly felt very cold and shivered visibly.

"You cold?" and said, "Lenny, close the bloody door will you?"

Lenny was standing just inside the door and closed the door tight.

"Sorry boss."

"You are getting worse. You been skiving off the junk I give for the customers and your brain is skittled."

There was silence inside the shed. Dev was too scared to speak. Just when he thought the guy must expect him to say something, the gruff voice said.

"I want you to deliver the junk to my customers at the club and the central motors. You'll get your cut too."

Dev started to protest, "but, but. I am not really cut out for this sort of thing. You see, I am only a …."

He was cut off again midsentence.

"Or else your mate Lenny will pay for it." There was a sound of something being drawn out of a sheath. "I know where you live and your sweetheart too. She doesn't know about your boys, does she now?"

There was no menace in the voice. It was said in such a casual voice and could have been talking about the weather. But it still frightened Dev. His mouth was now completely dry and could not speak. He just nodded his head.

"That is better. Now get out both of you. I need my sleep."

Lenny quickly opened the door and walked out, saying "Come on Bro."

Dev walked quickly out of the shed and walked towards the basketball court. He could hear the metal door shut with a creak and a loud bang. The whole tenement block must have heard, he thought. Dev was sweating by the time he reached the car. He got into the car and drove to Mowmacre hill where he dropped off Lenny. Neither of them spoke during the drive. Dev drove off without saying a word as soon as Lenny got out of the car.

The first box arrived at the care home a week later. It was delivered to the office in an innocuous looking cardboard box, the size of a small shoe box. He knew what it was the minute he set eyes on the box sitting on his desk at the office. He sat down staring at the box for a minute without touching it. His heart was racing as he called out to the secretary.

"Sheila, can you come here a minute please?"

Young Sheila, who worked as his secretary as well as manager for the care home came inside.

"Yes, Dev. What can I do for you?"

"Do you know who brought this box here?" His voice shook as he spoke. She looked at the box and was about to pick it up when Dev put his hands on her wrist to stop it.

"Sorry." She looked surprised. "I don't remember the box coming in at all. It definitely did not arrive with the post as I took the post from the postman. Out delivery is not due till later in the afternoon. What is it?"

Dev picked up the box, trying hard not to show the shake in his hands and said, "I am not too sure. A friend had said he would send me some samples."

"It does not have any markings on it apart from your name."

"It must have been hand delivered by one of his boys." Dev tried to sound flippant. "That is ok Sheila. I just wanted to know if he came down himself to drop it off."

"I wouldn't know Dev. I can ask around if you want?"

"No, that is fine. I will speak to him. Don't worry."

No one at the office could recall who delivered the box. He hid it in the cupboard as soon as she left the office. He waited until he had sorted out all the daily routines of the Care Home before he dared have look inside. He locked the door and closed the curtains before picking up the box from the cupboard and opening it.

There were twenty plain brown paper packets neatly arranged inside. There was nothing written on the paper packets either. He emptied the box to see if there was a note underneath. There was nothing. He was a bit lost. He did not know who to deliver the packets to and how much money he was expected in return. He got through the day filled with apprehension. He kept looking at the front door of the Care Home half expecting the man from the shed to appear. But no one came. He stuffed the box into his bag and took it down to his car at lunch time to take it home. Once inside the house he hid it in his wardrobe under all his clothes. Nothing happened the whole of next day to and he was beginning to think he might have to find Lenny and give the box to him. Finally the phone call came as he was getting ready to go to the temple the next day.

"Did you get the supply?" The gruff voice of "the gaffer" was unmistakable. There was no small talk. "Have you looked inside?"

Dev was taken aback for a minute and stuttered, "Yes, Yes I did."

"You better remember what I tell you and not make any mistake." The voice continued as if Dev had not said anything. "All you got to do is take it to the Central Motors and the guys have been told to pick things from you."

The line went dead. He looked at the phone to see if he was mistaken. Nothing. He tried the call back and he got an operator's mechanical voice saying "number not recognised."

He took the packets in a plastic bag that night to the "Central Motors" not really sure what to expect. The public toilets under the Belgrave flyover had the infamous name of "the central motors." No one knew exactly why it was called that. It was frequented by druggies, drug pushers, pimps and prostitutes plying their business after dark and sometimes even during the daytime. It was quite big, windowless building right under the flyover lit up with tube lights. Most of the lights had long been broken by those who frequented the place for nefarious activities other than using it for toilet purposes. The council had long given up replacing the bulbs. No sooner were the bulbs replaced, they would be broken within 24 hours. Bright light was not conducive for the kind of business that took place there. The place was made darker by the red painted walls, which had become darker over the years. No one had complained and the council had not bothered to repaint the walls. It suited the users perfectly.

Dev could not see anything as he entered the dingy toilets. He stood just inside the door trying to adjust his eyesight to the darkness. His eyes lit up when he saw Lenny lounging in the shadows of the toilet.

"Thank goodness you are here." Dev exclaimed as soon as he saw him. "I did not know what to do with this stuff."

Lenny pulled him into the corner and put his finger on his mouth shushing him.

"Not so loud." Lenny whispered. "You just stay here and they will find you. I will let you know who the customers are when they get here."

"I am doing this as a favour to you Lenny. Don't expect me to do this for very long."

"Thank you Bro. You are doing me a big favour. I won't forget it." Lenny had replied. "It is only till he gives me back the job. It won't be long, I promise you."

His expensive Rolex watch showed midnight when the first customer rolled in. He had not seen the young weedy guy come inside. He was not aware of him until Lenny nudged Dev and whispered, "Give him the stuff." Dev was taken aback and didn't know what to do for a minute as he stared at this apparition who had turned up out of nowhere standing next to Lenny. The guy would not look up at either of them and was constantly shifting his feet.

"Go on, give him the bloody stuff." Lenny whispered again, this time a little louder.

Dev fumbled as he tried to get his hand into the inside pocket of his jacket to get the stuff out. He tried to pull out one brown paper packet and got his hand stuck in the process and dropped several packets on the ground.

"Bloody hell, Bro. What is the matter with you? Get a grip on yourself man."

Lenny whispered loudly as he bent down to pick the packets

up from the ground. He pushed one of the packets to the guy's hand and said "Go on, shove off now."

Dev found his hands were shaking uncontrollably and he was sweating profusely. He tried to speak but only managed a croak in the process.

"You will be fine Bro. First time is always the hardest. These guys are all harmless. They are so full of drugs and weak, that they can't hurt a fly." Lenny said to reassure him. The next client came in a few minutes later and Dev had finished distributing all the packets within an hour. As Lenny had said the next ones were not so bad. But he was still very glad to get it all over with. He wiped his face, which was now dripping wet with sweat and shook Lenny's hand before rushing back to his car which was parked half a mile away on a side street.

It did not take him long to familiarise himself with the "customers." It was during the third "drop" as Lenny would say that he noticed two men in dark hoodies at the Central motors. The two men had entered the toilet together and did their business. They took their time to wash their hands and dry their hands, which was a bit unusual, Dev thought. Clients visiting those toilets did not bother with the water generally after urinating. It was more common for them to spit at the toilet or the corner of the room rather than wash their hands. Neither of them said a word nor looked at Dev who was standing in the dark corner of the large toilets. He watched them walk out of the toilets with increasing tension. There was something about the two, which made him nervous and afraid. As he walked out of the toilets at end of "deliveries," there was no sign of them anywhere. He kept thinking about them as he drove home that night. There was no sign of them the next time he went to the central motors and he soon forgot about them.

He would get a new box delivered to the care home office now and then with little brown paper packets inside. Dev never saw the "gaffer" again. The man was very prompt with his payments and there was always cash in the box after the first shipment. This went on like a clockwork every fortnight for a couple of months and then started to go down first in numbers and then in frequency. It went on for about six months before completely drying up. Dev was glad to see the back of it.

It was an unusually bitter September night when he was shivering inside the toilets trying to keep himself warm by pushing his hands deeper into his pockets when there was a prod on his back.

"Don't look around mate. But this is a warning from the gaffer. He is not happy with your work. You have cost him his business."

Dev tried to turn around to protest when the hand pushed him down.

"I said don't, didn't I?" The menace in the voice was unmistakable. "We are taking over the business from Lenny now and you better hope it picks up. Or else, my friend Big Luke here will give you a visit and you won't like it. You won't like it at all."

The hand came off Dev's shoulder and he was gone. Dev did not dare turn around to look. He couldn't remember how long he was standing there until eventually his desperate urge to use the toilets himself made him run to the nearest one. His hands shook violently as he tried to unzip his trousers and nearly wet his trousers. He was still sweating profusely as he walked out of the toilets.

His friendship with Lenny strengthened during that six months and they would meet up in the Quebec. Lenny's addiction to 'junk' deteriorated at the same time and he became one of Dev's "regulars." The two men from the Gaffer had started back his supplies with "the specials" meant for chosen customers. The numbers were very few and far between.

When it finally dried up completely, Dev breathed a sigh of relief and swore never to get involved with the business again.

He had bought a supply of the little brown paper packets "for future use."

Lenny had become increasingly reliant on Dev to supply him with the junk as he flitted from job to job. He appeared to be permanently broke. His girlfriend, Sharon had thrown him out the house when he lost his last job as labourer. He had been unceremoniously kicked out by the manager when he found Lenny spaced out and weak as a kitten one morning and could not even lift a brick. He had persuaded an eighteen year old girl, Jodie, to take him in (more out of sympathy than love) into her council flat. She had a small baby of her own and worked in the local supermarket.

Lenny had introduced him to "the guy" who could get him as many of "the poppers" as he wanted. It was not long before Dev would swing by the Central Motors first to pick up Lenny and then they would go to the club together.

It must have been a couple of weeks of starting the delivery job that Lenny dropped another request.

"I like you Bro. You know I can do other things for you too."

"What do you mean?" Dev was feeling quite light headed after going through half a bottle of a "popper."

"I am much cheaper than those boys you pay for at the club."

Dev had stopped in his tracks and looked at Lenny. He could not really focus his eyes and just laughed.

"You? You really can do it with me?"

That was the first time Dev took Lenny to the house on Harrison road.

THE TEMPLE

Dev watched the young lad out of corner of his eyes as he performed the evening Aarti. He had been coming to the temple regularly now for a while. Dev had noticed him for the first time during the havan after yet another thread ceremony on a Sunday afternoon.

It was a fast disappearing tradition which marked the entry of a boy into adulthood among the upper class Hindus. The boy this time turning into teens and had a lot of his friends had thronged the temple with their parents. All the boys were ribbing the young novice who was in a bright red silk *dhoti* and a bare chest. That is all except this one boy who sat in the corner alone staring at the fire of the *havan* throughout the afternoon. He had slipped out of the side door with his mum chasing after him without waiting for the customary meal that followed.

He came back again a couple of weeks later. But this time on his own. Again, he sat in the corner of the temple the entire evening and disappeared before the *Aarti* was completed. Dev saw him in the temple almost every Saturday evening after that and his behaviour was exactly the same every time. Dev thought he looked very much like Sanju, maybe a little smaller. He missed Sanju badly. His visits to Central Motors and Abbey Park gave him a buzz, but not satisfying like what he had with Sanju.

Dev decided to speak to him next time he turned up. He delayed the *Aarti* one Saturday waiting for him near the door.

"Hello, young man. How are you?"

He was startled by this and started to back off towards the door. Dev was too quick for that and placed himself in front blocking the exit. The boy stared at him without saying anything and his eyes were wide open, unblinking. Dev could see the stark fear in his eyes. He smiled and put his hand on the boys shoulder. Soft, yet firm. Reassuring yet stopping him from moving at the same time.

"Don't be afraid." Dev continued still with his disarming smile. "You are in a temple. You are quite safe. No one can touch you here."

For a moment, the boy seemed reassured and opened his mouth to say something. But stopped again and started to wriggle out of Dev's grip. The door behind Dev opened and an elderly couple walked through distracting Dev for a minute. As he smiled at them and said,

"Namaste, uncle. Please come in, I'll be with you in a minute."

As he turned around, the young lad had disappeared out through the door. It was several weeks before he came back to the temple again. Dev would keep looking at the door every Saturday evening hoping the boy would return. He would peer out of the door several times to see if he was hiding outside. He even started to feel slightly disappointed when the boy didn't turn up. It was probably a couple of months later when he had nearly become a memory that he reappeared in the temple. Dev had smiled at him through the *Aarti* but he didn't make any attempts to speak to him even though he was quite desperate to talk to the boy. This time the boy stayed back for the *prasad* after the *Aarti*. Dev was surrounded by the members of the Hindu Council that evening and they wanted to talk to him about the upcoming elections to the council. Dev could see the boy standing leaning against the back wall as he took the council members into the back room. By the time he had finished with the meeting the boy had gone. He did not see him again.

Dev's visits to the Quebec reduced somewhat with the Hindu Council elections for a short while. He was appointed the president of the council to the delight of his father. His mother insisted in arranging a special *havan* at the temple to celebrate this. It was a grand occasion with most of the Gujarati community of Leicester attending. It had attracted the local newspapers too. Meera Ben was so impressed when the local TV news crew came to interview his son. She would tell anyone willing to listen, how regal his son looked on the TV.

Ramcharan had sold the little grocery shop on Harrison road as soon as Dev started to work as a priest at the temple and the attendance went up. Neither he nor Kishen had time to run the shop. Dev had never shown any interest in the shop from the beginning and Ramcharan had not forced it on him either.

Dev had become popular among the priestly community in Britain for his outspoken views on several issues, including his treatment of widows. He was in the news more often than not fighting for the disadvantaged, particularly among the Hindu community. He was quite successful in raising awareness among the political circles of Leicester and he was very friendly with the local Member of Parliament, Fred Homuz. Homuz would consult him for matters involving the Hindus, not just of Leicester, but the whole of the country. Dev would attend meetings at the local surgery on a regular basis, either taking a petition on behalf of the disadvantaged Hindus or on invitation by Fred Homuz to discuss local and national issues. When he was invited to the Member of Parliament's house for dinner, he knew he had made it.

He was climbing the social as well as career ladder quite rapidly, which had its own effects. He had a lot of friends within the Hindu community as well as outside. He had made several enemies within the temple too, as well as outside. Some of the elders, particularly, Nathuram Godse, an elderly statesman of the Hindu community of Leicester, thought his views were too modern and radical and he was going against the ancient sages of Hinduism.

"Our sacred scriptures were meant to be spoken in the language of the gods which is Sanskrit. That is why it was called 'Shruthi' – spoken by the gods. Dev Sharma is causing blasphemy by saying that the hymns can be read in English."

Nathuram made his views quite plain during the Hindu Council meetings. He was not impressed that ~~he~~ Dev was "only a secretary" of the council. He felt that he was more qualified to run the Hindu Council than Dev who was "an upstart with sacrilegious views." He had never really understood why Dev was beaten up by some people.

"There must be a reason why he was beaten up. Such people should not be made priests of our temples." He would repeat to every given opportunity. His intense dislike of Dev was well known among the community.

He was also made the secretary for the Society of Hindu Priests of the UK much to the chagrin of Nathuram Godse. It also meant some amount of travelling for Dev across the country and he was often quoted by the media on issues concerning Indians in general and Hindus in particular. His views appeared to matter to the wider public and the news media would quote him on issues ranging from racial discrimination to religious bigotry and even the refugee crisis in India.

The attendance in the temple grew during those years and most Sundays the temple was packed to the brim. The three brothers were kept busy officiating within the temple and also outside with many religious Hindu ceremonies – naming ceremonies, weddings and sacred thread ceremonies or "Upanayana." The three of them found themselves running around the city from one function to another during festival days.

The Temple itself was doing quite well with more than a regular income. His father did not take part in any of the ceremonies now. He would come and sit in the temple on a chair watching his children perform with pride. His vision and mobility were still pretty good and he would walk to the Belgrave shopping area every day to buy vegetables. Younger brother, Vijai still lived with parents and there were plans to get him married to a~~n~~ young nurse at the Royal Infirmary. Dev would take great pleasure in ribbing Vijai off as he was the shiest of the three brothers and he would blush bright red every time Revathi's name was mentioned. Everything was right with the world and Ramcharan was content and extremely happy with himself. Meera Ben had finally stopped complaining about moving to the "cold and depressing foreign country!" She would come into the temple on Sunday afternoons for the *havan* and sit on a stool listening to the hymns. She had taken to sit in the corner on a chair with sacred beads reciting hymns under her breath some evenings until Dev would come and say it ~~is~~ was time to go home.

The festivals, of which there were several, became bigger by the year. Some of them such as *Diwali* and *Krishna janmashtami* became so big that the police commissioner came down to discuss special traffic arrangements for the festivals. One of the local schools agreed to let the visitors use their car park for the visitors during the festivals.

Dev joined hands with some of the local charities to help raise the awareness of the poor and disadvantaged within the Asian community in Leicester. He would spend hours with Fred Homuz discussing the help government could give them.

A helpline started for Asian gay community, as a small offshoot of the main Gay helpline and it became a full institution with several volunteers working in it now, with Dev leading the group.

The temple had grown in size to when his father had started it all those years ago. They had bought the property next door and converted it into a function hall big enough for weddings with two hundred guests. Dev had set up a social club of sorts where youngsters and unemployed Hindu youths could come and spend time. He had managed to get some local artists to teach youngsters Hindi language and Indian music. He had even managed to sign up some kids to learn Sanskrit under the tutelage of his elder brother Kishen. The temple was thriving in all directions.

Bowing down to the pressures of the local Gujarati community, a Temple Committee had been set up to oversee the functioning of the temple, much to the disappointment of his father, Ramcharan.

"I built this temple with my own two hands only to be snatched away by strangers." He grumbled when Kishen told him about the move. "Where were all these people when we were struggling to keep the lamp lit in the temple?"

"I know how you feel father." Kishen had replied. "But, the council pays an endowment towards the upkeep of the temple every year and we need the money to maintain the running of the temple now. We can't rely on donations by the people anymore."

Ramcharan sighed. "I know son. There is no faith among the people anymore. Most of the businesses from Belgrave used to be so generous in the past. These youngsters nowadays want to spend their money on expensive cars and holidays. God doesn't exist for them anymore."

It had taken some time to convince Ramcharan that they would not be losing "control of the temple," but instead gaining some help to run it. He had finally agreed reluctantly to go along with the plans for election.

"Don't expect me to be there for the elections." He had said before retiring to his bedroom that night. Kishen had felt sorry to see the back of a stooped figure of his father walk slowly away from him.

Nathuram Godse was thrilled when he was appointed the secretary of the Temple Committee. He took the office like duck to the water. Dev was surprised to see some serious interest among some youngsters in the election of the office bearers. The young guy who was appointed to committee, Vasudev Batra, seemed familiar to Dev. But he could not place him. He was a young man of thirties, full of energy and self-opinionated. Dev remembers the first meeting of the committee where

Vasudev was quite vociferous in his opinions, particularly about the sanctity of the Hindu religion in general and that of temple in particular.

The words "sanctity" kept ringing in his ears for many hours after the meeting. He was quite certain that he had seen Vasudev somewhere before. There was something he had said during the meeting that convinced that he had seen him somewhere before. It bugged him all evening and even on the way to Quebec that night only to forget after the first few minutes of opening the first bottle of the poppers.

PLAYBOY OF ASIAN WORLD

The temple was more crowded than usual. Men and women were standing around in groups and there were heated arguments going on. Dev stood up at the side of the altar and picked up the microphone. The disturbance of the speakers was quite loud from the cheap speakers the Gujarati Radio inc had installed. But it had the desired effect. Everyone stopped talking and Dev said,

"I think we are all here for prayers and we should concentrate on those first and discuss the issues of the day after prayers."

He had always been extremely articulate and knew how to get attention of people. No wonder he had been made the Secretary of National Council of Hindu Priests at the young age of thirty five years old. His charisma had not gone down over the years. In fact, he had become increasingly popular. He had made a connection between the older Gujarati population with their rigid views and the younger generation with a more modern outlook on life. He could easily identify with both the groups without even attempting. The young thought he was cool as he would wear designer jeans and smart casual shirts and go out with them to the clubs and bars after the *aarti*. He spoke their "lingo" as it were. He did the prayers in English so they could understand. He spent time to explain what he was doing during any of the ceremonies. This impressed not only the younger crowd but also some of the older ones who had never had the proceedings explained to them at any time. He was one of the most popular priests among all the temples in Leicester.

His father led the prayer that night and Dev stood in the background helping. At the end of the prayers, he signalled everyone to sit down and took the microphone.

"I know that there is a lot of disquiet among our people. The Leicester Haymarket Theatre have advertised the opening of their controversial play." Everyone started to speak together and it was becoming a pandemonium. Younger hot headed ones wanted to take sticks and "burn the theatre down for blasphemy." The theatre had announced the opening of a play called "Krishna Lila – A Play boy of Asian World." The connotation of their god, Krishna, considered by many to be the 'supreme god-head' to be some sort of a 'Play boy,' was abhorrent to, not only the Hindus but also the Krishna Consciousness sect of Leicester.

Dev continued, "This is exactly the type of reaction they are expecting. And, it will not help. If you let me continue, I can update you on the state of play today."

There was an immediate silence from the gathered devotees. His brother Kishen spoke up.

"Dev has been speaking to the Theatre Company on all our behalf and let us hear what the outcome was."

"Thank you." He said to his brother and turning to the crowd he announced, "I have had a meeting with them and tried to persuade them to stop the play being opened next week. Unfortunately that is not possible due to financial reasons. The company apparently has spent a vast amount of money so far and they are not prepared to shelve it at this late stage. However, they are offering to change the name of the play."

The noise that started was tremendous. Everyone was speaking again and Dev's vice despite the loud speakers was being drowned. The younger ones started a loud chant in praise of Lord Krishna and clap their hands in rhythm. It was gathering momentum and reaching a crescendo when Dev's now elderly father walked up to the main bell of the temple hanging from the ceiling in front of the deities, slowly with a walking stick and started to ring loudly. The huge brass bell could drown any noise. The crowd started to quieten down again.

"If you continue to behave this way, we will not get anywhere. Will you please let Dev finish what he has to say?" Dev's father was almost pleading now.

"Thank you father. Yes, as I was saying. However, they are prepared to change the name to 'Krishna Lila : A Play of Asian World.' I am sure you will all agree that it is a more appropriate title. We all know of the childhood pranks of our Lord Krishna and is of course a 'Play of the Asian world.' I have not agreed yet with the management until I get the approval of our devotees. Now, what do you say?"

The crowd was very quiet for a minute and then one of the elders at the back stood up and said,

"*Pandithji*. If you think it is appropriate, I have no objection to that."

As others started to speak again, Dev raised his hands and continued.

"I know how these big companies work. They would have invested a lot of money into the project. If we keep objecting and make a lot noise with demonstrations, placard, disruption and general mayhem, we will play right into their hands. That is exactly what they want. A lot of free publicity. More people would want to see the play which has caused such a controversy and it will be a hit. I am sure you agree that is not what we want. We want the teachings of Lord Krishna to take centre stage, not some smutty interpretation of profit mongers."

That appeared to hit the crowd and there was a lot of nodding of heads and general agreement. Dev smiled to himself and looked at his father and brothers. There was an imperceptible nod of satisfaction. The three of them knew that Dev had agreed that a change of name would be sufficient to pacify most of the Hindu population of Leicester. There had been several demonstrations with large placard decrying the Haymarket theatre company and the police were in force outside the theatre. The main actress Parminder Nagra and the director

Nona Shepherd were asked to use the deliveries door instead of the stage door to enter and leave the theatre.

Next day there was a telephone call from a BBC reporter. She wanted to interview Dev. He agreed with one condition. That he has to see what was going to be shown on TV.

That evening, a young girl called Tanuja Solanki turned up at the temple with a cameraman. The interview took about an hour.

"What is the one message you would want sent out with this bulletin?" She asked.

"It might be correct according to the producers in the Haymarket Theatre and people who wrote this play, but we have to also make sure about what messages we are giving out to people at large." Dev had said. "We must think of the sensibilities of the community as a whole."

"The producers maintain that they are only portraying the Rasa leela of Krishna. What do say to that?"

Dev's face became very serious as he spoke.

"Those poems were composed as a metaphor for his love of people. You have to take the essence of the theme and not take the story literally. It portrayed the mutual love of people and Krishna. Unfortunately the world has changed and such love is seen in a smutty view point. It was never meant to be and never been portrayed as such in our scriptures."

The strength of feeling in his answer took the reporter by surprise. The interview on the local news helped calm many of the people in Leicester and a potential conflict was avoided. The play opened to muted response with a few people demonstrating outside the Haymarket theatre with placards and very little news coverage. The play itself petered out after a few shows because of poor attendances.

That was not the first time Dev was on the TV, but it was still exciting for his mother, Meera Ben. She would tell anyone who was prepared to listen to her to watch her son on the TV. It was the following year when one of the gay clubs in London decided to open its doors with the name of Kali. Dev lead the petition against the club successfully and even went to the Parliament to stop the club's name.

When the local Member of Parliament, Fred Homuz found out about his Good Samaritan act towards the eastern European refugees, he asked Dev to join the interfaith group to help stabilise the harmony between several religious groups including Christians, Muslims and Jews.

It was several weeks later when he eventually had a chance to see the young boy again.

"Thank you for your advice last night." He said.

Dev could not understand. He had not seen him for a while.

"You are welcome." Dev replied, still unsure of what he was talking about.

"Your advice on the phone was very helpful. Now I can understand what is happening to me."

It suddenly clicked. It must have been one of the callers on the Asian Gay helpline he was manning the night before. He had spoken to a few, but could not really recognise his voice over the phone. Dev smiled and felt his heart beating faster.

"Why don't we go into the back office and have a quiet chat?" Dev said touching the young boy's elbow and leading him into the room at the back of the temple.

"What is your name?"

"I am Ankush."

"Nice to meet you Ankush." Dev continued as he got the young Ankush to sit on the chair facing the window. "There is nothing to be ashamed of or worried about who you are. We spoke briefly last night over the phone. You can tell me everything and I can help you."

The story was all too familiar for Dev. Born in a staunch religious family, with severe set of rules for behaviour for both the young boy and his sister. They were accompanied everywhere they went and there was always a chaperone for everything. They were essentially muzzled from birth. Elder of the two siblings, he wanted to rebel against the authority of his parents, who were "suffocating" his feelings and emotions. He had only begun to realise he was not like other boys in his school very soon after reaching teenage years. He was strongly attracted to a boy in school, who unfortunately turned out to have a girlfriend of his own. That had come as a blow to him and he was torn between letting his parents know or ignore his primal urges. He was so desperate that he had considered taking his own life. He did not know who to turn to until he saw the little poster in the community hall he had gone for a birthday party.

Dev was warming up to the Ankush as he spoke. They talked in the room for a while and agreed to meet up again outside the temple. It was Sanju all over again for Dev. His rendezvous at the care centre office became quite regular and his visits to the Central Motors was almost completely stopped. He would still frequent the Quebec and enjoy the poppers and dance away till the early hours of the morning.

His charisma and influence at the Council and Stuart's entrepreneurial skills had paid off and they owned three care homes now. Two in Leicester and one in Milton Keynes. Money was rolling in. He would be seen driving everywhere in his silver BMW, which became his pride and joy. He was seen flaunting designer jeans and watches in the clubs after finishing work at the temple most nights.

He clicked extremely well with the younger crowd within the temple with his modern ideas and excellent command of English and his ability to explain the rituals to both the young and old in a language they could understand. He could slip from Sanskrit to Gujarati to Hindi to a colloquial English with aplomb.

SHEENA

Sheena was slowly settling in at her job in Leeds and was climbing the career ladder... The routine of coming home on Friday night and driving back on Sunday night in her new car was almost clockwork. Dev would spend the weekend doting on his wife like any dutiful husband. She would accompany him to the temple for the ritual havan on Sunday afternoon and they invariably went out for a movie or a dinner on Saturday night. This routine continued for more than a year.

Dev was surprised to find her car parked outside their little terrace house on George Street on a Thursday night when he got back from the Quebec quite late. Panic set in as soon as he saw it. He fumbled in his pockets to get his keys out and nearly dropped them in the gutter outside. As he entered the dark house the lights came on and Sheena was standing in the sitting room door with one hand high up on the door frame.

"It is two o'clock in the morning." She said in a matter of fact voice. "You were not in the temple tonight. Vijai didn't know where you were. You did not pick up your phone either."

Dev came forward to give her a hug. She pulled back out of his reach. He looked sheepish when he said, "There was a meeting of the association and a dinner afterwards. One thing led to another. I did not realise the time. You know how these things go. Once they start to talk, you can't stop them."

He was quite surprised at the ease with which the story came out. Sheena was quiet as she turned and went inside.

"Come on sweetheart. It is so nice to see you. I wasn't expecting you today. It is ~~a~~ such a pleasant surprise."

"I bet it is." The sarcasm did not go unnoticed by Dev.

"Your eyes are blood shot and you have a foul smell on you. What kind of place were you in?"

"You must believe me Anju. You can call Nathu Bhai if you want. He was with me all the time." He hoped she would not call Nathuram Bhai, the secretary of the Hindu Society. He kicked himself for not using Stuart's name. He would have covered for him with no questions asked. Sheena did not say another word as she went upstairs to the bedroom. He could hear her footsteps on the stair and the bedroom door shut. There was suddenly a deathly silence as if a heavy downpour had stopped. She had not raised her voice and there was no tantrum. But the effect was equally as loud. He took his phone out of his pocket. He noticed that his hands were shaking. He managed to switch the phone on after the third attempt.

"Shit!" He swore under his breath. There were three missed calls from Sheena and two from Vijai. He had kept the phone on vibrate in his jacket pocket, but had not felt it while he was dancing away. He was quite high on 'poppers' too. He had emptied an entire bottle that night. It was a wild night indeed. He had taken a boy to the little house on Harrison road and he was exhausted when he had finished with him.

The house he had bought on Harrison road needed plenty of work. He had hired some builders to get the house back in shape so that he could rent it out. He had managed to get upstairs completed and they were working on downstairs with a new kitchen. He was quite pleased with the way the three bedrooms looked now. Sheena had been busy choosing fittings and paint during the weekends she was in Leicester. It was coming along quite well and he was hoping to have the house ready soon. The three bedrooms upstairs were all done up and had been put to good use frequently by Dev. The two of them had put in a lot of effort to choose the furniture for the bedrooms. He wanted them all in wood to remember his days in Kenya. Sheena had put her foot down for the furniture for sitting room and insisted on sumptuous sofas. They were yet to be delivered. There were a couple of old green settees left by the previous owners – made of synthetic material and stained beyond recognition.

"I want them to be comfortable and warm. Wooden furniture is ok for a warm country like Kenya. Not very good for this cold country."

When he went upstairs to bed, Sheena was already asleep. He could not get any sleep that night. He tossed and turned till finally falling asleep with sheer exhaustion in the early hours of the morning. He was woken up by the front door slamming shut.

"Anju. Is that you?"

There was no reply. He got out of bed and went downstairs to check. There was no sign of Sheena. He looked out of the window to see her car was missing too. He looked at the clock. It was still 8'O clock. *'Where could she have gone at this time of the morning?'* He thought about the previous night and started to sweat as the panic set in. He picked up the phone and dialled Nathu Bhai. There was no answer. His panic got worse and he was sweating profusely. He was not sure what to do. 'Has she gone to meet Nathu Bhai?' He knew very well Nathu Bhai would not cover for him. He had never forgiven Dev for beating him in the Hindu Society election. He was the senior figure in the society and felt that it was unthinkable that anyone would oppose him in the election. He had made his displeasure quite clear from the start. When he was beaten by what he thought was a young upstart, he was furious.

He went to work late to find Stuart was waiting for him.

"You are late. You look like death warmed up. Dev, I am telling you to slow down."

"Don't start. Please Stuart. I am not in a mood."

Stuart looked at him for a minute and said, "Come, let's go for a coffee first."

When Dev hesitated, "I am sure they can do without you for another half an hour. They are not going to miss you anyway."

They walked in silence to the little café round the corner from the council offices. Stuart did not say anything until Dev had his first sip of the coffee.

"Do you want to tell me anything?"

Dev looked up. He could feel the sensation of panic coming back.

"No. Why do you ask?"

"Are you sure?"

"Yes. I'm quite sure …" There was a hint of hesitation there in his voice.

"I can only help you if you tell me what is going on."

"Why? What do you think is going on Stuart?"

"You tell me Dev. I have known you for a long time and you are my friend. I wouldn't like to see you get hurt."

Now the panic set in. He could feel the heat under his collar. Stuart could see the fear on Dev's face.

"Sheena came home last night."

"And you weren't in?"

"Yes." Was the brief reply.

"You were at the bloody club, weren't you?"

Dev did not reply. He bent his head down and sipped his coffee.

"Don't tell me you took a boy home last night?"

"No. No. I would not do that. I was at the Harrison road house."

"You silly clown." Stuart exclaimed. "How many times have I told you? You are risking your reputation and career with these stupid escapades."

"I know, you have Stuart. I will change. I promise."

"You have said that in the past. But you have never changed." Stuart paused. "Now, things are more serious. Sheena has been calling around. She called me this morning and looks like she has been talking to someone at the Hindu Society too."

Stuart could see beads of sweat appear on Dev's forehead. He loosened his collar and stopped drinking his coffee.

"What did you tell her?"

"What could I tell her? Nothing." Irritation in Stuart's voice was obvious. "I didn't know where you were or what you were up to. You are sunk if she speaks to that old man Nathu from the Hindu society. He doesn't like you one little bit."

"No. He doesn't."

"In fact he hates you with a passion. He will get you into trouble if he can."

"You are not helping me Stuart. Tell me what I should do."

"That is rich! How many times have I told you to behave and slow down?" Stuart's sarcasm did not go unnoticed. "You just won't listen. Is it worth losing such a lovely wife? And you tell me you are planning to have a family too?"

Dev looked up at Stuart. He looked desperate. He promised he would stop going to the Quebec and frequenting Abbey Park or the Central Motors for picking up boys. He had to find a way for getting out of the clutches of the drug dealer somehow. Dev was not sure how he got through work that day. When he got back home that evening there was still no sign of Sheena. He called her mobile.

"Hello."

"Anju, where are you?"

"I have been out. I am coming home now."

Her voice was brusque.

"OK. I thought I would let you know that I am going to the temple now."

"That is fine."

Her reply was brief and curt. He thought he could hear some male voices in the background. Asian male voices. He wanted to ask who she was with, but bit his tongue in the last minute.

The temple that night was busy with it being a Friday. Both Kishen and Vijai were already there. They looked up as he entered the hall. He looked at them to see if they suspected anything.

"Bhaiya, where were you last night? Bhabhi was worried sick. I called you too and you did not pick up the phone."

Dev gave a weak smile and replied, "I was at Harrison road with Stuart and the builders. I had forgotten that my phone was on silent. Sorry."

"That is OK. You should switch your phone back on when you get out of your office." Kishen said.

"I normally do, Bhaiya. I must have forgotten last night."

Sheena did not come to the temple that night or any time during that weekend. She was fast asleep by the time he had gone back home. There was a just a peck on the cheek for goodbye on Sunday evening as she left for Leeds.

Dev spent most of the Monday throwing 'poppers' out of the Harrison road house and cleaning up. He stopped going to the club and the Belgrave toilets. Stuart noticed a change in Dev, but he did not say anything. He had ignored messages from Ankush. Until one Monday night a few weeks later, when he turned up at the temple just as he was closing the doors along with his elder brother, Kishen.

"Hello, young man." Kishen had noticed him first. "The temple is closed now. Come back a bit earlier tomorrow."

Dev looked at Ankush and felt guilty at seeing his sad face. It looked like he had been crying with bloodshot eyes. He immediately went forward and put his arms around his shoulders.

"What is the matter Ankush? What are you doing so late on a school day? Come I will drop you home." Turning to Kishen, he continued. "Bhaiya, this is Ankush. I have known his family quite well. He does not look very happy. I better take him home."

Kishen looked closely at the young boy and nodded his head.

"Yes, I think you better do that. It is quite late at night for a young boy to be on his own."

Dev had gently ushered Ankush towards his car parked on the far side of the road. Ankush had not said a word till he shut the door.

"You are not answering my calls or texts."

"I am sorry Ankush. I have been busy at the temple. It has been hectic with Diwali coming soon."

"I missed you. I went to the care home and they said you had not been there for a while either."

"I missed you too." Dev started the car and set off in the direction of Ankush's house. "We will make up for it after Diwali."

"I sure hope so." Ankush replied with a sullen look on his face. Dev dropped him off at the corner of his street with promise of a rendezvous at the care home next day. He had missed the buzz of excitement for a while now. He could feel the urges coming back. It did not matter how he hard he tried, they were there pushing him towards the young boys and the inevitable 'poppers' and an odd visit to the club. He had not managed to get away from Lenny's friend the drug supplier completely.

Sheena appeared to be distant most of the times. She still came home every weekend. The previous camaraderie was missing. They were still a happy couple for any onlookers. At home it was a different matter altogether. Dev would be on his best behaviour. Sheena would be quiet and did not respond to any of his amorous advances. It was about a month after the surprise visit from Sheena, that Stuart dropped another bombshell.

"I saw Sheena last night." Stuart had said. "I thought she only came during the weekends?"

Dev nearly dropped the cup of coffee he was holding.

"No. You must be mistaken, Stuart. She is not due back till Friday night. I spoke to her last night and she is still in Leeds."

"Are you sure?" Stuart asked. "I could swear it was her last night. She was coming out of the coffee house with a couple of men. I did not recognise the men. I was driving and could not stop in the traffic."

"No, Stuart. You are definitely mistaken. She is still in Leeds."

"Are you sure?"

"I am quite sure." Dev was not so sure now.

"What men?" he asked as an afterthought.

"Two guys, I think. Asian, must be in their twenties or thirties. I could not recognise any of them though. I was driving in heavy traffic and couldn't take my eyes off long enough to look at them."

"Well, you must be mistaken then. Sheena is not due home till Friday."

He tried to convince himself that Stuart was wrong. But a seed of doubt had entered his head and it bugged him the whole day. He called Sheena as soon as he got a chance, but could not get through to her till evening. She told him that she would be home on Friday night.

"Stuart thinks he saw you yesterday at the Leicester centre with three men."

There was silence at the other end of the phone for, what Dev thought a long time.

"No, I wasn't in Leicester yesterday. I have been in meetings here all day yesterday. Stuart must be mistaken."

"That is what I thought. OK, Anju. I will see you on Friday night."

Dev was not entirely convinced. There was a nagging doubt at the back of his mind, which would not go away. 'What if she has been checking up on me?' He shrugged his head, 'she wouldn't do that. She is not the type.' He said to himself. His visits to the Quebec and the Central Motors became infrequent. The Abbey Park was shut down partly due to lack of clients and partly on the advice of the police.

Sheena did not get home that Friday till quite late. Dev had made an effort to get the house cleaned up and cooked her favourite dish, pasta with pesto sauce. She did not speak to him when he opened the door. Instead, she went straight to the bedroom and locked herself from inside. Dev went upstairs and knocked on the door.

"Anju. Are you OK? You must be tired after the long drive. I have cooked your favourite pasta."

There was no reply for a minute. Just as he was about to knock on the door, she said.

"I am tired now. I don't want any food. I had something before leaving Leeds."

Dev found that she was distant throughout that weekend. He tried to make small talk at breakfast with no success.

"It is funny Stuart mistook someone for you in front of that pizza place on Wednesday." Dev laughed as he said.

Sheena looked at him for a minute and smiled.

"Yes. He was mistaken. I had a very tight schedule this week. The firm is busy with a big case. Barristers from London had come."

"I thought so too. Stuart sometimes ~~gets~~ lets his imagination run away with him."

Her mobile rang as he replied. She went into the kitchen and closed the door before answering the phone. She had never done that before. He could hear her muffled voice through the door. He was desperate to hear what was being said. The coffee was cold by the time she finished her call and came back.

"I have to go out for a meeting. I'll clean up when I get back."

Before Dev could say anything she had picked up the cup and her bowl and dropped into the kitchen sink.

"I will make something for lunch. Or shall we go out for lunch somewhere nice?"

"Ok." She said as she went upstairs. She was changed and back down in minutes. She turned around as she picked her car keys and said,

"I'll call you when the meeting is finished."

And she was out of the door before Dev could say anything. This left Dev feeling very uncomfortable. He cleared the dining table and cleaned the dishes in the sink and kept himself busy to take his mind off. It did not help. His mind was in a turmoil.

'Stuart has put a seed of doubt in my mind.' He thought. *'I am making a mountain of a mole hill. She had gone out for meetings on weekends before. This was nothing unusual.'*

He paced up and down the house and felt increasingly restless thinking about Sheena's behaviour and Stuart's words. He finally decided to call up Stuart.

"What is up, Dev? You sound anxious." Stuart had said.

Dev explained Sheena's behaviour and his suspicions. Stuart just laughed.

"Now you are being silly. You are reading too much into the situation. You know her company has clients in Leicester and she has had meetings before. How many times you have complained to me that she is working too hard and does not rest even during the weekends?"

"But you said you saw her in Leicester in the middle of the week and she says she wasn't here at all?"

Stuart laughed again.

"Oh, that. I must have mistaken. If she says she wasn't, she wasn't. Don't be paranoid now."

Dev felt a little relieved after that conversation. Sheena called him around noon and they met up at her favourite Italian restaurant in the centre of town. She appeared to be her usual self and was talking about the furniture for the house at Harrison road. She wanted to see the progress at the house and they had driven down in her car. Dev had spent time explaining the progress in refurbishing the house and she seemed quite happy at the progress. They had spent nearly an hour at the house and as they came out of the house, she stopped abruptly. Dev was walking to the car and turned back to see why she had stopped. She was staring at the back of someone who was walking briskly away from them. It was a youngish Asian guy in jeans and trainers.

"What is the matter Anju? Are you OK?"

"It is nothing. I am fine. I thought I recognised someone."

Dev smiled. "That is not surprising as we are pretty close to the temple and you must have seen someone you had seen before. There are an awful lot of people in this area who visit our temple regularly."

"Yes, you are right. That must be it."

But she was quiet throughout the ride back home after that. There were several phone calls to Sheena that weekend and she would go into a different room to take her calls every time. The temple was very busy that weekend with preparations for the Diwali the following week. There were many volunteers who worked throughout the day getting the temple decorated and ready for the big occasion of the year. One of the local restaurants had donated colour lights and the engineers were busy fitting the lights both inside and outside the temple.

"This is beginning to look more like Diwali we used to have

back home in India and even Mombasa." Ramcharan had said when the lights were switched on for the first time for testing. "It is a good thing we have so many people helping this time. I knew this day would come. I must be thankful to my dear departed uncle for making this happen."

There were tears in his eyes as he spoke. He frequently spoke of his uncle who had helped the family settle down in Leicester, initially with the grocery store and then the temple.

"I miss Mombasa though." Kishen said. "It was always warm there. It never gets really warm here."

Ramacharan sighed deeply and replied,

"God moves in mysterious ways. Maybe it was written in our fate that we should live in England. I can't complain. We have a good life here."

"I agree with father." Dev said. "Mombasa was nice. But we have a good life here and we are all happy now."

He was looking at Sheena as he spoke. She was busy talking to some young men, giving instructions about something. Sheena spent a lot of time in the temple that weekend and Dev was very busy at the temple trying to get it ready for Diwali. He was looking forward to the big day. The local TV channel wanted to televise the occasion for their weekend news bulletin.

"Sheena seems to be enjoying herself." Kishen said. "She is always telling some young men something to do."

"I have never seen those three men she is talking to before in the temple. Must be some new comers. There is an influx of Indian students into the university this year." Dev said.

"I have noticed. It is good that young men are coming into the temple and showing interest in our culture." Ramacharan said. "I am very impressed with what you did about that play on Krishna. It could have turned really ugly if they had continued with the same name."

"Yes, the name 'playboy of Asian world' was completely inappropriate. I am glad the producers saw sense and changed the name to 'the Play of Asian world.'

"Not everyone was satisfied with that." Kishen who had joined them just then said.

"It is Nathu Bhai particularly. He is from the traditional background and takes things literally." Dev replied. "The world is changing and we have to change with it. Otherwise we will be left behind."

"You have to be careful Dev. There have been several threatening phone calls to the temple over the last few months. These calls are getting worse as we get nearer Diwali." Kishen said.

"You are right. It is worrying. The police are not really interested." Ramacharan said. Dev was quiet for a moment before saying,

"They must be some fundamentalist elements who don't like God Krishna included in the play at all." He could remember one particular caller who had insisted that he speak to Dev and had gone on a tirade once Dev said hello. He was screaming down the phone with ugly names.

"You dirty faggot. You have no right to be a priest. You will rot in hell." The tirade had gone on for a while ending in '*We are watching you. We will get you one day. You better watch your back.*"

Such phone calls including death threats at Dev became more frequent as the day of Diwali approached. Police had turned up after a note was dropped through the letterbox of the temple. It was a printed sheet asking the "temple committee" to throw out "queer priest." The threat was quite clear – they would 'kill the faggot' if he continues to officiate in the temple. The police had questioned everyone at the temple and had taken away the letter for "forensic analysis."

One police officer, Mark Henson had visited the temple on a few occasions with more questions. They had left two police officers to patrol the street outside the temple. When nothing happened for a couple of weeks, they were withdrawn. The nuisance calls continued unabated. Since the attack outside the Quebec all those years ago, there had been few episodes where he was followed by men and abuse hurled at him. He made sure he was always in a group when he visited the club. He managed to hide his visits to the club and the "central motors" from his family. He was still working for the Gay Helpline and spent a lot of time helping gay Asians both over the telephone as well as personal meetings.

"The play at the theatre has finished now. I don't think you will have any more problems." Officer Mark Henson had said when he came to tell them that the police watch was going to be removed. "If you get any more problems, please give me a call."

He had left his card with Dev. When he was called after the next threatening call, he said, "I suspect these crank calls are made by the same guys and chances are they are harmless. Keep me posted." And had hung up.

"I think we should all be careful." Ramacharan said "There will be a lot of people during the festival and we don't want any problems. I think you better give that officer another call and ask him to post some men outside the temple during the festival days."

Mark Henson was good to his word and had agreed to post a couple of men over the three days of the festival. He came to the temple that evening as they were closing up.

"I caught you just in the nick of time." He said to Dev. "Have you got a minute?"

Dev was looking forward to get home quickly and get changed before going to the Quebec.

"I am on my way to meet some boys in the city. Can you make it quick?"

"Yes, sure. I just wanted to touch base with you about the security arrangements for the upcoming festival."

"I think my father has become a bit paranoid since that threatening letter."

Dev laughed.

"I don't think we should take any chances with so many people attending the temple around the festival days." Mark said. "I will speak to your father if he is in the temple."

"My father is not in today. But you can speak to Kishen. I really must go now."

As Dev was about to shut the door, Mark said, "I would not use the public toilets at the Belgrave flyover at night if I were you. It is not quite safe."

Dev's heart was beating fast as he walked to the car.

HARRISON ROAD

The noise of a telephone ringing woke him up. He tried to go back to sleep as it sounded distant. He could not go back to sleep as the sound became increasingly irritating. '*Why does not someone pick up the bloody phone*' he thought to himself. It kept ringing incessantly and he decided to do something about it. As he stumbled out of bed he noticed the nude form of the girl half covered by the sheets next to him. For a minute he could not remember who she was. Then a smile spread on his face. He had met her a few weeks ago in one of the pubs and for a change she had not wrinkled her nose at his unkempt appearance. In fact she had gone out of her way to get friendly and ended up in his bed before long. She must have been in her thirties and was obviously well educated. That surprised him the most. His exploits generally had been young school drop outs or middle aged frustrated alcoholic housewives. It was his first Asian conquest. He wanted this to last.

He was going to thump on the wall to shout at his neighbour to pick up the bloody phone when he realised it was his own phone. He fumbled around the desk which was littered with pizza boxes and empty beer cans looking for the phone. It must be here somewhere. I can hear it. He picked up the girl's skirt from the chair and threw it down on the floor. There it was on the chair hidden under the skirt. '*This better be important to wake me up in the middle of the night.*' He looked at his watch. No watch on the wrist. He remembered giving the watch to the shop guy for the four cans of beer. 'Shit, this is worse than I thought' and picked up the phone.

"This better be important. Tell me you are dying or someone is trying to kill you. If not, I'll come around and bloody kill you."

His voice sounded gruff from lack of sleep and too much beer.

"You better get your ass down here now, Sean." Said the voice on the phone. It was Peter Marshall, the sergeant from his precinct. "We have a stiff down here. He has been done in."

"Shit. What happened?" He was wide awake now. He shook his head to clear the cobwebs off his brain. "Where is this?"

"It's in Harrison road. It looks like a slaughter house down here. Blood all over the place. They tried to burn the place down. Can hardly see anything with the smoke."

"Nobody touch anything!" Sean shouted down the phone. "Nobody moves a muscle until I get down there."

He slammed the phone down and moved back to the bed where the brown beauty was still fast asleep. He roughly pulled the sheets off and slapped the exposed hip.

"Come on sweetheart. Wakey wakey. It's time for you to go."

She tried to pull the sheets back over her nakedness and mumbled,

"It's middle of the night. Leave me alone. Where do you want me to go?"

"I don't care. It's time for you to go home. I have to go out to work."

"It's all right, you go. Let me sleep. I will be here when you get back."

Sean pulled the sheets off again and said,

"No. You won't. Now come on be a sweetheart and get dressed. I have to go now."

He did not want to upset the girl as he had enjoyed the night and did not want to end it there.

"OK, Ok. Hold your horses." She shouted as she got out of bed and picked up her clothes on the way to the bathroom. "You men are all the same. Don't come crawling back to me again later," and slammed the bathroom door.

Sean sighed deeply as he pulled his trousers up and started looking for his shoes. He was out of the dingy apartment before the girl come out of the bathroom. He felt dizzy as he walked down the dimly lit corridor towards the lift in the corner.

'Bloody hell. I better pull myself together or I will have an accident.'

He stopped at the water cooler in the corner and poured himself a glass of ice cold water. He felt somewhat more human after the third glass. The cold October air outside the apartment block gave him a shock. The easterly breeze was not strong but freezing cold. He pulled his jacket collar up and tucked his arms under as he walked towards the car, which was parked around the corner in a side street. It was still quite dark outside and the car was covered in a slight frost. He was not going to pay fifty quid a month to park in the apartment car park. By the time he reached the car, he was out of breath and shivering.

Too many beers and cigarettes and too little food and exercise was showing. He cursed himself as he struggled to fit the key into the door of his old banger. A ten-year old Ford was the only one he could afford. It spluttered to life at the third attempt, just as he was cursing the car and the fate that he firmly believed was the cause of his present state. He could not afford to be a member of the AA and he would have had to call his sergeant to pick him up again. That would be the fourth time this month. He hated doing that. It took him another five minutes to scrape the frost off the windscreen and get going. The clock on the dashboard said ten past four.

By the time he reached Harrison road, there were two patrol cars, a couple of fire engines and an ambulance parked on the roadside kerb. He did not have any trouble finding the house with the flashing blue lights visible for miles. There was already a small crowd of onlookers despite the early hours of the morning.

The front of the house had been screened off with police ribbons stopping onlookers from getting too close to the scene. The incident van pulled up as he was getting out of the car. The bobby standing outside the door recognised Sean and gave him a weak smile. His reputation on the force was wide spread and there were bets running as to how long before he gets the sack.

"Morning Sean."

"Morning. Don't let them get inside before I have had a look first."

"You won't like what is in there." The bobby said. "It is a mess. You need to go around the back."

"How do I get there?"

"There is an alleyway just down the street. That will take you to the back of these houses. You can't miss it."

Sean just grunted in reply and walked down to the tiny alleyway littered with garbage and fallen rubbish bins. The bobby was right, there were two more cops hanging around the back of the house with more ribbons and more sheets. There was a rickety iron gate leading up a stone path to the back door. The back garden was filled with rubbish from renovation work being done inside – broken bath, toilet, sink and even some old furniture littered the back yard. There was no "garden" as such that he could see. As he pushed the back door open to go inside, acrid smell of smoke and gas hit him and he wrinkled his nostrils involuntarily. All the lights were on and he could still see wisps of smoke coming out of the living room. Sergeant Peter Marshall was talking to the fire crew, turned around and saw Sean.

"Welcome to the slaughter house. Mind your step though. There is blood all over the place."

Sean nodded at the fireman and smiled at Peter.

"Not something you want to see at this time of the morning."

"You are right Sean." Peter replied. "It is in the front room. You go through the dining room."

"I hope none has moved anything?"

"The firemen had to move a few things to get inside. The whole place was covered in smoke when we got in."

Sean grunted something under his breath and walked through the dining room towards the sitting room door. He stood at the doorway without moving and took in the scene. There was a half burnt settee on its side, near the front door, still smoking. The fire extinguisher foam covered part of the settee. Part of the front door was on the floor in pieces. A thick plastic sheet screened off the doorway. The front wall of the room was black covered in soot. Then he saw him. He was lying face down in a large pool of blood which had spread around him. The left hand was hidden underneath and the right hand was stretched out in front of him. As he glanced down on the floor, the carpet was stained in several places. Nondescript colour and the gaudy pattern hid some of the stains, but he could still make out the stains across the floor. It looked as if either the body had been dragged on the floor or the dead man had dragged himself along the floor. Closer inspection showed hand prints on the wall just below the window. The curtains were mostly burnt leaving a tiny skirting at the top. The paint of the window frames was burnt and flaking off. It looked as if he was trying to reach out for the window. 'Was he trying to open the window? Call for help?' Sean thought.

He knelt down to have a look at the body on the floor. First thing that stuck him was the fair complexion of an Asian man, tall well-built and well dressed. The bright pink shirt was soaked in blood and the light blue jeans was stained in places. Black shiny shoes looked expensive. There was an Armani jacket hung over the large settee against the wall.

There were two other cops standing round looking bored and a bit annoyed at being hauled up in the middle of the night. Peter who had followed Sean, turned to one of them and said,

"Go and make yourself useful. Get the neighbour in here for Sean."

"Sure will do Sarge. I'm sure he will love me to wake him up again."

"Little chance of that. He would be peering out of the window to see what is happening. He looks like a nosey bugger to me."

"Who is the stiff? Do we know?" Sean asked Peter.

"We don't know. Not really. We are waiting for the forensics to come before we touch anything." Peter replied. "The neighbour who called the fire brigade said he saw some fire but ~~don't~~ doesn't know who the house belongs to. Or more like he doesn't want to tell us."

"What do you mean? Is this guy not the owner of the house?"

"I have already asked the guy who called the firemen. He says that all he knows is that some Asian guys have been coming around for a while trying to renovate it."

"I'd better go and talk to him. Don't let anyone touch anything until I come back."

"What about the forensics?" Peter shouted as Sean left through the back. Sean stopped, turned around and said,

"Tell the buggers to be careful. I want to examine things myself. I don't want anything being moved."

The cop had brought the neighbour along to the back of the house. It was a portly guy in his pyjamas stained with last night's dinner at the front and fingers dark brown with nicotine stains.

"This is Mr James Maddison. He is the neighbour who called us." The cop introduced the guy. Sean shook his hands and said,

"Thank you for helping us Mr Maddison. We are ever so grateful. I am Detective Inspector, Sean O'Connor."

"It is no problem, Inspector. Glad to be of help." His voice was guttural and his breath still reeked of stale beer. Sean was used to foul smells, but a combination of strong curry, sweat and stale beer was a bit too much even for him. He took a step back before continuing.

"I am sure you have already told my colleagues. But can you tell me what you saw please?"

"Sure. I was woken up by a dog howling incessantly in the early hours of the morning. That is when I smelt smoke. I sleep with the window open you see. I've done that for as long as I can remember." He said showing his nicotine stained teeth which were rotting away. "I looked out of the window and saw the smoke."

"Where was the smoke coming from Mr Maddison?" Sean prompted.

"It was coming from under the front door of the house. I had heard a car drive up last night and voices coming from the house. So I quickly ran outside and knocked on the door. There was no reply. Bill from the opposite house heard me and came across. We both were shouting and knocking on the door for a while. When we did not get any response, I called the fire brigade and the police. I was sure the fire would spread to our houses." He was gesticulating wildly by now. It just made the smell emanating from him worse.

"What time do you think you saw the smoke Mr Maddison?"

"I can't honestly say for sure. But, it must be after four in the morning. Cause, the milkman came around just as the fire brigade arrived."

"Did you know the people living in this house?"

"I can't say for sure. It had been empty for a while. I think this Indian bought the house and was getting it made up. There have been workmen on and off for the last six months at least."

"You never met the owner?"

"He said hello a couple of times, but never really talked." Maddison said. "Good looking lad, tall for an Indian I thought. I've seen a couple of other Indian guys come and go once or twice."

"Do you know where he lived?"

"No. We never really spoke."

"Thank you Mr Maddison." Sean said forcing himself to shake his hands again. He had to fight hard not to wrinkle his nose as he did. "Is it all right if I come back to you if there are any other questions?"

"Sure." He replied. "Is it true there is a dead body inside?"

"I will let you know what has happened soon Mr Maddison. Rest assured that the fire has been taken care for now."

"Yeah. The firemen were very quick in coming." Maddison said. "If there is nothing else I better get back home. I got to get ready for work."

"Thanks again, Mr Maddison." Sean said as he turned to go back inside again.

The forensic team were already in the sitting room. There was Tanya, in her usual blue jeans, a black jacket and gloves going around spreading some white powder on the walls and furniture to get fingerprints. There was a young guy, looked just out of school with a camera bigger than him taking photographs of anything and everything.

"I hope you guys haven't touched anything?

They hadn't noticed Sean coming in.

"No chief." They said in unison.

"Sean, meet Charlie Sands. He is the new photographer. Been with us for a month now." Tanya said introducing the young kid.

Sean just snorted in reply and shoved his hands deeper into his pockets.

"Good. Let me know when you have finished. I want to have a look around." Turning to Charlie, "and you, be careful what you touch. Tanya, you better keep an eye on him. This all I need. A rookie at the start of a murder case."

Sean left them in the sitting room, staring at each other and went into the dining room. He had worked with the girl,

Tanya, before. But the kid was someone he had not come across before. There was pine dining table in the middle with a couple of chairs pulled out and one of the chairs was lying on its back. He called out to the sergeant.

"Has anyone been touching anything here, Peter?"

"I don't think so, Sean."

The sergeant wandered over into the dining room and looked at the scene. "We could not get in through the front door and got in through the back through the kitchen. Nobody has been into this room yet. Apart from the fireman, that is. I don't think they have touched anything here. Looks like something has happened here too."

"Yeah. Looks like it. Get the forensics to get prints off here as well." Sean said as he scanned the room slowly.

Apart from the chair on the floor there was nothing out of the ordinary. There was a sideboard with a couple of empty glasses on it. A damp patch on the dining table caught his eye. He bent down to take a closer look. The smell was unmistakable despite being masked to some extent by the strong smell of the smoke. He had smelt enough junk in his life to immediately recognise it. He took his nose down almost to touch the table and make sure. That is when he noticed the spoon on the floor. He knelt down on the floor and there they were, a syringe with the needle still attached and a burnt out candle. The candle must have been still lit when it had fallen on the floor as it had dripped on the floor and stuck down with wax, which had solidified. The spoon was still facing up and he could see a tiny bit of brown residue in the spoon. He crawled around on all fours around the table look for any other clues. Nothing. He got up and turned to the sergeant,

"Get Tanya in here please Peter and the photographer kid too."

He stood there surveying the scene while waiting. 'There's something missing here.' He thought, but couldn't put a finger on it.

"I have the forensics here Sean."

Sean turned to the photographer and said, "Does that camera shoot a video?"

"Yup, but not a very good quality one." The kid said. "But I have a good one in the car. I can go and get it."

"You do that. I want you to take a video of the whole house starting with the sitting room in the front." Sean said. And turning to Tanya, "I want to show you something."

He knelt down again signalling the girl to do the same.

"Once these have been photographed, I want you to send these to the lab."

She looked at him wondering why. "That looks like a spoon with a bit of Marmite left …." Stopped half the sentence when she noticed the syringe. "Oh. I see what you mean. Do you think that is what I think it is?"

"Yeah. I do." Sean replied. "If it is, we will have the drug squad goons trampling all over here. I want to get as much info as I can before they get here."

He had been taken off the drug squad ever since the investigation the year before. They had not found any proof for their claims of misuse of confiscated drugs. But he was still taken off the squad.

"It would be the best, for your own benefit. The force has lost its confidence in you." The commissioner had said after the enquiry was finished. His own chief, James Stoker also had come in for criticism and both of them had been moved to homicide full time. His job had gone to a Mick Mills, 'half assed upstart,' according to James. Sean had no confidence in Mick Mills capacity as a drug enforcement officer.

"Looks like there is enough residue in the spoon to get what we want. I'm sure the syringe and the needle will also give us enough to see what was inside."

"That is good. Has anyone been through the dead guy's pockets?"

"No. Not yet. I am finished with the powder in there. I'll see what I can get out of his pocket."

"Thanks Tanya. That might tell us who he is."

Both of them went back into the sitting room and Tanya took out a couple of steel forceps from her bag and knelt down next to the body, avoiding the wide pool of blood around the body. It had spread almost up to the middle of the room. The bulge on the back pocket of the jeans meant a wallet. She had difficulty pulling the wallet out of the pocket down with the forceps at first. There was caked blood on the back of the jeans and the wallet was stuck inside. She took a knife out of her bag and started to scrape off the dried blood from the pocket opening. It took her nearly half an hour to get the pocket open and pull the wallet out. The wallet was bulging with twenty pound notes sticking out and several bank cards. She managed to pull them out and took it over the coffee table in corner to dust it for prints. She took out the cards and the money with forceps along with a colour photo of a beautiful Indian girl and dusted them for prints as well. The driving license said his name was Dev Sharma of George Street, Leicester.

"He is from Kenya!" Tanya exclaimed.

"Yeah. There are a lot of Indians here who have come from Kenya. Mainly shopkeepers." Sean said.

"So, do you think he is a shopkeeper?"

"Could be. It is not the first time we have come across some shop keepers who also did a bit of drug peddling on the side."

Tanya was examining the Armani jacket on the large settee. She was going through the coat pockets as she spoke.

"Wow! Look at this chief!" She exclaimed. She was holding a wad of twenty pound bills in her forceps and finding it difficult to grasp as it was so thick. Sean's eyes widened.

"There must be at least a thousand quid in there!" He said.

The photographer kid had just come into the room then and whistled loudly.

"Bloody hell. That's a lot of money." Sergeant said loudly. "Guess that rules out robbery as the cause."

"We got a Sherlock Holmes here." Sean said with an undisguised sarcasm. "I better call the chief and fill him in."

He called Philip Stoker on his mobile. He must have just woken up as his voice sounded groggy over the phone. Sean filled the chief with what he had learned so far.

"So, you think it could be drug killing?"

"I am not sure, chief. There is something missing here. I can't put my finger on it." Sean replied.

"What do you mean?" James asked.

"It somehow does not add up. The dead guy is a well-dressed bloke from what I can see. He is wearing expensive clothes and there is an Armani jacket. Not the kind you would associate with this place. The neighbour thinks the owner must be a shopkeeper. I don't know many shopkeepers going around in an Armani jacket either! I think there maybe drugs involved."

"They are getting more sophisticated Sean. Keep looking till I get there." James replied and as an afterthought continued, "I suppose you got to tell that idiot Mick Mills. I can just see him streaking back to the commissioner about homicide interference."

"I have not done it yet, chief. I was going to wait till I been through the house once properly. You know how they are. Bull in a china shop. We won't get any decent clues or prints once they romp through the house."

There was a noise on the other side of the line, like a muffled cough.

"I did not hear you say that Sean. You better let them know as soon as you can." The phone went dead before Sean could protest. He just grunted to himself and went back to the sitting dining room where Tanya and Charlie were still busy.

"Tanya, have you finished dusting the sitting room?"

"Yes, Sean. You can go through them if you want to."

"I'll be careful." Sean said and went into the sitting room.

The smell of the smoke was still quite strong in there. He dare not open the windows yet. He started to go through the little chest of draw in the corner and the draw under the coffee table in the middle. Nothing. They were completely empty. There was a three seater settee against the far wall of the room with a brass stand next to it. He knelt down on the floor and took out his little torch he always carried in his jacket pocket. There was nothing under the settee either. He lifted the seats off the settee. There it was. Tucked under the middle seat cushion, yet another wad of money. He did not pick it up. He wanted Tanya to dust it for prints. He left it there and looked up at the stairs in the corner of the sitting room at the stairs leading up. The stairs creaked as he went upstairs. There were three bedrooms, two of them still bare, with no furniture. The master bedroom had a double bed, a large pine cupboard, desk, chest of draws, a dressing table and mirror.

He stumbled on the little stool in front of the dressing table and nearly fell over. Cursing he leaned forward to pick up the stool from the floor. That is when he noticed that the cupboard door was partly open and the bottom draw of the chest was also open. He walked over careful not to touch anything and opened the cupboard door with his torch. The cupboard had a couple of designer shirts and jeans neatly hung on the rails. There was a neat row of polished shoes on the floor of the cupboard. Just as he was turning away from the cupboard he noticed that one of the shirts was out of alignment and sticking out a bit more than others. He tried to push the shirt back into line with no luck. There was something stopping it going back and was stopping the door from closing properly. He gently pushed the jacket sideways to see what was stopping it going back. There was a row of card board shoe boxes neatly piled up at the back of the cupboard.

'Hmmm. That is interesting. I wonder what that could be?' he said to himself under his breath. The boxes might have his socks and cufflinks. He had noticed the sleeve of the dead guy downstairs with silver cufflinks under the jacket. 'Better get Tanya up here to get some prints.'

He moved onto the chest of draws with a half open bottom draw. He knelt down on the ground to take a closer look. He opened the draw using his torch again and shone the torch inside. He whistled again. There were underwear, socks and handkerchiefs neatly folded and a stash of cash in twenty and ten pound bills.

He was sorely tempted to open one of the boxes to see what was inside. He had to force himself to get up and walk downstairs to get Tanya and Charlie. He was very thoughtful as he came off the stairs.

"What is the matter Sean? What did you find upstairs?"

"I am not sure yet. Have you found out who this Dev guy is, yet?"

"I have been making some calls Sean. No one has come back to me. It is still a bit early. They are looking at the driving licence records. We should know who he is soon."

"Tanya, we got some more work upstairs." Sean said turning to Tanya. Both of them trouped upstairs to the bedroom. "Can you dust those boxes and the cupboard for prints please? I want to have a look inside those boxes before the drug squad arrive."

"Sure Sean. It will only take a few minutes."

As soon as she finished ducting the boxes for fingerprints, Sean took out one of the boxes in the cupboard and opened it. It did not really surprise his to see ten little brown paper packets arranged neatly inside the box. He opened one of them carefully to find a very fine white powder. He took a pinch and tasted to the horror of Tanya watching him closely.

"Just as I thought. It's got to be pure Heroin. There's plenty of stuff for your lab here Tanya."

"Don't you think we should wait for the drug squad, before we take anything?" She was getting worried at Sean's brazenness.

"Of course we should. The boss should be here any minute too." Sean replied, wishing she would go away. That stuff looked premium class. He would not mind slipping a couple into his pocket. There was plenty in those boxes for the drug squad, he thought. The other three boxes turned out to be empty. "Come on, we better get downstairs and wait for the rest."

He put the packet back into the box as he found it and quickly walked downstairs just in time to hear vices coming up from downstairs.

"Why wasn't I called before?" Unmistakable gruff voice of Mick Mills berating the young sergeant, Peter Marshall. "I hope you buggers haven't messed up everything."

"No, Mick. Only the forensics have been dusting for prints and taking pictures. No one has touched anything."

"Are you sure?" Sean could make out the smirk in his voice. "I am sure that …"

He cut short in midsentence when he saw Sean come down the stairs.

"You are sure of what Mick?"

"Nothing. I was just making sure these guys haven't messed up any evidence."

"No, they haven't." Sean would not disguise his irritation in his voice. "Everything as they were when the first police came here."

Mick did not reply, but turned to the sergeant and said, "What is this about drugs then?"

"There were some in the dining room floor and there is some upstairs too." Tanya replied standing in the corner where she had been since coming downstairs watching the two men.

"Have you run them through yet?"

"Give me chance. We have only just found them an hour ago."

"What else have you found?"

"There is plenty of cash stashed away in the house." Tanya replied again. Sean had lost interest and hoped Philip would hurry up.

Mick continued his questioning Tanya and the young sergeant while Sean wandered around the house aimlessly before eventually walking out at the back. He thought he would go for a walk. The winter was already setting in and the sun was yet to come up. There was mist in the air and a freezing cold breeze blew away the remnants of uneasiness he had felt since Mick had walked in. He pulled up the collar of his jacket and pushed his hands deep into his pockets as he walked briskly down the alleyway. Instead of turning into Harrison road, he continued down George Street. That was the name on the driver's license in the dead guy's wallet.

It was yet another suburban street lined with neat terraced houses with a tiny yard in front masquerading as a garden and a small steel gate. At the far end of the street there was a corner shop selling groceries. Despite the area being considered a ghetto for the Asians, it was quite cosmopolitan in appearance. The first large building he came across was an old stone built church, with the year 1908 carved on the front and a spire, which had seen better days. The grey tiles over the roof had been had green moss at the edges. As he passed the church on to the next street there was the Sikh temple with orange flags flying on top in cold October breeze. He turned right and decided to go back on the next road, Wrexton Street. As soon as he turned into the street he saw a larger building with saffron flags flying on top. The entire building was decked with colourful lights and buntings everywhere almost covering the front. It must have been a community hall in the past turned into a Hindu temple. There was a yellow board on the wall proclaiming it to be "Sri

Krishna Mandir." It is the festival of lights for the Hindus. The area of Belgrave would be decked out for the festival and the main shopping area would be closed off for festivities. 'Not much of festivities in Dev Sharma's house this year.' He thought to himself.

Sean stood in front of the temple for a minute wondering what was inside. It was completely deserted at this time of the morning but would be heaving later in the day for the festival. He had never been inside a Hindu temple in his life despite being in Leicester for the past twelve years. 'There must be at least ten of these in this area alone', he thought. He walked close to the front of the temple. There was a small car park at the front with large steel gate with a heavy padlock stopping anyone getting to the little front door. He stood there for a minute holding onto the cold steel gate. He took out a crumpled packet from his jacket and lit a cigarette.

He stood in front of the gate with the cigarette in his mouth, started thinking about the dead body in the burnt house. There was something not quite right, he thought again. But could not put his finger on it. He scratched his head and nearly burnt his hair in the process. But still nothing. There was this dead body wearing designer jeans and an expensive pink shirt, Gucci shoes and a Rolex watch in a dilapidated house, in a rundown area of Leicester. Whoever had killed him were not after his money or the drugs in the house. They had plenty of time to go through the house and steal anything they wanted. They had enough time to try and set fire to the place. He had not seen any signs of forced entry at either the front or the back door. The dead man obviously knew the killers.

'This is too much for this time of the morning' he thought. He was beginning to get a headache again. He stubbed the cigarette on the ground and started to walk back to Harrison Road. There was an army of cars and vans in front of the house by the time he got there. He looked at his watch. It was turning eight. 'My god. I have been here nearly three hours!' he said to himself.

The street was now cordoned off with police ribbons everywhere and a large crowd had collected just outside the cordon. He recognised a couple of journalists among the crowd, who recognised him and started to walk towards him.

"Sean." One of them shouted. Sean tried to ignore him and increased his pace. She ran towards him still shouting. "Is it true someone has been murdered inside that house?"

The other journalist also started to run towards him.

"Come on Sean, you can speak to us."

Soon there were a couple of photographers pointing their cameras at him with flash bulbs going off in his face. He covered his face and didn't say a word. He had learnt to keep his mouth shut in front of the journalists. He had not forgotten the mess that they landed him in a drug heist a couple of years ago. He ignored the front and went straight to the alleyway and the back door. Philip was already there talking to Mick Mills as he entered the sitting room.

"Where have you been?" Philip asked as he entered the room.

"Out." Sean replied.

"What was all that noise outside?"

"The press is already outside." Sean replied. "I saw those idiots from the Chronicle and the Mail already with their photographers. It won't be long before the TV is here."

"Why all the media interest?" Philip asked. "What do we know about this dead guy?"

"We know his name. It is Dev Sharma and he lives in George Street according to the driving license and he is loaded."

"What do you mean?"

"It is exactly what I said. He is obviously loaded. He is wearing expensive designer clothes, wearing an even more expensive Rolex watch and there was at least a grand in his jacket pockets." Sean replied.

"Wow!" Philip said. "That is not someone you would find in a place like this."

"Exactly, chief. It does not add up."

By the time Sean finished briefing Philip it was another hour, as he wanted to see everything for himself. Mick Mills rather uncharacteristically kept himself in the background. His team had already loaded the cardboard boxes from the upstairs bedroom into the yellow police boxes and carried them into the van waiting at the front. The forensics had moved the body to the morgue for post-mortem. They were still waiting for the guys at the headquarters to get some info on the dead man's driving license.

"I suppose we better speak to the press outside." James said as they neared the front door.

"I got a couple of leads I want to follow chief." Sean said. "I will file a report later."

"What leads?" Mick wanted to know.

Sean just looked at him without answering.

"You carry on Sean. I'll see you later at the headquarters."

LENNY

It had taken Lenny nearly an hour to walk to David's apartment. He did not know where to go. He could not very well go to his girlfriend's flat. Not after the recent fight after losing the last job. She had thrown him out of the house screaming never to come back. David and Vanessa were good friends and they would take him in, he thought. It was still early in the morning and all the lights were out. He had to knock several times before he could hear movements inside the house. There were already a few irate neighbours shouting down to stop the racket. Vanessa opened the door bleary eyed, with the chain still on the door.

"Who is it?"

"It's me Lenny, open the door please, Vanessa. I am desperate."

There was sound of chain being moved and door opened with Vanessa standing looking bewildered in her nightie and rubbing he eyes.

"Who is that, Vanessa?" John's voice from the bedroom upstairs sounded gruff. "Do you know what time this is? It is 5'O clock in the bloody morning."

"It's Lenny, love." Vanessa said as she pulled Lenny inside and shut the door. Turning to Lenny, she continued "What the hell are you doing at this time of the morning? Is that blood on your hands? Are you hurt?"

Lenny stumbled into the apartment and collapsed on the settee covering his face with blood stained hands.

"I think I have killed someone, Vanessa." He sobbed. "I think I have killed Bro. I have killed him. Killed my best mate."

He was stuttering by this time and his sobs got worse as he went on. Soon he was sobbing like a baby and Vanessa could see his thin chest heaving through the shirt.

"What the hell are you talking about?" David had come into the sitting room by then still in his pyjamas. "What do you mean killed someone?"

"I am telling you Dave. I killed Bro. My best friend Bro." Lenny was shivering violently now. "What am I going to do now?"

"Tell me what really happened. How can you kill someone?" David was getting a bit irate now. "You can hardly swat a fly let alone kill someone. What happened to your jacket? You got blood all over your shoes too."

Lenny stared at his blood stained hands and his shoes.

"I don't know Dave. I can't remember a thing. It's like a nightmare." Lenny had stopped sobbing now, but the words were still coming out slowly at first and then a torrent flooded out. "I can see him lying there with his throat slit open and blood all over the floor. His eyes! I can still see his eyes staring at me Dave. I can't get them out of my head. I can see them even when with my eyes shut. How could I have done that Dave? How could I kill my Bro? He was my mate and I killed him. He was the best thing that happened to me. Where will I go?"

"Wait a minute." David said, trying to stop the torrent and make some sense out of what he was saying. "Tell us what happened from the beginning. You left us in the evening stone cold sober."

Lenny stopped and looked at David and then Vanessa as if he could not understand the question.

"Tell us where you went from here."

Vanessa prompted.

"Uh. Oh." He stuttered again and looked blank for a minute before starting again. "I needed a fix. So, I went to Sharon's to see if she got some stuff. I knew she always kept some at home. I was desperate for some, you see."

He was almost pleading.

"Yes. What happened then?"

"She didn't have any. Lousy bitch. I am sure she was lying. She wanted it all for herself. That's why I went looking for Bro. I called him from Sharon's. He said he would meet me at back lane of near the Garage. I remember getting into his car and picking some mates of his on the way to the house. He had the good stuff. I tell you, Dave. It was really good stuff. You have never had anything like it. He called it the special. I remember him mixing it. I tell you, he was good. I tell you ….."

"You are rambling Lenny." David was getting impatient. "Get to the point. How did it happen?"

"That is it. I don't know. I don't know for f**k's sake. Stop grilling me." Lenny looked blank. Tears started rolling down his cheeks. "You don't believe me, do you?"

There was a desperate plea in his eyes.

"We believe you Lenny. You got to tell us everything if you want us to help."

"I could not have killed him. Do you think I could have killed him? Do you? Do you?" He had his head in his hands again. He could not stop the throbbing. Why doesn't it go away? "But I woke up with the knife in my hand. And it was my knife. There is blood all over me. There was no one else in the house. I must have killed him."

Lenny started to sob again. David could see his thin chest racking with every sob.

"You are not making any sense. Where is your jacket? Go and get yourself cleaned out." David said and turning to Vanessa, "Give him a towel and I'll get some tea for us in the meantime."

Lenny looked at himself and shrugged his shoulders.

"I don't know. I must have left my jacket and cap at the house."

"What house? Whose house?"

"It's Bro's house. Been there before for my fix." Lenny said. There was a look of desperation in his face.

"Get yourself cleaned out and let's talk about it." Vanessa said handing him a towel.

Lenny came back from the bathroom a few minutes later as David walked in with the teas.

"Get this down you and start at the beginning and tell us what happened."

Lenny took the mug of tea gratefully and sat on the settee taking a sip before speaking. The story unravelled in spits and spats. And he was stuttering most of the time. David had to prompt him repeatedly.

"There is not much to tell, Dave. After I left here last night, I went to Sharon for a fix. She would not give me any. I was bad. Real bad. I needed a fix quickly. I called Bro and he asked me to come over to the usual meeting place. I don't remember much after that. It is all fuzzy. I remember it was dark and I got into a car."

He was staring at the wall behind David, trying to concentrate.

"Go on. Where did they take you?"

"I don't know. I .... There were others too in the car." He stopped and David could see drool dripping from the corner of his mouth. "Wait, they were waiting for us."

"Who was waiting for you?"

"And there was that cat." Lenny's eyes were glazed and he could not focus. "I tell you David, the cat was a monster. You haven't seen anything like it before."

"What are you talking about? What cat? What is it got to do with it?"

"I tell you it was a monster and it attacked me. If I didn't have my knife it would have killed me."

"Did you kill a cat?"

"No, I could not kill the cat. But it was a monster and kept attacking me. I thought I was a goner, David."

"You are not making any sense Lenny." Vanessa said. "Take your time and think carefully. Tell us slowly what happened from the beginning."

It was no use. He was babbling again and it was difficult to understand what he was saying. David went up to him and put his hands on Lenny's shoulders.

"Lenny, look at me." Lenny stopped mumbling. "No, I want you to look at me."

Lenny looked up and there was terror in his eyes.

"You are safe now. You are in our house and there is no cat here. We will look after you. I won't let any cat get at you."

"We went in a car to his place in Harrison road."

"Whose place?"

"Bro's place." undisguised irritation in Lenny's voice. "Been there before for other things."

David and Vanessa looked at each other.

"What other things?" Vanessa asked.

"You know things. Things that Bro likes doing. He was good to me. Bro was a good man and I killed him."

"Stop saying that, for God's sake. You haven't killed anybody. You can't kill anybody."

Lenny was sobbing again uncontrollably. His thin body shuddered as he sobbed.

"I must have killed him. I can see his eyes now. It is as if he was asking why?" He suddenly stopped and looked up at David. "Why did I do that? He was a good man."

"What happened next?" David asked. "Did you go in his car?"

The throbbing headaches came back and Lenny put his hands on his head, squeezing his temples. He sipped his tea again before saying anything else. He thought he could see Bro's eyes in the tea cup. He squeezed his eyes shut and put the mug down on the coffee table.

"I don't know. I think there were two more men in the car. Why can't I remember?"

"It is important you try to remember Lenny." Vanessa pitched in.

"These headaches have come back. It is throbbing. I can't think." Lenny was squinting his eyes and trying to concentrate which made his headaches worse. He started to massage his forehead and eyes started to water. He shook his head violently before continuing. "I think it was a big car. I definitely remember there were other blokes in the car."

"Who were the blokes? Did you recognise any of them? Are you sure there were only two of them?"

"No. I never seen them before in my life. They must be his mates. They seemed to be pally like. Bro said it was alright."

"How many were they?"

"I think two others. I am not sure there may have been more."

"Was it Bro's car?"

"I can't remember. Bro was there with me. We went to his house. I remember getting into the house with him. I remember sitting at his dining table while he got me the fix. That's all I can remember. It was good stuff Dave. It was really the best. Next thing I remember is ...."

His voice tapered off to a grumble and neither David nor Vanessa could make out what he was saying. He was rambling on about ghosts and blood and eyes. Lenny stood up and started to wave his arms about. There was a terrified look on his face and the eyes appear to be focusing on something miles away. Soon sweat was pouring out of his face and mixed with drool from the corner of his mouth started dripping all over the floor.

For Lenny, the demons had come back. Dark clouds seem to engulf him and the only thing he could see were those blood shot eyes of Bro, staring at him. He thought he could see blood squirting out of the eyes. They seem to accuse him of something. He thought he could hear the eyes shout out 'Why?' repeatedly. But eyes can't talk. Can they? Suddenly that cat was back. It was still huge and had angry eyes spouting fire and claws open to attack him. It hissed at him and it sounded more like a growl. It had come out of the dining room and was poised to jump on him when he screamed.

"Stop them, Dave! Stop the cat! He is going to kill me! Shoo! Go away. I'll kill you if you come near me." He screamed. Staring at Vanessa. He struggled to get his hand into his trouser pocket and brought out empty. He looked at his empty hand stupidly. "Oh my god. Where is my knife? Someone stole my knife. Dave, someone has stolen my knife. I can't kill that cat monster. You got to help me now."

"There is no cat here, Lenny. That is only Vanessa coming in from the kitchen. She brought you some headache tablets. You better take some." David said trying to control him with his hands on Lenny's shoulders. "You know we have never had any cats here in our house."

But there was no use talking to him. His eyes were again focused miles away and he did not seem to hear anything David said. He wriggled out of David's grasp and started to ramble again. He had his hands squeezing his head tightly as he kept staring at Vanessa without focussing. But it was not Vanessa he was seeing in the room. He could see him clearly. He tried to scream as the hand holding the knife came down on the back of Bro. But no sound came out. He was so desperate to warn him. The knife came down on his back again and again until he collapsed in a heap on the ground. It was a frenzied attack with blood spurting out of his back. As he collapsed, he turned around to look at Lenny. He reached out to Lenny. But he could not move. It was as if he was nailed to the ground. Then the knife came down and slit his throat, in a deliberate and swift move. That is when he heard the hiss again. It was not the cat this time. It was the last breath of Bro as blood bubbled out of his mouth and eyes kept staring at Lenny. That's when Lenny screamed finally and collapsed onto the settee.

"Where is my knife, Dave? Have you taken my knife?" Lenny screamed again shooting out of the settee. "You have stolen my knife. I'll kill you for that"

Lenny tried to lunge at David and ended up falling down again helplessly. David and Vanessa helped him up and tried to get him onto the settee. He started to struggle again and mumble.

"For god's sake, please stop them. Why me? What have I done? I didn't mean to kill him. I didn't mean to kill anyone. Somebody make them go away. I can't stand it anymore."

He was pulling at his shirt and the buttons started popping off and there was the noise of tearing. He had the shirt off and threw it on the ground. He tried to pull at the zip of his pants and got his fingers stuck and he screamed in frustration. David came and tried to restrain him and pulled him down on t the settee. Lenny was struggling and the two of them managed to get him to lie down on the settee. Lenny was waif of a man and it was not too hard to control him. He was thin and quite fragile. He used to be called a 'string bean' while at school and since leaving school he had lost even more weight, particularly after starting on the heavier stuff.

Vanessa got a blanket to cover him. He curled up under the blanket and started to shiver violently. The two of them looked at each other not knowing what to do next. They had seen him like this before, but usually when he was off the stuff for a few days. This is the first time they had seen him like this so soon after a fix. Neither of them were not sure what to do next. They would not dare call the ambulance for the fear of questions being asked.

They still had the blood stained shoes on Lenny. He might have some blood on his clothes too. David picked up his shirt from the floor and started to look carefully for blood stains. He was a bit puzzled to see no sign of any blood on the shirt apart from the ends of the sleeves. By this time a gentle snore could be heard from under the blanket.

"I think we better have a good look at his clothes when he wakes up. We will have to get rid of his clothes somehow." David said looking at Vanessa. "I don't know what he got himself into this time. I had told him not to carry that stupid knife with him. He wouldn't listen."

"You are right." Vanessa replied. "Let's hope we can get some sense out of him when he wakes up. I better get his shirt washed up. I bet he will have blood on his trousers too. Your clothes won't fit him. What are we going to do?"

"I am sure Sharon would bring some clothes for him here. Give her a call and see."

"What am I going to tell her? Lenny is not with Sharon anymore. You know he has been fooling around with that teenager for a few months. That is why she has kicked him out of the house."

"I know, Vanessa. But she still loves the idiot for some reason." David replied. "I am sure she would help and won't sell him to the pigs. Give her a call and see what she says."

Sharon picked up the phone at the third attempt.

"Yeah. Who is it?"

She sounded rough and in a foul mood.

"It is me Vanessa, Sharon. How are you?"

"I'm up to my eyeballs with this kids. I have had enough. What do you want?"

'Not very friendly' Vanessa thought. Wonder what Lenny sees in her. She was much older than Lenny too and foul tempered.

"It's Lenny."

"Yeah what about him? I haven't seen him for a couple of days."

"He is in some sort of trouble."

"What has he done now? The creep was round here last night asking for dope."

"I know he keeps some of his clothes at your place. Can you bring a pair along please if you can?" Sharon said doubtfully.

"Why should I? The creep can rot in hell." Sharon was screaming down the phone line. Vanessa could hear one of the kids screaming in the background. "He has left me for that floosy who is barely out of school. Why don't you ask her?"

Vanessa was quiet for a minute before replying.

"You are right Sharon. She lives with her mum still. You know I can't ask her. Chances are, she does not keep any of his clothes at her place. It being her mum's place anyway."

"Go and stuff yourself. Ask that creep to get lost."

"Come on Sharon. For old times' sake. He treat you well when the going was good wasn't it?"

"For ......" the voice trailed off and there was no sound on the line for a minute or two. Vanessa thought she had been cut off. She looked down at the phone and it was still connected.

"Hi Sharon. Are you still there?"

Vanessa could hear some kids screaming on the other side and sound of glass breaking. There was a lot of swearing and more screaming from the kids.

"Yeah. I'm still here. I am bloody sick of these kids. I am going to kill them or they will kill me." Sharon said exasperated.

"You are right. He was good to me when he had some brains. That dope has rotted his brain now. I don't know what he sees in that skinny bitch."

"He is in a bit of trouble now. He needs your help."

"What has he done now? Is the police involved? I don't want to get into trouble with the pigs."

"No. The police are not involved." Not at the moment anyway, Vanessa thought. "We don't know what has happened. He is zonked out and filthy. I can't really get him out of the house in his state."

"OK. Hang fire. I'll have to get Mom to come over and keep an eye on the kids before I can bring some clothes over."

The line was disconnected before Vanessa could say anything. David was quiet listening to the conversation.

"Is she coming over?"

"Yeah. She wasn't going to at first. Not that I blame her too, the way Lenny has treated her over the last few months.

"What are we going to do about the sleeping beauty now?"

"I would let him sleep it off for now." Vanessa replied. "I might as well get ready to go to work now. No point going back to sleep."

"You are going to work?" David said. "We can't leave him behind in this state. We don't know what he can get up to when he wakes up. I can't afford to stay off. You know that. I'll get sacked even if I miss one more day now."

Vanessa was not too pleased with that.

"I should not have opened the door to the bugger. I can't afford to miss either. I don't get paid for days I'm off. Anyway, he is your friend not mine."

She worked as a cleaner at a local factory on a contract basis and got paid only for the hours she worked.

"Sweetheart, I'm sure you can catch up over the weekend. I don't want to lose my job."

It was finally agreed that Vanessa would stay back to keep an eye on Lenny, who was snoring away on the settee.

"It does not look like he is going to wake up for a few hours anyway. I might as well get some housework done in the meantime. If Sharon turns up early, I'll see if I can persuade her to keep an eye on him."

It was not to be. Sharon did not turn up till after lunchtime and she was still in a foul mood. If anything, even worse mood than that in the morning. She was carrying the baby in her arms with a large bag full of nappies and baby stuff. She dumped the big bag on the floor as soon as she entered the house.

"I'm sick of this shit. I had to lug this baby and her stuff in two buses to get here."

Vanessa wanted to ask why she had brought the baby, but decided against it on second thoughts.

"Thanks for coming Sharon. Can I get you anything?"

"Cup of tea would be great. Where is that bugger?"

"He is sleeping on the settee in the sitting room. Has not woken up since he came in at around 4 this morning."

"At Four? That is middle of the bloody night for God's sake. What the hell he's been up to? I bet it can't be anything legit. One of these days cops will catch up with him and that'll be the end of it."

Vanessa did not say anything as she got busy making a cup of tea in the kitchen.

"Are you gonna tell me what's he done?"

"He thinks he has killed someone."

Vanessa's voice was calm and soft as continued to stir the tea. Sharon put her hands to her mouth and collapsed on to the dining chair. It was lucky that the baby's basket was on the dining table. It could have ended up on the floor. She found difficulty getting words out of her mouth.

"What …..? when ….? Are you sure?"

Vanessa sighed before replying.

"We don't know for sure. He keeps saying that he has killed someone and he keeps calling out for someone called 'Bro'. Difficult to get any sense out of him and he still has not woken up to ask questions."

"Have the police been looking for him?" Sharon was shouting. "I knew one day he would get into serious trouble."

"We don't know for sure what has happened, Sharon. He was still under when he came in and could not get any sense out of him."

"I'll tell you it is that bitch got him into this trouble. I told him she was trouble. The bugger wouldn't listen." Sharon did not seem to take any notice of what Vanessa was saying. "Did you say Bro?"

"Do you know anyone called Bro?"

"Yeah. I even met him once. Nice bloke. Indian or Pakistani I think." Sharon replied. "He was helping Lenny get a job or something. I am not sure."

"Anyway, he now needs help. We have calmed him down now and he is sleeping it off." Vanessa said. "I got to get to work soon and so does David. You have to keep an eye on him for now."

SEAN

Sean did not go straight back to the office from the Harrison road house. Instead, he had knocked on the neighbour's back door. A middle-aged lady opened it. She looked at Sean and gave him a puzzled smile. She was a slim lady, looking rather jaded and tired. He could see she would have been a stunner a few years back. The years had not been kind on her.

"Yes? Can I help you?"

Sean took out the badge from his wallet and showed it to her.

"I am sorry to bother you. I am Sean O'Connor from Leicester Constabulary. I am investigating what happened next door."

"I was not here last night officer. I already told the police man who came to ask me questions before. My husband is not at home, officer. He has gone to work." She said.

"I am sorry to intrude again. But I came to see you Mrs Maddison." Sean said. "Do you know where the milk man who did the rounds this morning lives?"

"I don't know where he lives. He has his farm somewhere outside Leicester." She replied. "But, I have his phone number if you want."

"Yes please. That would be very useful.

Mrs Maddison went inside and came back with a scrap of paper with a telephone number on it.

"Thank you so much Mrs Maddison. I really appreciate it."

"You are welcome. Hope you find whoever did it." She said and started to close the door as Sean turned to walk back out of the back gate. He stopped at the gate and turned around to see

Mrs Maddison through the frosted glass of the back door staring at him. It unnerved him a little, but he kept going. Something made him turn back and look at the door after a few steps. She was still there staring at him. He decided go back. She opened the door as he stepped through the back gate.

"Is there anything else I can do for you officer?" Sean saw the smile did not go to her tired eyes.

"I am sorry to bother you again." Sean was feeling uncomfortable under her stare. He adjusted the collar of his jacket as he continued. "Can I ask you some questions?"

"I am sorry officer. What did you say your name was?"

"It's Sean. Sean O'Connor, Detective Inspector of the Homicide squad."

"I am Mandy, Mr O'Connor. As I was saying, I have just come home after a busy night shift at the hospital. I have only been back a couple of hours ago and was about to go to bed. Whatever happened next door, it happened when I was at work. I don't know how I can help."

That made Sean cringe.

"I am really sorry. Maybe I should come back another day."

He started to leave when she stopped him again.

"That is OK, Mr O'Connor. Another few minutes is not going to hurt. I have the rest of the day to sleep as Jim won't be back till tonight. Come in and have a seat."

Sean smiled with a relief as he sat down on the settee in front of her.

"Thank you. That is very kind of you. I know you probably were not here when the incident took place. What do you do?"

"I am night sister at the accident department at the Royal Infirmary."

"Did you know the people who owned the property next door?"

"Yes, I do. It is owned by that nice priest from the Hindu

temple on Wrexton Street. He is here most days with the workers. They have been working on it for a few months now. Very nice man, and very pleasant. He is always very courteous and helpful. I saw his wife too once. Stunning girl. Make a very nice couple."

"Do you know his name?"

"I think he was called Dev. I can't remember the wife's name." Mandy replied. "I hear someone has been killed next door. I hope it is not that nice man."

"We are not sure yet Mrs Maddison. We are still making enquiries." Sean said. "Is there anything else you can tell me about the man?"

"Not really. He was always well dressed and seemed to be well off. He drove a flashy car."

"Can you remember seeing anyone else with him?"

"No one apart from the workers. They seemed to have their own keys and came and went most days." Mandy replied.

"Thank you Mrs Maddison. You have been very helpful. If you remember anything else, please call me." He took out a card from his wallet and gave it to her.

"I'll certainly do that officer."

Sean stood up to leave and as he was crossing the door, she stopped him with and said,

"You probably know that he was beaten up badly couple of years ago."

Sean stopped in his tracks and turned around closing the door again.

"No. I did not know that. How do you know that?"

"Sorry. I probably should not have told you." She suddenly appeared nervous.

"I am glad you did. Any information however trivial you think it maybe is important to us." Sean said. "Please tell me what you know."

"He was brought into the accident department where I work

a couple of years ago. I can't remember any details now. I think he was beaten up outside a club or something." Mandy replied hesitantly. "I was working that night at the hospital. Please don't repeat this to anyone. I will get into trouble. I should not be telling you this as it is confidential information."

"Don't worry Mrs Maddison. I will not put this in my report and it will remain confidential. I can ask the hospital for the information officially."

"Thank you. I really should not have told you this. Now you better leave Mr O'Connor."

"Thanks again Mrs Maddison. I really appreciate you taking time to talk to me after a busy night shift. And please don't worry, your information will not go past me. Can you remember approximately when the attack took place?"

"I think it was in summer two or three years ago. But I can't be sure." Mandy said opening the door again for him. "Now you must excuse me. I am sure you can get all the information you need from the hospital."

Sean walked back to the car deep in thought. Once inside the car he took the piece of paper Mandy had given him with a phone number on it. There was a name on it too – Joe Bamborough. He took out his mobile phone from his jacket pocket to find that the battery was on the way out and the signal was not too. He was not sure if there was enough battery to last a call. He called the number anyway. The phone rang for a long time and just when he thought he was going to get an answer machine a sleepy voice answered.

"Who is it?"

"I am very sorry to bother you Mr Bamborough. My name is Sean O'Connor from Leicester Constabulary." Sean replied trying to sound as apologetic as possible as he just realised that he must have woken up the milkman who had probably gone to bed just then. "I would like to ask you a couple of quick questions if you don't mind."

"I do bloody mind." The irate voice on the other end. "I have just got to bed after a tiring milk round. Call me in a few hours' time."

"My Apologies Mr Bamborough to disturb your well-deserved sleep. We are investigating an incident on Harrison Road either late last night or in the early hours of this morning. I just wanted to know if you saw anything unusual this morning on your rounds."

There was silence at the other end for a minute. Sean looked at the phone to see if he had been cut off.

"I don't think I saw anything out of the ordinary this morning. Just the usual morning jogger and the dog walker I see every morning."

"Thank you sir. If you remember anything at all even if you think it is unimportant, please give me a call on this number."

"OK." And the phone went dead.

Sean was a little disappointed. He was hoping to get more out of the milkman. He decided to knock on a couple of more doors in the vicinity and ask some more questions. He spent next couple of hours knocking on several door on either side of the house with nothing. He had noticed a newsagent shop at the corner of Harrison Road and Moira Street. The doorbell tingled as he pushed the door open and walked in and an elderly man with a long grey beard looked up. There was no one else in the shop.

"Good morning. It is a bit quiet this time of the morning" Sean said, more of a statement than a question. The elderly Asian shopkeeper smiled showing his dirty yellow teeth.

"It is always quiet at this time of the morning around here. We were busy this morning though. Someone has been killed down on Harrison Road and the place has been heaving since morning with ghoulish interest in such things." He laughed.

"But it is good for business. I am not complaining."

Sean smiled in reply.

"I am Sean O'Connor, one of the policemen investigating the death. Can I ask you a few questions?"

"You certainly can officer. I know most of the people in this area as I have had this shop now, let me see … for over twenty years."

"Thank you. Do you know the people that live in number 77, Harrison Road?"

"Now let me see." He stroked his beard as he spoke, as if in deep contemplation. "77? Did you say? Is that the place where they found the dead body this morning?"

"Yes. It is." Sean replied.

"I don't think anyone lived there. It was up for sale for a long time as it needed a lot of work. If I remember right the priest from the temple on Wrexton Street bought it." He said stroking his grey beard. "Now, what was his name? A very nice young man. Not married for long. Popped into the shop a couple of times with his beautiful wife."

"Would it be Dev Sharma by any chance?" Sean prompted. The shopkeeper's name lit up.

"Yes. Yes, that is him. Don't tell me he has been killed?"

"What time did you come into the shop this morning Mr…?" Sean asked.

"Abdul. I am Abdul Parikh." He replied. "Now let me see, it must have been just after 5 this morning, just as the newspaper guys dropped off the load."

"Where do you live Mr Parikh?"

"I live in Mowmacre Hill and I walked down. It only takes me less than half an hour to walk down, you know. It is good for me, as I don't get any other exercise nowadays. Getting old is not good for you."

"So you must have set off from home around 4.30 this

morning? Did you see anything unusual?"

"You are right. Let me think." He was stroking his beard again. "Hmmmm. I don't think so. The usual milkman and an odd drunk going home, or should I say swaggering home?" He laughed.

"Are you sure you did not see anything else?"

"I am not sure what you are getting at officer. But I don't think I saw anything else unusual."

Sean pulled out his card and gave it to the shopkeeper.

"If you remember anything. Anything at all, please give me a call on that number."

Just as Sean was opening the door, he was stopped by,

"There was this guy who nearly knocked me over this morning."

Sean turned around and came back inside.

"Yes?"

"He was not really drunk. He looked confused and dazed and he was talking to himself. But I don't think it is important."

"Why do you say that?"

"Because it was in Mowmacre Hill, not on Harrison road. It happened just as I set off from home."

"Yes. You are probably right. But I still would appreciate it if you can tell me anything more about this man."

"Not much to tell really. I did not take any notice of him. These drunks are best left alone. If he had not nearly bumped into me, I would not have seen him at all." He said stroking his beard furiously now. "It was quite dark you know at that time of the morning and you can't be too careful."

"I understand Mr Parikh. Is there anything you can tell me?" Sean insisted. "Was he young or old? Was he Asian or white? Anything?"

Mr Parikh paused for a minute in deep thought.

"Well, I think he was a white lad, tall and skinny. But I can't be too sure."

Sean gave up after a few more questions and left the shop with the shop keeper staring at his little card.

MEDIA

Flash bulbs went off in his face as Philip walked out with Mick tagging behind along with two other cops. Philip looked up to see the crowd standing behind the police cordon. There was a sizeable local population who had already gathered to watch. The police were in force trying to keep them behind the lines. Sheila Blacklock, the public relation girl had turned up by then and came over to speak to him.

"How do you want to play this chief?"

"We don't really know much at this stage to tell the press."

"You have to talk to them. They won't let you go without speaking to them." Sheila replied. "Why don't you give out a statement without any questions?"

Philip agreed.

"There are the usual suspects from the Leicester Herald, Mercury, the Mail, Evening Chronicle and the some independent reporters. No TV yet." Sheila said. "I will get them across here."

She wandered off to get them from behind the police line as Philip turned to Mick and said,

"I don't think we should say anything about the drug find."

"Sure, if that is what you want." Mick replied. "Why?"

"I got to think how to play this card. I don't want it to backfire later. Not until we find out more about the dead guy yet."

"If that is what you want." Mick was obviously not very happy. He was losing his chance to get his name in the papers. Sheila came back with a few reporters and a couple of cameramen.

"Superintendent Stoker is going to make a statement. No questions please at this time."

There was a string of protests at this statement. The photographers clicked away with the cameras. Philip put his right hand up and started.

"Thank you for your patience. All I can say at this stage is that we have found a body of adult Asian male in the house behind us. The family have been informed. We are awaiting forensic tests before confirming the cause of death. The incident appears to have occurred in the early hours of this morning. I would appeal to anyone who had noticed anything unusual around this area during last night and early this morning to come forward with any information they have. I can assure you that any information given to us will be treated with utmost confidence. You can do that either over the telephone or come into the headquarters personally to talk to one of our officers. There are trained officers manning the telephone line ready to take your calls. Unfortunately I cannot take any questions at the moment as I don't have any answers yet."

Philip paused for a moment before continuing. His voice was grave when he said, "It is important that the public works with us in this case. When I talk to the press, I am talking to the killer."

He turned to go back inside the house when the reporters started to shout,

"How was he murdered?"

"Is it true he was a priest?"

"Is it a drug killing?"

Philip did not say a word until he was inside. Sheila could see his face getting redder as more questions were thrown at his receding back. As soon as he was inside, he turned on Mick.

"How the hell do the press know more about this dead man than the police do?" and before Mick could reply. "Is there any truth in what those guys are saying?"

"They are shooting in the dark chief. You know how these reporters are."

"When are you going to get any info on this man? It has been now ..," and he looked at the watch before continuing. "... six hours since the first cop got into this house."

"We should be getting some info anytime soon. They have been at it now for a few hours."

"I am off to the HQ. Call me when you get some info. I hope that Sean has got some news by now."

He walked through the house and through the back door where his car was waiting. He slammed the car door just as Mick was about his mouth to say something.

"Where to chief?" The driver asked.

"Let us get back to the headquarters and make it fast."

The morning peak hour traffic did not do anything to Philip's mood. He was seething by the time he reached headquarters. The reporters' parting question kept ringing his mind all through the journey. Sean was waiting for him in his office. He threw a sheaf of papers on the desk as James sat down.

"I have been busy. There is a lot more to Dev Sharma than we think." He started. "He is a priest. He is a Hindu priest during the day, married to a solicitor. He works in a Hindu temple on Wrexton Street. He is also a Social worker for the Leicester city council working with disadvantaged people."

Philip stared at Sean for a minute before saying anything.

"You said Priest during the day. What do you mean?"

Sean hesitated before continuing.

"As I was saying, he is a priest by the day married to a solicitor. But he spends his night at the Quebec, Central motors and the Abbey Park."

"Then those reporters were right?" James said. "What about drugs? Is he involved in drug peddling?"

"Yes and no."

"What do you mean?"

"I don't think he is really a drug pusher in the broad sense of the word. He is only a carrier for someone else." Sean replied. "We did find a cache upstairs in the house. We also found a wad of money too."

"So he is a drug pusher then?"

Sean hesitated before replying. "I am not convinced about that. There is something not quite right here boss. I can't put my finger on it. It looks too neat. It looks like a package delivered to us. Whoever did this want us to believe that this was a drug kill."

"And you think it is not?" Philip said looking over his glasses at Sean. "Why?"

"I can't explain chief. It does not look very professional to me. Why have they left neat packets of drugs still in the house? We found it within half an hour of getting inside. They had more than enough time to take the drugs away. And the cash. I don't know exactly how much money there was in the house. But there was an awful lot of it stashed everywhere. The thief would have had plenty of time to take all the money." Sean paused. "Look at the fire. A professional would have made a good job of setting the place on fire. It just does not look like a professional job to me. It is almost as if they wanted us to find the drugs and the cash."

"Maybe that is what they want us to think."

Sean did not reply. It suddenly occurred to him that he might have been on the wrong track all along.

"Anyway, let's wait and see what the forensics dig up before we jump to conclusions." Philip continued. "In the meantime keep digging. Try your contact and see if there is anything."

"You are right boss. I have already been speaking to the neighbours."

"Did you say Abbey Park?"

"I know what you are thinking chief. The thought crossed my mind too when they said his favourite haunt was the Quebec."

Sean replied. "It is possible that he is gay."

"Did you not tell me he was married to a solicitor?"

"Yes, that is right." Sean replied scratching his head. "I wonder if he played for both sides?"

Philip looked at him and smiled.

"It takes all sorts I suppose. You better check out all the gay clubs and see if there is different angle to this murder."

"Yes chief. I will do that tonight. They usually come alive around midnight."

"If they have left the drugs and cash, we have to look for something else as motive for the murder."

"Yes, it could be a jealous lover."

It was a thoughtful Sean who left the chief's office. He did not notice the usual smirks from the office staff as he walked out into the cold October air, heavy with moisture from the previous night's rain. It had started to drizzle again. He pulled his jacket collar around his neck as he felt the chill in the air. He hated this time of the year when it is neither summer or winter and rained most days. He hated the cold rain. The breeze did not help and he was cold and wet by the time he reached his car. 'Not much point going to the Quebec or the Abbey Park at this time of the day. A visit to the hospital to check out Mrs Maddison's story may be useful,' he thought. He turned the car towards the Leicester Royal Infirmary.

The receptionist at the Accident and Emergency department was not the most helpful. She got him some forms to fill out to get information about a patient. He had done this before and was not surprised to see that the twenty page document now had grown to thirty four pages full of policies and procedures. Now it also needed a signature from the Superintendent too.

"Can you tell me when a Mr Dev Sharma attended your department please?"

The homely fat girl at the desk smiled at him.

"You know better than that officer. I can't give you any information about any patient without authorisation."

"I just need to know the date of attendance so I can fill out this form you have given me." Sean turned on his best charm. No good. It just washed off her. Nothing he could say would change her mind. He returned to the office to fill out the dreaded form and get signed by Philip Stoker. It took him all afternoon to fill out the form. He was about to leave the office when his mobile rang. It was the milkman.

"Is that Mr O'Connor?"

"Yes it is, Mr Bamborough. Thanks for getting back to me. Just give me a minute and I'll go outside where the telephone reception is better."

That was partly true. There was nothing wrong with the reception. He did not want the office spies to hear his conversation. He walked quickly outside and turned the corner into the car park.

"Yes, we can speak now. The line is quite clear here."

"I just remembered something about last night. Or should I say early this morning?" Mr Bamborough said. "I am not sure if it is important. But I saw three Asian guys getting out of the alley behind Harrison Road as I turned into Wrexton Street."

"That is good Tom. Can I call you Tom?"

"Sure you can. I did not think much of it at the time. But after your phone call this morning, I could not get back to sleep. I went over my route in my mind when I remembered the three men."

"Why do you think it was odd?"

"Well it was very early in the morning. I think it could not have been more than 4.30. Usually there is no one at that time of the morning around that area. Three men coming out of a back alley was strange I thought."

"Yes, it is odd." Sean replied. "Did you get a good look at them?"

"It was dark at that time of the morning. There were three guys wearing hoodies. I thought one of them looked a bit chunky. Did not get close enough to see what they looked like. Sorry."

"That is OK. Did you see which way they were headed?"

"They turned into Harrison road and got into a big car and drove off."

"What kind of car? You did not by chance look at the registration?" Sean said with a glimmer of hope.

"Sorry. No. I know it was a big car. One of those van like cars. I thought it was a taxi at first." Tom replied.

"Was it a taxi?"

"I don't think so. It was one of those big family cars."

"Did you make out the colour or make of the car?"

"I think it was dark maroon. It may be a Ford or a Volkswagen. I can't be sure."

"Thank you very much Tom. You have been most helpful. Is there anything else you can remember?" Sean asked.

"Not at the moment officer. I will give you a call if I think of anything else."

Sean was not sure what to make of that call. Are these three men involved in the murder? They were near enough at or around the time of the murder. He decided to check out the Quebec and the Abbey Park. The drizzle had continued and it was quite dark by the time he got to the Quebec. It was still too early for any of the customers at the gay club. The staff were still cleaning and rearranging the furniture when he walked through the front door of the club. No one took any notice of him walking in. The guy at the bar was busy cleaning the shelves when Sean walked up and sat down on one of the stools. Sean cleared his throat and said, "Excuse me."

The barman could see Sean's reflection in the glass shelf. He stopped cleaning the shelves and turned back.

"The club is not open till six tonight. Come back later." A gold tooth glittered in the light under the false ceiling of the bar when he smiled. Sean raised his hands in supplication and smiled back. He took out his badge from his jacket and flashed it in front of the guys face.

"I am not here for a drink mate. I just want some information."

The two men who were rearranging the furniture stopped and looked at Sean.

"What kind of information? We run a respectable establishment officer. We don't want any trouble."

"I am sure you do." Sean said adjusting himself on his bar stool which he found to be extremely uncomfortable. "I just want some info on one of your customers."

He took out a photocopied image of Dev from his jacket and placed it on the counter, straightening the folded paper as he did so.

"Have you seen this guy in your club before?"

The two men came over to the bar when they heard the question and peered over Sean's shoulder. Before the barman had a chance to reply, one of the guys said,

"I have seen him here. He was only here last night."

"Are you sure? Who was he with?"

"I am quite sure. He comes here regular at least once a week. And he always has a posse with him."

"What do you mean, a posse?" Sean asked.

"You know, he always got these young men around him, mostly white guys. He is almost never on his own. Good customer. Good tipper too." He said with a broad grin on his face.

"Can you remember who he was with last night?" Sean asked.

"Not really. They had a few drinks and danced away till quite late. I am not sure what time they left." The guy answered. "Why are you asking these questions? Has anything happened to him?"

"We are investigating a death of someone and his name came up. I can't say more than that. If you think of anything else, please call me." Sean said handing one of his cards over to the guy.

"I will certainly do officer." He said looking at the card intently.

"Is he gay?" Sean asked without looking up. There was a silence for a moment. Sean looked up at the guy.

"Most people coming to this club are very friendly people and they enjoy each other's company. We don't ask questions. He has a regular boyfriend I think." The guy sounded surprised at the question for some reason.

"Do you know him? What is his name?"

"I have no idea. He was always hanging out with many guys, but this one seemed to cling on to him most of the time. He must be the boyfriend."

"Tell me more about this boyfriend then. Is he Asian or white?

"He is white guy alright. He is always with young, good looking white guys. He had good taste." He replied. "If you come back later tonight, he might even turn up."

Sean looked around to the other two and said.

"What about you guys? Have you seen this man before?"

Both of them nodded their heads denying it. Sean gave his cards to the other two guys as well before leaving. He suddenly realised he was starving. He had not eaten anything the whole day. He turned his car towards The Swan. Abbey Park and Central Motors can wait till tomorrow.

The car park was in darkness as he drove in with very few cars parked. Daisy gave him a smile as he walked into the bar and slid on to his favourite stool. He always got a welcome smile from Daisy.

"You are a bit early Sean." She said wiping the counter in front of him. "Are you OK?"

Sean smiled back, more of a grimace than a smile. "I have had better days Daisy. I am starving. Hope you have something to serve me nice for tea."

"The cook has done a fab job with fish today. I am sure you will enjoy it. Take a seat and I'll send Judy over to you."

She signalled the waitress who was at the back of the restaurant part. A petite young girl came over looking nervous. Daisy turned to Sean and said, "It's her first day here at work. Just out of school. Be nice to her."

"You know me Daisy. I am always nice." Sean laughed.

"Not that nice. I have heard stories about you being nice to girls!" Daisy also laughed. That seemed to make the little girl even more nervous. "Judy, this is Sean. Look after him. He is not as bad as he looks. Let me know if he misbehaves and I will take care of him."

"Hi Judy. Don't listen to her. I am harmless. And I am starving as well."

"Do you want your usual while Judy gets the fish for you?" Daisy asked.

"Yes please." Sean said and walked over to a table in far corner away from the glare of the bar lights. Daisy brought over his beer and a bowl of nuts. He had not finished the beer when a guy in a worn out grey jacket and a nondescript crumpled hat slid into the seat in front of him.

"Mind if I sit down here?"

Sean shrugged and said "It is a free country." And looking around the nearly empty pub, he continued "There are plenty of empty tables too."

The guy took off his hat and said offering his hand to Sean, "I am sorry. How rude of me. I am Derek Jacobs from the Herald."

Sean did not take the offered hand and instead said, "I think you better find another table mister. I don't speak to the press."

"Come on Sean. Don't be like that. You are in the middle of a big case which is about hit the national headlines and you don't want to talk to the press?"

The African accent was unmistakable.

"I am not going to repeat myself. Bugger off."

"You could do with some good publicity right now. You are barking up the wrong tree. You want to know where the priest was before he came to Leicester." When Sean did not say a word, he continued, "I know about your trouble with the Internals. I just want to ask you a few questions."

Sean could feel the heat rising under his collar. He had stopped drinking and stared at the guy in front of him.

"I am not going to repeat what I said."

He pushed his chair back to get up when Daisy walked over.

"Come on mister, leave Sean alone. He has come here for a quiet meal. I can get you a good table."

Derek got up and pushed his card out in front of him on the table.

"If you change your mind, give me a call."

Sean sat down and pushed the card back to him "I won't change my mind."

Derek started to walk towards the door with Daisy following him and turned back at the next table.

"There are things about this case that you don't know and it is not likely the cops will ever get the real story."

Sean did not say anything and appeared to be concentrating on something at the bottom of the beer mug. Derek turned back at the door, stuck his badly discoloured hat on his head and said,

"For what it is worth, I think you should to talk to the grieving widow and a couple of r mates. Don't leave it too late mate. Remember, you scratch my back and I will yours."

The door swung shut behind him as Sean looked up to say something. He was not sure what to make of the reporters comment. This case was getting more confusing and it has only been a couple of days, he thought.

THE HUNT

The conference room was buzzing on the morning, three days after the body was discovered on Harrison Road. Leicester was going through a particularly bad patch with a string of murders and robberies over the past few months. There was pressure from the home office in London "to get their act together." The police chief had come pretty down hard on Philip Stoker the night before and wanted some action as quickly as possible. They had a lot of information about the dead man but no leads. Stoker had called a news conference the day after the discovery of the body and appealed to the public to help with information. There were several calls the first day and they soon dried up to a trickle.

The news conference was held at the headquarters this time and was packed with news media including the national channels – BBC and ITV as well as Channel 4. Stoker was accompanied by Mick Mills and the press officer, Sheila Blacklock. Dev's two brothers were there on the podium too. Stoker started off with a statement telling them what they had found out so far, which was very little. They knew quite a bit about the dead man but they were struggling to find a motive. As soon as he finished there were a lot of questions thrown at him.

"Is it true he was gay?"

"I would rather concentrate on finding the killer than on his sexual preferences, if you don't mind."

"Why do you think he was killed?"

"Obviously somebody did not like the work he did. The motive is obviously jealousy of the work he was doing." Krishen replied.

"Did you know he was gay or bisexual." The reporter from the Mercury persisted.

"People loved him for the way he delivered his services. He was more casual, more sociable. He mixed with a lot of young people and attracted the younger ones amongst us. He felt that the Hindu priesthood was not delivering enough to the younger generation, he believed there was work needed so that the younger generation would know their heritage."

"With respect sir, you did not answer my question."

Stoker lifted his hand to object, but Krishen continued.

"No we did not."

"Is it true that he was killed because of he was gay?" Yet another tabloid reporter this time. Krishen did not answer straight away.

"We still don't know the motive for the killing. Speculation will not get us anywhere." Stoker replied. "The information that we have got is that he had a lot of men friends he used to meet. He socialised in the gay scene and in gay clubs of Leicester."

"Our teachings tell us not to reject people regardless of their faith, lifestyle or anything else. My advice to people who are saying things like this is to go back and take another look at the religion. I cannot think of any reason why anyone would want to hurt him." Krishen said with a voice full of emotion and tremor. "Everyone we have spoken to has nothing but good things to say about my brother. There is nothing to suggest why he was murdered, especially like this. My parents feel like lightning has struck. We are all devastated. We have no idea at all what could have happened. He was such a warm, caring person. He honestly wouldn't hurt a fly. Even his tone of voice was soft. He had no aggression."

There were tears in his eyes as he paused. There was a deathly silence in the audience. He did not wipe his tears but continued.

"That's what makes it so shocking. How could he have enemies? His popularity was so great among the community as a whole, not just the Hindus. He fought for equal opportunities, for people with learning disabilities and for widows, who are often left behind in the Asian community. He brought them forward, saying they have the same rights to live life to the full. He fought for everyone who was weak and couldn't have their say. He used his power to help them achieve their rights. He was there for anyone who had problems, not just Hindus. He was the community in himself."

Jai who was quiet all this time, added: "All we can do now is have stone hearts and pray for justice. We know his time has finished here. Probably God needs him somewhere else, to look after humans in other parts of the world."

There was quiet after that emotional outburst until another reporter piped up.

"Do you think it was racially motivated then?"

"We just don't know anything about that yet." Stoker replied.

"Does the police believe that the victim was a bisexual then?"

"I have not ruled anything out. It is one line of inquiry we are investigating. We know that he led a double life. He had a happy domestic home life but also had a separate social lifestyle. We need help from associates in both these facets of his life and I can assure people that we treat any information sensitively."

"Is it true you are looking for some Asian men?"

That threw Stoker off balance a bit. He had only found out about the three Asian guys the night before from Sean.

"Three young men were seen near Harrison Road around the time of the incident. We would like to speak to them to rule them out of the investigation."

"Are they suspects in this case?"

"No one is a suspect at this stage. We just want to talk to them at present."

"Is it true that you found lots of drugs in the house?"

Just then there was commotion at the back of the hall. Sheena had entered the room in a flourish with a young guy in a smart suit with lawyer written all over his face. Flash bulbs went off and TV cameras were swinging rapidly to get her pictures. Almost everyone on the floor were poking their microphones at her shooting questions all at once. She marched towards the podium without flinching and saying a word. She knew she had everyone's attention on her, not just because she was the wife of the deceased. She looked stunning in a black trouser suit, figure hugging jacket and high heels. She walked in as if she owned the place. It was not a grieving widow at first sight. She marched up on to the podium staring at Stoker. Sheila put her hand out to welcome her on to the stage. A limp and brief handshake and she was next to Stoker.

"Thank you so much for coming Mrs Sharma. You don't have to speak to the press if you don't want. We can field the questions and his brothers are doing extremely well."

"I want to make a statement if you don't mind."

Stoker looked at Sheila Blacklok, who nodded. Stoker turned to the press and said, "Mrs Achar will be making a statement. I will not allow any questions at present."

Sheena stood up and walked to the front of the desk and spoke without referring to any notes.

"Dev was a loving and caring husband. He made us happy. He was a truly godly person. He took away the darkness and brought in the light wherever he was. We were very happily married and deeply in love. When you love someone that love is unconditional." She paused and looked around to see the response as it were. "I miss him. I miss him very much. We were planning to have a family soon."

At this her voice broke and she nearly collapsed. Stoker rushed forward to stop her from falling. He guided her to the nearest chair as Sheila took over the conference and ended the reporters' questions. The police were completely taken aback by the sudden appearance and the outburst of the grieving widow. The media exposure managed to generate some more calls to the switchboard but nothing of consequence.

Everyone, including Stoker, was taken aback by the previous day's news conference. The commissioner had decided to scrap all the initiatives on new traffic and burglary and even the long running drugs investigation programme to concentrate on the case. At the last count, there were more than a hundred officers working on it.

Stoker had called the entire homicide squad as well as the drug and burglary squad to be present for the meeting that morning. There was hardly anywhere to sit inside the room. Sean had slid in through the side door and sitting quietly at the back trying to look as inconspicuous as possible. He had not had any more luck after the first day. Stoker walked in with a sheaf of papers under his arms. He stood on the little platform at the top end and tapped on the desk in front to get everyone's attention. The room became instantly quiet.

"Thank you guys. I am sure you must have heard quite a bit of rumours about the murder on Harrison road by now. There is a lot of media attention already and I have a suspicion it is only going to get worse. We need to get some answers quickly. Both Sean O'Connor and Mick Mills have been working hard since the discovery of the body." Turning to Sean sitting at the back he continued. "Sean will brief us about what he found at the scene and Mick here will fill you in on more details. Sean why don't you come up here and give a brief account of what you saw yesterday?"

Sean hated this part of the briefing. He did not fancy standing in front of these idiots knowing that they would be laughing behind his back. This had gone since the Internals investigation five years ago, which still had not concluded. His name was still under a thick cloud and his every movement was being watched. The Police Union were supporting him and the rep, Johnny Walker, kept telling him that the Internals don't have a case against him every time there was a 'conference.' All his reports were scrutinised and he was not allowed to go on a watch on his own.

He stood up and walked to the front reluctantly. Mick was already there at the front waiting to say his piece. Philip Stoker nodded at him encouragingly as he faced the crowd of officers sitting in the room. Sean went over the murder scene and talked about the drug and cash find. He left out his interview with Mrs Maddison and others.

Mick Mills took over once Sean had finished. He was his usual eloquent self and embellished the scene of the murder. He had interviewed the "entire neighbourhood" over the previous three days with his officers with no substantial information. When he finished, Philip stood up and said, "I want you guys to talk to your contacts and dig up anything about this man Dev Sharma and his links to the drugs. I want you to look into your contacts in the Asian and Gay communities and get as much information as possible. It won't be long before the big chiefs from London start jumping up and down. It is going to get hotter as the news hits the TV tonight. I would bet my bottom dollar that this will hit the main national news tonight."

He had winced at the news report on the local TV the night before when the reporter had dug up the numbers of unsolved murders within their precinct area over the previous twelve months. The national channels were represented during the last night's conference and there was no reason why it would not form the main news tonight. He looked at both Sean and Mick and said,

"Both of you in my office now."

The three of them walked back to Stoker's office as the conference room burst into jumbled conversation.

"We have to get this case sorted ASAP. I am getting a lot of flack from upstairs on this one. Have you got anything for me before I go and see the commissioner?"

Stoker said as he sat down at his desk. Mick started off with, "My men have spent the last three days interviewing people around the neighbourhood. I am still going through their reports chief. But I got a report from the Forensics."

"And what do the Forensic guys tell you?" A gentle hint of sarcasm did not go unnoticed by Sean.

"The cause of death is due to stab injury to the neck. They think he died between two and four o clock in the morning. They are still checking his blood to see if there was any drugs or alcohol in the system. I was on my way to the lab to get the rest of the report."

"You do that Mick and let me know what they find." He waited till Mick had left the office before turning to Sean and raised his eyebrows. "Well?"

"Yes chief, I have been busy too. It looks like you were right. This guy Dev is bisexual. He is married to this solicitor, Sheena Achar and he also has a boyfriend. He is a regular customer at the Quebec and probably also at the Abbey Park. There is still nothing about drug use or drug dealing. The underground has gone quiet on this one. I can't get anyone to say anything about this guy. I know that he used poppers while at the clubs." Sean took out his little notebook from his worn out jacket. "The milkman says that he saw three Asian men coming out of the alley behind Harrison road around the time of the murder. But he could not identify any of them if any of the guys were shown to him. Too dark, he says. I also know that he was beaten up a few years ago by someone outside the Quebec. Well, you know that already."

"So, what do you think?"

"It could be either a homophobic hate murder or a jealous boyfriend? You know what I think about a professional hit."

"You don't think it is racially motivated?"

"There is nothing to suggest it is."

"What about your contact, the druggie?"

"Strange, chief. He has gone quiet too. Says he does not know anything about this man. The clients in both the Quebec and the Abbey Park shut up as soon as they see me coming." Sean paused for a moment.

"What is it Sean? You are holding on to something."

"I am not sure if it is important. But this reporter guy came looking for me at the pub last night. He says he knows something that we don't."

"What do you mean? Did he say what it was? Can you trust him?"

"That is it. I can't trust the bugger. So I did not encourage him."

"Hmmmmm. It may be something you may want to pursue. We seem to be going up a blind alley with every lead." Stoker said and pulled out a folder from the pile of pares on his desk. "This came from the hospital this morning."

It was a thick folder with photocopied pages neatly stapled together.

"I can't believe it!" Sean exclaimed. "It has been only a couple of days since I put in a request."

"Looks like the commissioner has been speaking to his mate, the chief exec at the hospital." Stoker smiled.

"Let me go through this. Might get some leads to his enemies if he had any." Sean said picking up the folder and leafing through it. "Do you think those three Asian guys have anything to do with the murder?"

"At the moment we can't rule anything out. See if you can find anything in those records."

A LITTLE RED NOTEBOOK

Sean's mobile phone rang for the third time in ten minutes. He could not recognise the number that was calling and no one spoke when he picked the phone up. The first time he thought it must have been a wrong number. The second time he knew there was definitely someone on the other end of the line. The third time, someone cleared her throat.

"Hello, this is Sean O'Connor. Who is this? Don't be afraid. You can speak to me in confidence whoever you are."

There was silence and the line went dead. Must be a crack caller, Sean thought. He thought nothing of it as the phone went quiet for rest of the morning. Just as he was about to get into the car an hour later, the phone rang again. This time the caller spoke before he has a chance to say hello.

"Is this Officer O'Connor? Are you alone now?"

A husky female voice, very subdued and barely audible.

"Yes, I am. I am in my car and there is no one about. Who is this?

"I want to show you something which might help you in solving the murder of Dev Sharma." The voice of a female, but could not recognise as it was muffled.

"I am listening." Sean's heart skipped a beat as he replied.

"As I said, I have something to show you."

"What is it?" Sean was trying to rack his brain. He thought he had heard the voice before somewhere, but could not place it. "We could meet up somewhere."

"No. I don't really want to meet you. It is not safe."

Sean paused for a minute not sure how to respond.

"We can meet wherever you want. Somewhere discrete and I promise to keep it confidential."

There was a long pause at the other end. He thought the line was disconnected and said "Hello. Are you still there?"

"Yes, I am. I will have to think and call you back." And the line went dead. Sean scratched his head and did not know what to make of it. He was busy through the rest of the afternoon sifting through the papers that were piling up on his desk over the previous few days. There was a lot of rubbish information with several crank callers blaming anyone and everyone for the murder. There were calls from right wing activists claiming it to be the hand of foreign terrorists to Gay activists claiming it to be an anti-gay murder. There was the usual number of calls from people claiming it to be race motivated murder and there was one claiming it to be an "act of God reprimanding the soiled priest."

Sean had been trying to get some more information out of his contact, Johnny. He had become elusive and had not returned any of his calls. He had finally got a message through and arranged to meet him at the usual place near the Canal. He had not met Jonny for a few years now. There was no need to, since he had left the Drug squad under a cloud all those years ago. It was getting quite dark by the time he reached the canal bank. He sat in the car thinking about the telephone conversation waiting for the battered red car, he was so familiar with, to come around. He was nodding off when there was a knock on the car window. Sean wound the window down and said looking at his watch,

"Where the hell have you been? I have been waiting for ages."

"I have to be careful."

"Anyway, get in the bloody car then."

Johnny opened the door and slid in to the front seat.

"This is a blast from the past. I thought were not working with the drug squad anymore?"

"I don't. I am with the Homicide team now."

"I don't have anything to tell you. Everyone seems to be stressed out. Cops nosing around too much."

"I am in the middle of a murder case now. It looks like there is a strong link to drugs."

"What murder are you talking about?"

"Have you not seen the news or read the newspapers?"

"The priest who was killed on Harrison road?"

"Yes, it is the priest killed on Harrison Road. Have you heard anything?"

"Was he involved in drugs?"

"We don't know yet. He might have been."

"I have not heard anything about a hit." Johnny said looking out of the car window.

"You would tell me if there was a contract out, wouldn't you?"

Johnny turned back in his seat.

"You know I would boss."

"I know you too well, Johnny. I don't trust you as far as I can throw you. Getting anything out of you is like getting blood out of a stone."

"No boss. I promise you. I have not heard anything. I will make some calls and see what is happening." Jonny said trying to sound convincing. "Can I go now?"

"Yeah, get lost. But remember if I find out if you have been holding out on me what will happen."

"I would not do that boss." Jonny said as he slid out of the car. Sean gunned the car as soon as the door was shut. He was driving into the pub car park when the phone rang. He looked at the number to see if he wanted to pick it up. It was the same caller from this morning. He stayed inside the car and answered the call.

"Hi, Sean O'Connor here."

"Mr O'Connor, will you meet me near Indigo Restaurant on Melton Road in an hour?"

"Yeah, sure."

"Do you know where it is?"

"Yeah, I have been there before."

"Good. I will be waiting for you in the car park outside the restaurant. One hour. Don't be late." And the line went dead. He looked at the phone slightly annoyed. 'How the hell does she think I can recognise her?' He called the number back to ask. There was no answer and the call was "declined." That irritated him even more. He looked at his watch to see if he has time for a quick drink before driving. 'At this time of the night it shouldn't take more than half an hour to get there. Time for a drink.'

The pub was already full and Daisy was busy with customers. She came over to him as soon as he managed to get to the front of the bar.

"That reporter guy, Derek, was here looking for you." She said as she placed his usual pint of bitter on the bar. Looking over his shoulder at the heaving mass, she continued, "He may still be here. Let me know if you want him out."

"Thanks Daisy. I'll take care of it."

Daisy smiled and moved on to the next customer. Sean leant on the bar sipping his drink mulling over the woman on the phone.

"You need to talk to me if you want to crack this case."

It was said in a hushed tone next to his ear. Sean turned around to see the reporter. It did not look like he had changed since that day. Same grubby jacket and jeans. And that crumpled hat that made him look like a poor version of Indiana Jones.

"I am sure I don't need your help."

Sean got up and walked towards an empty table to sit down. Derek followed him.

"You are looking at the wrong people and wrong places."

"And how is it that you are such an expert on this case?"

"Let us just say that Dev and I go a long way." His African accent was even stronger today.

"Let me finish this drink and we will have a chat outside."

Derek pulled a chair up and sat down without saying a word and waited for Sean to finish his drink and get up. The two of them walked outside to the car park before Sean spoke.

"You have two minutes to tell me what you know. I got to be somewhere else."

"I grew up with Dev in Mombasa. His family were forced to emigrate after a scandal."

"What kind of scandal?"

Derek appears to be thinking for a minute before replying. "Let us say that one of the Jesuit teachers in the local school took an extraordinary interest in little Dev."

"What is it got to with his killing?"

"Have you spoken to his wife?"

"She is grieving as you probably know. Yes, I have spoken to her. Obviously she is heart broken."

Derek laughed. A hollow cynical kind of laugh.

"She is good, I give you that."

"What are you trying to say? Has she got something to do with her husband's killing?"

"I am not saying she has or she has not. But our paths have ~~been~~ crossed before and she is not what you see at first sight."

Sean snorted and replied, "Just because she got the better of you in something does not mean she killed her husband. Now if you will excuse me, I have to be somewhere else in a hurry."

"The two of them knew each other for ten years before they got married and get this. She knew he was bisexual when she married him. I heard what she said at the press conference."

"So she lied about him being Gay. I need more than that."

They had reached his car by then and Sean opened the door and sat inside. Derek knocked on the window. As Sean wound down the window, Derek said.

"Think about it. I would not put it past her to bump him off when she found out that Dev had not changed after the marriage. Have you ever thought about who got the priest beaten up for being Gay all those years ago?"

Sean closed the window and started his car without a reply. He could see the reporter standing in the car park, a lonely figure in a pool of light in the dark car park. He felt sorry for him. He had not considered Sheena as one of the suspects so far. 'Maybe there is something to this reporter, worth checking out.' She had very cleverly evaded questions about the priest being gay or bisexual at the news conference. She had shut the reporters by stating that she did not know that he was Gay. He reached the Indigo restaurant just before nine. He had been there once before. It was in the outskirts of Leicester, an old derelict pub converted into an Indian restaurant with a Chinese twist. It still had not caught on with locals as it was a bit out of the way and the restaurants on Belgrave road were too well established with regulars. The car park was lit up at the front with a line of cars near the entrance. He drove to the back of the car park, which was in darkness. He sat there not sure what to do next. The voice on the phone had not said whether to meet inside the restaurant or not.

He was about to open the door when one of the cars in the front came to life. The lights did not come on as the car drove to the back of the car park to near where he was parked. He sat in the car waiting to see what happened next. The car stopped at the back of the car park in the far corner, away from him. There was quiet again. He was getting a bit restless when his mobile rang.

"Is that officer O'Connor?"

"Yes it is. I am parked in the car park at the back."

"OK. Stay in the car."

The line went dead. He could see someone get out of the car in the far corner and walk towards him. She was tall and slim, wearing a tight jeans and heels. She had her head covered in a scarf, which went over her face half way up just exposing her eyes. Even in the darkness she struck a note and made his heart race. He liked the sway of her hips as she walked across and was glued to her figure when she knocked on the window and signalled him to open the back door. She slid into the back seat behind him.

"Don't turn around please."

He could smell her perfume, quite strong and yet subtle.

"Can I ask who you are?"

"It is not important who I am. I have something to show you. It will help you in your investigation. But I don't want you to show it to anyone else or make it public."

"That depends on what it is. I can't promise you not to use it as evidence if I think it is necessary."

She became very quiet at this. Sean tried to turn around to see what was happening, when she hissed,

"Don't! Whatever happens, you are not to turn around."

Sean could feel the hair on his back stand up. There was something in her hushed voice, which made him shiver. He reluctantly turned back to face the darkness out of the windscreen.

"If what you show me has any incriminating evidence, I will have to use it. It is the law."

"I have a notebook where Dev has been keeping a dairy of everything he did since childhood. It is his little red notebook. There is a lot of personal information there and I don't want innocent people dragged into this."

"How did you come across it?"

"I am not going to tell you. I will let you read it and you have to promise to give it back to me. I can only let you have it for twenty four hours."

"Yes. I can give it back to you tomorrow, I am sure."

"What guarantee do I have that you will return it to me tomorrow?"

Sean smiled to himself. Two can play at this game, he thought.

"You just have to take my word for it. I can't say any more than that. I can get it back to you here at same time tomorrow."

There was a silence from the back seat. There was a noise of zip opening and some tearing from the back.

"Don't turn around. Just pick up the book from the seat after I have left. I will be here tomorrow at the same time."

Sean could hear the door handle turn and the door creaked open.

"Don't be late." And the door slammed shut.

He watched her hips sway as she walked across the car park. She knew he would be watching as she got into the car and drove off without switching the lights on. He could barely make out a head covered in scarf and not much else. He could not wait to see what she had left on the seat. He leaned over to pick up the package. He grabbed the package and managed to pull it over from the back of the seat where it had slid. He switched on the overhead light to take a closer look. It was a red notebook that was badly crumpled at the edges. The cover had been carefully sealed in thick clear plastic which had become a dirty yellow colour with usage. He turned over to see that pages had been stuck in with glue at the back making it twice the size it had started off with.

Whoever's it was, they had looked after the book very carefully over the years. It was obviously very old. He gently opened the notebook to see the first page. There was an old black and white photograph to boys standing on a beach somewhere. One was an African boy with a thick afro flock of hair. It was hard to read in the dull light of the car. It appeared to be a child's scrawl talking about a new country and new people. He turned the pages to the middle at a random page and what he read shook him. He quickly closed the book and looked around to see if anyone had seen him. There was no one around nearby. He was still parked in the darkest part of the car park. He could not wait to get the book home to read. He stopped at the local Indian take away to pick some curry and rushed home.

He spent the next four hours reading the notebook. He did not notice that the curry had gone cold while he was reading the notebook. It was a fascinating story of someone's life from childhood to almost the day he died. By the time he finished the book, he felt repulsed at the man and at the same time a subtle admiration for what he had achieved.

A little lost boy displaced from his childhood home because of a sexual scandal in a foreign country, not of his own making, reaching the top of his chosen career was amazing. He had grown from a sullen and confused little boy to a charming and charismatic leader. It was a story filled with intrigue, sex, drugs and shenanigans that would put Borgias to shame. He did not appear to hide anything in the book in most places. The people involved were mentioned by their first names or nicknames – such as Sanju, the Gaffer, the rent boy and Nathu. It would take years of searching to actually identify anyone. One thing that was not consistent was the dates. Not every entry was dated. His adult life had started off being a Good Samaritan helping the needy, the helpless and gay in the Asian community and progressed to blackmail for sex. He loved his new car and his watch, but most of all he appeared to love sex. He appeared to have a voracious appetite for sex. Sex with young boys, both Asian and white. He had been a runner for someone called 'the gaffer' supplying drugs for a brief period. He was not addicted to drugs, but would enjoy a bottle of popper whenever he visited the gay clubs. He had started off with the now defunct Spots club and frequented places like the Quebec, the Abbey Park and the Central Motors to pick up boys.

When he finished reading the book, Sean felt drained. Until a few hours ago, he could not understand why anyone would want to kill a well-known and charismatic Hindu priest. After reading the book, he was surprised that he lasted that long. There were many people who would want him dead. He appeared to have control over all of his victims. Except one. His Achilles heel was his wife, Sheena Achar. He had kept his sexual orientation a secret from her, or he thought he had. What started off as an infatuation had turned into a fanatical love. He had poured out his love for Sheena in some detail. It was almost as if he was trying to justify his bisexuality. He had made sure that his fight for the Gay community was out in the open and as public as possible. So much so that anyone would think he could be nothing but straight. Bit of a contradiction in terms, Sean thought. He dreaded her leaving him. There appeared to be some friction towards the end and he was beginning to suspect that she might have found out.

He picked up the little square, black and white photograph that had fallen on the bed, to take a closer look. It was obviously taken in a hot country somewhere on a beach. He could just see shadows of some palm trees in the background. The picture was already fading and slightly discoloured due to time. One of the boys was definitely an African grinning widely as did the other boy. What struck him was that the boys were not facing the camera, but embracing each other face to face. They could not have been older than five or six years at the time the picture was taken. He could not figure out who the second boy was. One of them, could even be the African boy, must be a Peter, the writer of the notebook kept talking about.

He picked up the notebook again to examine it. Something else stuck him. Some pages at the back appear to have been carefully removed – not just torn. There was discontinuity in the text between some of the pages. He scratched his head. For someone who had spent so much time and attention in the care of the book over decades, he appears to have been clumsy in his entry to remove some of the pages. Unless of course if someone else had removed it. His mind started to race and did not matter how much he thought, he could not find an answer. He took out the huge lens he had in his desk, which he had never had a chance to use since becoming a detective, to examine the book a bit more closely. He had imagined himself to be a sort of modern day Sherlock Holmes when he had seen the lens in a car boot sale all those years ago. The back cover of the book appeared to be thicker than the front cover. He took it to the table lamp for a closer examination. There appeared to be few sheets of paper stuck between the back cover and the last page. He tried to prise open the back cover with his fingers. The plastic cover was stapled to the last page sealing the sheets inside. He picked up his penknife and prised open the staples holding the back cover. Numerous pages of very fine paper, each neatly folded into four fell out. He gently unfolded one of them trying not to tear the paper.

It was a hand written letter, in very neat handwriting from someone called Peter Ngyo. He was Dev's friend from Mombasa. Luckily all the letters were dated. The first one appeared to go back to 1964. The first few were like reading letters from teenagers in puppy love. There was fondness to be expected of two long lost friends and maybe a bit more. Peter was obviously deeply in love with Dev. The letter spoke about a Brother Francis and Kilindini Harbour and the beach and cricket. The Jesus fort appeared to have a been a special place for the two of them as well as their trips to the Brother Francis's room at the back of the school. There was a lot of recriminations against the grownups generally in first few letters. There was an invitation to ordaining ceremony of Peter in 1982. It did not look like Dev had made it to the ceremony. The frequency of letters reduced after that until it completely dried up around 1994.

His head was spinning as he looked at the clock. It was nearly four in the morning. He had been up most of the night reading the damn "little red book!" He needed a drink. He staggered up to the sideboard and poured himself a shot of whisky. He started to feel a bit more settled after the second glass. Tiredness and alcohol finally took their toll and he was fast asleep still in his street clothes, clutching an empty whisky bottle.

He was woken up by the sun burning down on his face. The late October sun was burning his cheeks as he had forgotten to pull the curtains the night before. He looked at the bedside clock.

"Bloody hell, it can't be ten already!" he exclaimed and jumped off the bed, only to fall flat on his face as he tripped over the whisky bottle lying on the floor. 'Shit, the chief is going have my guts for garters.' He muttered to himself as he pulled off his clothes on the way to the bathroom. The mobile phone rang as he was shaving and brushing his teeth at the same time. He ignored the phone and let it ring till it was picked up by the answering service. It was the girl in the car park.

"Call me back Mr O'Connor. I wanted to remind you to return the little red book tonight." A brief and terse message. He better call her. He was now quite convinced that it must be the wife, Sheena. Once he was dressed, he called her number. She picked up the phone after the first ring.

"Hello." Still a brusque tone. She had recognised his number.

"Hello, Mrs Sharma, this is Sean O'Connor."

There was quiet on the other end. After what appeared to be ages, she said,

"I would be very careful Mr O'Connor. You have no idea what or who you are dealing with. I will forget what you said just now and expect to see you prompt at eight tonight." And the line went dead. He was now convinced that it must be Dev's wife who had given him the notebook.

Sean faced a dilemma. He was not sure if he wanted to show the 'little red book' to the chief or anyone else. There was nothing in the book to use as evidence. He had made some notes during the night and noted the dates and names as they appeared for some of them. He was not sure if he could ever find out who the people were in that book apart from the priest's family. There was one person he could recognise outside of the family. Dev's business partner, in care home business – Stuart. He could not remember his surname offhand, but should not be difficult to get it. He struggled with his decision throughout the day. The missing pages was something he could not get out of his mind or understand. Something at the back of his mind kept telling him that it is not good idea to share the contents of the book with anyone. Not just yet anyway.

Returning the book was a quick affair and it was over before he knew what was happening. Her car was waiting at the back of the car park as he drove in. She was out of her car before he had a chance to switch the engine off and knocking on his window. He wound the window down and said,

"Hello, here I am as promised."

"The notebook please."

Sean took the notebook out of the glove compartment and held it out. She snatched the book from his hands and turned around walk across the car park.

"Excuse me Mrs Sharma." Sean was out of the car and

stood outside the car. “Mrs Sharma.” He called out again as she did not stop.

She stopped and half turned towards him and said, “Yes?”

“Some of the pages were missing from the red book.” He said trying to sound quiet. But it still sounded loud in the car park.

She turned around to face him still a few steps ahead of him.

“I had not noticed that Mr O’Connor.”

“I did. I just wondered if you knew anything about the missing pages.”

“I would not know Mr O’Connor.” She did not sound as confident as she did before, he thought. Or was he just imagining things? “Now, if you will excuse me, I have to be somewhere else now.”

Before Sean had a chance to respond, she was back in the car. Her car was out of the car park before he could realise what was happening.

THE GARRULOUS BURGLAR

It was three weeks since the body was discovered and the police were no further forward with the investigation. Stoker was getting increasingly stressed and he was taking it out on everyone else. Sean got the brunt of his wrath almost every morning when he walked in, late as usual with a tongue lashing. He was reluctant to pull back any of the hundred odd officers looking for clues for the murderer. They had drawn a blank on the drugs end. The entire drug mafia appeared to have gone underground and none of the contacts had come with any information. Mick Mills was convinced that it was a drugs hit.

Several of the gay officers had started mixing freely with the local and Asian gay community, frequenting bars such as the Abbey Park and the Quebec almost regularly. Men were visiting the Quebec, every Friday to check out the Asian gay community. No one seemed to know or heard anything about Dev Sharma.

The call centre was quiet with only fifteen calls during the first week petering down to just three calls this week. Stoker had sent some officers to follow up some of them only to be disappointed with either a hoax or exaggeration.

Sean was late as usual on the Wednesday of that week and he was getting the usual dressing down from Stoker when one of the secretaries put her head round the door and nearly got her head bitten off.

"What do you want? Can't you see I am busy?"

"Sorry chief, I thought you might want to take this call."

"Who is it?"

"It is Gemma Cornhill, one of the PCs who has gone to check out a lead on a robbery on Mowmacre Hill." The girl replied. "She says that the guy is confessing to killing someone."

Stoker snorted, "And why do you think I would be interested. It would be another crank trying to get his name in the newspapers."

"He says he killed an Asian man."

That got the attention of both Stoker and Sean. Sean was sitting with the chief going through the papers from the hospital and forensic reports.

"Get the line patched through to me then. Let see what this is all about."

Sean could see a ray of hope in Stoker's face as he sat down to take the call. The officer on the other end. Gemma, one of the new recruits, was gushing with information.

"Chief, this guy, Lenny, says he has killed an Asian man three weeks ago. We came to this flat looking for some stolen goods on a tip off."

"Where is this flat?" Stoker asked.

"It is one of the tenement blocks north of the canal."

Stoker looked up at Sean. Both of them knew those flats. They had visited those flats a number of times as part of the Drug squad in the past. It was notorious as a habitat for several of the drug runners and users alike. It was the place Sean had made ~~the~~ his first drug bust.

"You better bring him in and let us have a chat with him."

Stoker put the phone down and looked at Sean.

"We might have something here Sean. Do you want to handle this or shall I ask Mick to take the questioning?"

Sean scratched his head before answering.

"You better let Mick take this one chief. He thinks this is his case."

"You're right. Let us sit on this one."

He picked up the phone and asked for Mick to be sent for and got back to the papers. He picked up the notes from the hospital and waving at Sean,

"What do you make of this Sean?

"It is obviously someone who did not like the priest. It looks like a deliberate attack to me and not a robbery gone wrong. Looks like they had been waiting for him at the car park and pounced on him."

""It was at the gay club. Did you get anything out of the guys in the club?"

"It is all in the report chief. Not much. He was regular as clockwork every Friday night, which was the Asian night at the club. He had a regular boyfriend, a young white kid who no one seems to remember the name of. No one seems to have picture of him either. It was almost as if the boyfriend has disappeared into thin air."

"Did anyone remember anything about the day of the attack? Was there anything in the police report?"

"Sorry chief. Dead end, I am afraid. No one could remember the attack. It was a few years ago and the people working at the time have left now. There was nothing much on the police files either. Mark Henson has done the report. I spoke to him and he can't remember much about the incident either. Says he interviewed the priest at the hospital and he was called to the temple when they had some threatening letter and phone calls not long ago. The priest could not identify any of the attackers. Claimed it was very dark and he could not think of any reason for the attack."

"Jealous boyfriend?"

"Judging by the medical report, he appears to have been given a good going over. Must have been more than one guy beating him up chief."

"Drug gang?"

"There is nothing coming out of the drug scene chief. My contact says that he was a runner for a short period and seems to have merged into a background. He was known to use poppers at the club. Whether he actually used the heavy stuff we found at the house is not clear."

"Yes, what about all the drug found at the house?"

Sean was not sure whether he should answer the question. He would be treading on Mick Mills territory.

"I don't know chief. Mick probably has some ideas about it."

Stoker snorted at this and did not say anything.[22]

"If you ask my opinion, I think the stuff was for personal consumption. I don't think there was enough there for him to be a supplier or dealer."

"That is not what Mick Mills thinks." Stoker said staring at Sean. "What about those Asian guys seen near the house? Any leads on those?"

"No chief. Since we put out that bulletin about that, there have been several calls. Most of them were crank calls I am afraid. Mostly from right wing activists claiming the priest to be heathen and got his just punishment."

Gemma brought Lenny in hand cuffed and looking pleased with himself for some reason into the station about an hour later. Sean could see her marching a weedy looking tall lad in scruffy clothes and torn trainers across the hall into the interview rooms through the glass window of Stoker's office. Mick Mills walked into the office at the same time.

"You are just in time Mick." Stoker said to him. "One of the PCs have brought in a suspect who claims he killed the priest. I want you to question him."

Mick's eyes lit up.

"That is a bit of good news chief. We were not getting anywhere out on the field." Then he looked at Sean who was sitting on the desk and doubt crept in. "Not one of the cranks is it?"

Sean's face was noncommittal. Stoker replied.

"We don't know yet. I am sure you can get it out of him if he is a crank soon enough." The sarcasm was completely lost on Mick. "Come on let us go and find out."

The three of them trouped towards the interrogation room. Stoker and Sean slid in to the side viewing room. They saw Mick open the door of the room where Lenny was sitting with handcuffs hands on the desk and the PC Gemma standing beside him.

"I will take it from here constable, Thank you." Mick said dismissing Gemma without even looking at her. He pulled up a chair in front of the desk as Gemma left slamming the door.

Mick was never known for subtlety. Lenny looked at him still with a smug expression on his face. Mick saw a scruffy young man, thin, almost emaciated sitting in front of him. He had the typical drug induced haze in his eyes, not really focussing on anything in front of him. Mick was not immediately impressed by what he saw. He picked up the folder lying the desk and leafed through the papers.

"So, you think you killed someone?"

Lenny did not answer first. He continued to stare at Mick with a fixed expression still on his face. It almost looked as if he was laughing inside.

"Yeah, I did. That's what I been telling those coppers outside."

"Yes, I see. And you are Lenny? Have I seen you before somewhere?"

"I keep telling you buggers, I killed the bastard, cause he tried to rape me."

"He tried to rape you? Are you sure?"

Lenny pulled the sleeves of his jacket and shirt and exposed arms full of puncture marks and old scars.

"He filled me full of the stuff and tried to rape me." Lenny said with a squeaky voice getting irritated. "Mind you, it was good stuff. The best I have had."

There was a hint of a smile, which did not go to his eyes.

"Did you know the man you killed?"

"Yeah, I known him for a long time. Bro was good to me. Don't know what came over him. I don't like to be fucked by a man. No way. I had to protect myself. I got a girlfriend. You understand?"

Mick smiled and said, "Of course I understand."

"I hope so. Vanessa told me you would understand."

"Who is Vanessa?"

"She is David's wife. She looked after me that day. I was in a real state after I was attacked. And there were two of them. I had to use the knife to protect myself. I think I killed him."

He suddenly started to sob. Slowly at first and intensified with the sobs racking his thin frame. As Stoker and Sean watched through the glass partition, he started to hit his head on the desk. Mick tried to stop him with no effect and sat back watching Lenny continued to sob violently. He soon appeared to get tired and lifted his head back and closed his eyes. There were tears rolling down his cheeks and looked a pathetic figure.

"OK Lenny. I believe you. But tell me what happened. Why did you kill him?"

Lenny went into a rage and started to shout and scream. No one could understand anything he said. It was more of a rant than a dialogue. It went on for a while until he appear to tire and rest his head on the desk go to sleep. Mick looked up at the glass partition asking what to do next.

"I think we should get a statement from this guy once he has sobered up from whatever he is under now." Stoker said to Sean. "Get a medic to have a look at him and see what he thinks."

The two of them walked around the corner into the interview room where Mick was trying desperately to wake up Lenny.

"That did not go very well, did it Mick?"

"I think he is drugged to the hilt chief. I can't get any sense out of him."

"Better get a medic to have a look at him and wait till he dries out."

It was not till a few hours later when the Police Doctor had examined Lenny and given an injection so that anyone could have a sensible conversation with Lenny. He had slept for six hours after the injection on the hard bench, which served as a bed in the lock up.

It was nearly eight o clock at night when Lenny was sober enough to speak. They took him into the interview room along with a stenographer to take down his statement along with some recording equipment. Stoker and Sean introduced themselves and sat on one side of the desk while Mick sat with Lenny on the other side with the recording equipment in the middle. The typist was on one side looking rather dejected for having to work overtime.

"We would like to write down what you say and also record this conversation. Is that alright with you Lenny?"

Stoker asked with an inordinately soft voice, which belied his size. He could put the worst criminal at ease. He looked like a doddery old uncle who had just walked in out of the cold. Lenny just nodded his head in agreement.

"Can I ask you to speak out loud whatever you want to say please? It is for the recording equipment."

"Yeah, OK."

"Good. Let's start again. Lenny, do you agree for this interview to be recorded and you are making a statement?"

"Yeah. I do."

The initial responses were all pretty monosyllabic until he got into the night of the murder. A floodgate seems to open and there was a barrage of information the stenographer was struggling to keep pace with. Sean could not understand a lot of it in the beginning. He talked about a giant cat trying to kill him. His eyes lit up every time he spoke about 'Bro.' There seemed to be a genuine affection towards the man. It became quite obvious that the priest was supplying Lenny with crack regularly. There were references to sexual encounters and visits to the Quebec, the Abbey Park and the Central Motors. It was not clear if he was directly involved in the sexual encounters or not. A 'gaffer' was mentioned a number of times and it was not clear who this 'gaffer' was. He appeared to be central to the drugs.

Lenny claimed that the priest took Lenny to his house on Harrison road and picked up a couple of his mates on the way. He claimed that the three of them tried to rape him and he pulled his knife out in self-defence.

"Do you mean to say the three of them tried to rape you?"

Lenny looked confused at this.

"No, no. It was just the Bro."

"So what happened to the other two men?"

"What two men?"

"You said there were three of them remember?"

"What are you talking about?"

This went on for a while until Stoker decided to move on.

"I think you killed him to get more drugs and steal his money." Mick said.

"No." He screamed. "Why would I kill Bro? I loved him. He was good to me and he looked after me. I tell you it is that cat, which turned him against me. He tried to rape me. He has never done that before."

It was close to midnight by the time they finished taking down his statement. Sean felt drained as he walked out of the headquarters and sat in his battered old car. It looked like an open and shut case with a confession by the killer. It would be up to the judge and the jury to decide whether he meant to kill the priest or not. And yet, there was a nagging doubt in Sean's mind. There was something quite not right here. He could not put his finger on it. He kept thinking about the reporter and his claims about Sheena. There was nothing in Lenny's statement or the little red book to tie her down as a suspect. He opened a new bottle of whisky and was down to nearly half when he finally fell asleep only to be woken up by the constant knocking on the door. He staggered to the front door only to find Stoker standing outside leaning against the wall. He left the door open and staggered back inside without saying a word followed by Stoker.

"Where the hell have you been all day?"

Sean scratched his head and looked at his watch. It was nearly four in the afternoon. He could not remember when he had fallen asleep. He had a splitting headache and he was hungry.

"Mostly in bed." Sean replied.

"You live like a tramp." Stoker said looking around the dinghy little flat. "This place is not the same since Lucy left you."

Sean did not reply, but walked across to the window and pulled the curtains and opened the window. The cold breeze from outside woke him up and helped clear the cobwebs from his drink befuddled brain. He stood there looking outside at the park in front and the bench under the large oak tree. There was an elderly couple sitting there with a dog running around the park. His mind went back to the happier days when he used to walk with Lucy hand in hand along with Jimmy, their golden Labrador. His eyes misted over at the thought. She had taken the dog with her telling him, "You are not capable of love or dealing with another living being."

He turned back to face Stoker and said,

"Do you believe that guy?"

"Which guy?"

"Lenny."

"Seems straight forward enough." Stoker threw the clothes from the settee on to the floor before sitting down. "The guy confessed to killing the priest in self-defence. It is for the lawyers to fight it out about the motive"

"Aren't you least bit curious to find out why he killed the priest?"

"He told us remember? The guy was trying to rape him."

His voice belied his conviction.

"So you don't believe him then?"

"Did I say that? Are you not listening to me Sean?"

"Chief, I have known you long enough to know otherwise." Sean replied. "Why else would you be here?"

Stoker smiled as he picked up the half empty bottle of Jack Daniels on the side table.

"What do you think?" he said closely examining the left over whisky in the bottle.

"I am not sure chief. It looks too neat. There are so many strings attached, it is practically a cobweb."

"Is there anything you are not telling me Sean?"

"I don't know what you mean chief."

"Come off it. You know exactly what I mean."

"You have read my report."

"Yes, I have, Sean" Stoker said looking through the whisky bottle at the sun "Fascinating. Did you know you could see lots of colours when you look at the sun through a whisky bottle?"

"I don't think I have left anything out in my report." Sean said feeling a little unsure of himself now.

"Why is it that I don't believe you then? You know I usually believe everything you tell me."

"I think I know what you mean, chief. There is something about this case which does not add up."

"There is more than something Sean. Why did he leave all that money lying around? He had more than enough time to clean up the place. For a drug addict, he left a drug cache as big as anything. He could have kept himself loaded for the rest of the year with the stuff we found in that house. He could have stolen the almost brand new beamer. It was found abandoned a couple of miles from Harrison road at the end of an alleyway. We still have not found the keys for the car yet. He did not even steal the Rolex watch on his wrist."

"So Lenny did not go in the Priest's car?"

"Doesn't look like it. So why is he confessing to killing the man?"

"Beats me chief." Sean almost blurted out about the little Red book.

"And another thing. While you were sleeping off your whisky, we have been working. No sign of his knife yet. I have over a hundred officers combing the streets from the priest's house to Mowmacre hill and nothing has come up. Yes, we did find some blood stained trainers at his friend, David's house."

Sean looked at Stoker with a question.

"Forensics are working on it to see if it matches either the Priest's or Lenny's blood. The guy does not have a place to live. He crashes out at a girl's place most nights." Stoker said putting the whisky bottle down again. "I can't understand what that teenager sees in that wastrel of a man."

"Have you ever thought it could be those Asian guys who had killed the Priest and loaded Lenny's hand with his own knife?"

"Why do you say that? There has not been a peep out of any of the contacts so far on that front."

"Well, the Priest was beaten up by some guys a few years ago and there was a rumour that he was beaten up by one of the grooms he had officiated before who felt that the wedding vows was somehow tainted by the priest being gay."

"No one has come forward about those three Asian guys seen on the Harrison road around the time of the murder yet.

The regular boyfriend of the Priest appears to have disappeared into thin air. The gay community might be protecting their own. The priest appears to have made some enemies among them too." Stoker replied. "Any word from your contacts in drug scene?"

"No chief. I know the priest was a runner for a brief period a year ago when the regular guy was 'indisposed.'

"I don't think it would be drug killing. The killing was not really professional. It was more of a frenzied attack. They tell me the guy was stabbed thirteen times and the stab in the neck was the one that finally killed him."

"I agree with you chief. They would have cleaned out the flat and we would not have found any drugs in the house if it was a drug killing."

There was silence for a minute as neither of them spoke. It looked like they had run out of scenarios.

"I know you went meet her last week, Sean." Stoker had picked up one of the whisky glasses on the side table and holding against the light coming from the window, was staring at the dark lipstick mark on the glass.

"Who do you mean chief?" Sean's bravado was not convincing. He could feel the heat under the collar.

"I know you met her twice Sean."

"Are you having me tailed?" Sean tried to sound indignant.

"You know me better than that, Sean. But I have been reading the Internals' report. You do know they still have their eyes on you."

Sean snorted and ground his teeth as he replied, "The buggers don't have anything on me. The tribunal cleared me last year. Why are they still after me?"

"Once you are in their sight, they never let you go. They are like leeches. They won't rest till they have their fill with your blood."

"The sons of bitches." His knuckles were white and stopped himself from slamming his fist on the glass top.

"You still have not told me Sean."

"Yes, I did meet the Priest's wife. I swore to keep it out of the official records."

"That does not make any sense to me. Don't tell me it had nothing to do with the killing?"

"I really don't know what to make of it."

"What do you mean?"

Sean spent the next half an hour telling Stoker about the contents of the little red book. He could see the fascination in Stoker's eyes as he recounted the years in Mombasa and the story of a manipulative and yet an extremely charismatic man. The story of a little boy in a strange country, sexually abused as a child growing up to be one of the most influential characters of the community. He seemed to be quite pally with several public figures including the local Member of Parliament, Fred Homuz and senior officials in the government, media and even the police. There was a lot about Sheena. Quite mixed. Towards the end he appeared to be reticent about his entries on Sheena There were intimate details of his trysts with several of the "boys" as he liked to call them. They were all marked with letters x, y or z. No names. When Sean finished, Stoker was almost speechless. He sat there staring at Sean, who got up and went to the bathroom.

"It was as if he was scared of something towards the end. There were quite a few entries scratched off in the book ...." His voice tailed off towards the end from the bathroom. "And there was something else I could not get my handle on."

"Where is the red book then?" Stoker called through the bathroom door.

"I gave it back." came the mumbled reply.

"What do you mean gave it back? Why did you give it back?"

Sean came out wiping his face with a towel and hair.

"I had to. I had promised her. She said I could only have it for a day."

"I don't believe you Sean. This is a bombshell and you gave it back." Stoker was incredulous. "Sand what was that you couldn't get your handle on?"

"I did not think it had any useful information regarding the murder chief. Anyway we could not have use the book as evidence, as it did not give any dates and only the first names or nicknames of people." Sean said moving towards the bedroom door. "There were some pages missing towards the end. And a promise is a promise chief. You know very well, I could not get any contacts if I don't keep my promises."

"What do you mean pages missing? How do you know?"

Sean came out of the bedroom pulling on a fresh shirt. He described the discontinuity in text.

"I could not understand how come someone who had taken so much care in looking after the book is so clumsy in some of the entries."

"Maybe someone else has done it."

"That is what I thought. But who?

"We could have identified the people and questioned them without divulging the source.

"No chief. You know very well I could not do that."

"You are not going soft on the girl. Are you Sean? She is way out of your league."

Sean was flustered for a moment, but recovered quickly.

"She is some looker, isn't she?"

"She has a perfect reason to bump the Priest off. All that talk of loving and devoted husband and visits to the infertility clinic could be a cover up. I thought she laid it on a bit too thick at the press conference about the devoted wife part. I can just imagine her wanting to knock of her husband when she found out he was gay. Don't you think?"

"She knew he was bisexual before she got married to him." Sean said stuffing the shirt inside his trousers.

"Maybe he was cheating on her with a boyfriend. Remember he had a boyfriend at the club?"

"Who, no one can find anymore."

"What do you mean?"

"It could be a red herring chief. It could be a story of jealous lover. The guys who claim that, might be saying that because he would not sleep with them."

"But she would fit the bill perfectly for this case in all respects. She did not have to steal any drugs or money from the house and she would not have to steal her husband's car. How do you know she did not pay someone to beat her husband to stop him from straying into Gay clubs? Is that not what the reporter said to you?"

Sean did not say anything for a minute.

"Why would she show me the book if it was going to implicate her? She is too clever for that chief."

"Maybe that is exactly what she wants us to think."

"I was quite convinced she had the priest killed till yesterday. Now, I am not so sure." Sean was scratching his head. "I wish I had the book a little longer. Maybe I have missed something."

"Are you sure here was nothing unusual in the book?"

"I only had it for a night chief." Sean was thoughtful.

"Now. Why did she want it back in such a hurry."

"Maybe I should have hung on to it a bit longer." Sean was beginning to doubt himself.

"It does not matter now, anyway. We now have a confession for the murder. Was there any link between Lenny and the wife?"

"No chief. I don't think she had even heard of him before.

I have been through her statements a few times since I read the book. She looks clean on paper."

"Did the priest know that Sheena had seen the red book?"

Sean though for a minute, trying to remember the contents of the little red book. "I am not sure. Maybe he did. She told me that she found the book after his death."

Stoker stood up and started walking towards the front door.

"I can't help feeling we got the wrong man."

Sean pulled on his jacket and said, "I feel the same way chief. It is up to the lawyers now. Come on chief, let's eat. I am hungry."

JUSTICE DONE

The case dragged on for nearly nine months. Sean spent several fruitless hours researching Sheena's background and trailed through the names he could remember from the little red book. He was no further forward at the end of nine months when Lenny was brought to the court.

There were tentative links between the priest and the local drug dealer, he bumped into links with right wing activists and even links between the priest and several leading men and women of the society. One enigma remained throughout - Sheena Achar. He could not get into her story. She appears to have come into the Priest's life out of nowhere, a law student from a respectable Gujarati family and working as an industrial lawyer for a reputable company in Leeds. She seems to have targeted the priest from the time she set her eyes on him. She was the perfect girlfriend and a loyal wife. Maybe a little bit too perfect. Everyone he spoke to had nothing but praise for her and at the same time no details were coming out. It was as if she was there and at the same time she wasn't. There were gaps in her story that Sean could not fill despite talking to people in both Leicester and Leeds. There were veiled links to the brutal attack on the priest, a year after the marriage.

The Gay community, particularly the Asian side of it, were very quiet in the beginning. As the months rolled by, they became more vociferous. Most of them had nothing but praise for the priest, but there were many who were not enamoured by the man. He appeared to have alienated many young men and was considered arrogant and 'stand-offish' by several. But none of them had any particularly strong enough feelings to mean any harm to the priest.

Sean spent many hours and many meetings with his contact, Johnny, exploring the possibility of a drug related hit. He even managed to speak to 'the gaffer' on the phone without any luck. Yes, 'the Gaffer' did confirm that the priest worked for him for a brief period. But there was no strong attachment or enmity he could detect. The priest had been a successful runner for 'the gaffer' and there was no animosity. He appeared to have been a good customer.

He had spent a lot of time talking to the Lenny's two girlfriends and his mother, Lisa Mitchell. He had even spoken to the teachers at John Ellis Community college where he was called a "string bean." He would rather run away than confront anyone during school days. He had dropped out of college without finishing his course and held down jobs in labouring and decorating. Life on one of Leicester's problem estates in Mowmacre Hill meant that he began smoking cannabis at a very young age and graduated to harder drugs culminating in a heroin habit. He had made friends with the priest around one of the gay clubs and the friendship had blossomed over the years. Lenny had looked up to the priest for more than just material gain. Sean also found out that Lenny had introduced the drug dealer, 'the gaffer,' to the priest.

Lenny's mother told Sean, "I was ill with pleurisy when he was boy. He would run to the neighbours and ask them to call a doctor. Later he got into drugs, because there were dealers on every corner of our estate."

One of Lenny's schoolmates recalled a "caring boy" – how he helped nurse a friend who was suffering from cancer. His long term girlfriend, Sharon Green insisted that Lenny was not a violent man.

"He is not violent, he didn't even like me to smack the children. I insisted he carry a knife for protection. You have to, living round here."

Both Sean and Stoker felt frustrated at the lack of progress on many of the promising leads they had. By the time Lenny was brought to court nearly nine months later, both of them felt that Lenny may in fact be telling the truth.

Justice Hughes was the trial Judge in this case. The trial went on for seven days with twelve members of the jury. Lenny had sat through the trial without saying much. He repeated his name and address to the prosecutor and the defending attorney did not bring him back to be examined as normally is the case. He would sit in his chair throughout the hearing without saying a word with the same smug expression on his face, the detectives had seen when he was arrested nine months earlier. He was now an inmate in the secure psychiatric institution where the doctors were trying to take him through the drug withdrawal programme.

Sean was trying to stay behind scenes. He sat at the far corner of the courthouse watching the proceedings with increasing disquiet. He was watching the faces of the different actors in the scene. He sat at the darkest corner of the courtroom trying to blend into the background.

Joan Butler, Queen's Counsel, prosecuting, told how Lenny met Dev, and was aware he was an "extremely promiscuous" homosexual who would pay for sex.

"The defendant now admits he was carrying a knife," Butler told the court. "We say Lenny was picked up in Leicester by the deceased and there was going to be some sort of sexual activity for which Mr Deodhar Sharma was going to pay."

She then continued saying that Lenny was a regular heroin user who spent a considerable amount of money on drugs and "was often short of money."

She added; "Mr Sharma was in the habit of carrying lots of cash on his person and in his car. After stabbing him, the defendant took the money."

She paused for minute and walked towards where Lenny was sitting and said,

"Lenny Mitchell had so little cash on the evening of the murder that he had to borrow the bus fare from his girlfriend's mother. Yet the very next day he bought a pair of expensive trainers and also spent a lot of money celebrating his wife's birthday."

"Bugger wouldn't buy me a pair cheap slippers, but goes ahead and buys an expensive trainers for that floozy." The murmur from Sheena was loud enough to be heard across the room and the justice gave her a scowl.

The jury was shown a video footage of the body. The clothed body of the priest was shown lying face down on the lounge floor of a house in a pool of dried up blood and then the body lying on the stretcher on the way to a police van. His throat had been cut. Kishen and Jai were visibly shaken and their mother Meera Ben started to sob loudly. There were gasps of horror from the gallery. Jai and his father helped her out of the court room as the judge was about to slam his gavel on the oak desk.

The jury of eight women and four men watched the film in complete silence. There was no commentary on the recording. It showed the outside of the house and inside, panning around the downstairs and pausing on smoke damage from a fire, allegedly started after the attack.

Mr D'Costa, representing Lenny tried to vilify the priest, calling him "an extremely promiscuous bisexual, who would do anything for sex." He also stated that Dev was "a manipulative individual who blackmailed young men into having sex with him." The priest was painted as a drug abuser and an opportunistic drug dealer. D'Costa spent a while harping on the statement made by Lenny to the fact that the priest was trying to rape him along with his friends on the night of the murder. He implied that Lenny only defended himself against a vicious attack. He drew picture of a predator trying to take advantage of his client while he was most vulnerable under the influence of hard drugs and paid the price. D'Costa claimed that it was an act of self-defence and not a premeditated murder.

Lenny Mithcell was convicted by the jury on 9th July of murder committed on previous October 20th. He was sentenced to life imprisonment by the Judge, Justice Hughes.

"He is an "existing prisoner" within the meaning of schedule 22 to the Criminal Justice Act 2003. No minimum term has been set by the Home Secretary. Accordingly, it falls to me now to determine, pursuant to section 269 of that Act, the minimum period which he should serve before the early release provisions apply to him."

He paused, adjusted his glasses once again and continued.

"My recommendation to the Home Secretary on the minimum period the defendant should serve was 16 years, based upon the then operative letter of practice of Lord Bingham, dated 10 February 1997, that is to say a starting point of 14 years. That recommendation was endorsed by Lord Woolf ."

Justice Hughes stopped again, looked up to see the reaction of the crowd. There was a gasp from the left side of the hall where Sharon was sitting with David and Vanessa Hutchins. Sharon was impassive, but one could see her jaws clenching and her hands tighten their grip on the plastic handles of the court chair. The teenage girlfriend was missing from the audience. She stayed away throughout the hearing. A low murmur had started waiting for the judge to continue. He cleared his throat and bent his head down to see over the top of his glasses to see who was making the noise. The murmur died instantly.

"I have read written representations from Mr D'Costa, Queens Counsel, on behalf of the Defendant. He has not requested an oral hearing. I have read written representations from the family of the deceased, contained in a statement dated 3 December last year. I set out the summary of the case which I incorporated into my recommendation to the Home Secretary."

He paused and adjusted his glasses once more and looked up to make sure everyone was listening. He had a rather docile face for a judge. He looked more like an ageing farmer than a judge. When he was sure everyone was paying attention to him, he continued.

"The Defendant was a heterosexual heroin addict. The deceased was an outwardly reputable Hindu priest, who as well known to his family and associates led also the life of a promiscuous homosexual, who habitually picked up strangers for sexual purposes and who relished the danger of attracting heterosexual men, particularly when drunk, for the purpose of seducing them."

There was a gasp from someone in the audience where the priest, Dev's family were sitting. They were quite shocked by the brutal description of him. The judge stopped again and looked disapprovingly at their corner.

"Late at night in the centre of Leicester, in an area well known for casual homosexual encounters, the Defendant allowed himself to be picked up by the deceased, who was kerb crawling for homosexual activity. The Defendant must have known the purpose for which the deceased approached him. He permitted himself to be driven to a house kept by the deceased for inter alia such encounters. There the Defendant stabbed the deceased approximately fifteen times, chiefly in the neck and back, with a knife which he habitually carried as a weapon. He stole money from the deceased and took his car to escape. Before he left he started a fire in the terraced house and left the gas on. Fortuitously the fire burned itself out causing appreciable interior damage and it did not spread to adjoining houses."

He stopped again and took a sip of water from the bottle in front of him. He wiped his mouth with a cloth he took out of his voluminous gown and continued.

"The Defendant's motive was likely to have been to obtain money to feed his addiction, whether by gift or robbery. He left some bank notes in the pockets of the deceased and failed to find some more which were in the car; this suggested a degree of panic by that stage."

He paused a little to see if this had any effect on the listeners in the court. When there was none, he continued.

"The deceased was at no stage armed. Apart from a cut to his hand from his own knife, the Defendant was uninjured. The absence of defence injuries to the deceased indicated that, contrary to the Defendant's account at trial, the majority of wounds were inflicted when the deceased was helpless rather than in equal struggle."

There was a sob from Sheena, who was sitting stoically all along. Sean, who was sitting not too far from her, looked up and stared at her. There was no expression on his face as his jaws tightened and bent down to look at his hands. The gruesome description of the murder was hard to take. Kishen put his arms around her to comfort. The judge did not take any notice and continued.

"The Defendant abandoned the car a short distance away and in the ensuing days made partial confessions to a number of friends, as well as giving them false accounts of his actions. On arrest he asserted that he was not present at the killing, and then that he had been kidnapped by two men and had acted throughout in self-defence. At his trial he abandoned the story of kidnapping, but asserted that he had accepted an innocent lift home and had been in fear of rape."

There was a whispering at the back of the court. The judge put his papers down and scowled at the back benches, which was filled with media. All the major newspapers and Television journalists were inside listening and furiously taking notes.

"If there are any more interruptions, I will have to clear the court"

There was an immediate silence as he continued.

"The representations now made by Mr D'Costa, on behalf of the Defendant include the submissions. Number one, that his trial story was true. Number two, that the killing was not premeditated. Number three, that the killing was not motivated by robbery. Number four, that the fire was intended only to burn a rag which had on it traces of his blood. And as to those representations. Number one, the jury's verdict effectively rejected this account, and in any event I am sure it was false. Number two, I do not believe that killing was premeditated. Number three, I am sure that the Defendant sought money, and it is clear that he took some, but I am not sure if he killed for that purpose and finally number four, is possible, but the danger created was an obvious one."

He stopped and looked up to see if it had registered. There was a pin drop silence at this stage apart from faint scratching from the reporters jotting down notes furiously on their notepads. He put the papers down and took another sip of water. A bright pink cloth came out of his gown to wipe his face this time as he was sweating. The July heat was taking a toll on many. The court room was not air conditioned. Presence of so many people inside the room made it even worse. He took another sip of water before he continued.

"Accordingly, the following aggravating features of the case which I set out in my report to the Home Office remain the relevant ones. Use of a knife habitually carried as a weapon. Number and ferocity of wounds, chiefly to back and neck. The fire, with enormous risk to adjoining life and property and the influence of drink and drugs Murder on any view followed immediately by theft."

He adjusted his glasses which kept on slipping from a sweaty nose and continued.

"I repeat the mitigating factors. Number one, the conduct of the deceased. Number two, absence of demonstrated premeditation. Number three, absence of previous convictions for violence."

He looked briefly before continuing again, "But the Defendant had told a psychiatrist of a number of occasions when he had either been involved in fights or had felt impelled to destructive behaviour or to violence, against others as well as himself. Under the now operational terms of section 269 the starting point in this case, if the Defendant were now to be convicted of this offence, would be one of fifteen years. The same factors which I have set out would aggravate and mitigate the offence. Since he was convicted before section 269 came into force, the minimum term which I must set may not be longer than that which would have been set by the Home Secretary under the practice which he would have followed at the time."

There was a deathly hush among the audience.

"On review of this case, I can see no reason to alter the view expressed in my life sentence report. The appropriate minimum term is one of sixteen years. In my view that recommendation would have been accepted by the Home Secretary under the practice then prevailing. The appropriate minimum term in accordance with Schedule 22, paragraph 6 of the Criminal Justice Act 2003 is sixteen years, less eight months spent in custody on remand."

There was a commotion from the right side of the court where Sharon had sat quietly all this time with David and Vanessa. She had started to sob. David tried to control her with no success. The judge did not stop and continued.

"The term set is the minimum term. The Defendant may of course serve longer. The assessment of any danger he may represent in the future is for the authorities and not for me."

Jailing Lenny Mitchell for life, Justice Hughes told him: "It is perfectly clear to me that you were picked up by the deceased man in his motorcar.

"It is quite impossible to believe you were not aware of what he was after. What happened is not clear - if there was sexual activity or not I don't know. But there was some kind of altercation and the jury has decided it was not self-defence or provocation. It was a sustained attack from behind with a knife that you carried habitually."

The judge pronounced the sentence by bringing the gavel down hard on the oak desk.

"Lenny Mitchell, of no fixed abode, this court sentences you to life imprisonment, to serve a minimum term of sixteen years.

There was an immediate cheer from the priest's family and supporters. At the same time there were jeers from the left side of the courtroom and shouts of "injustice!" and "unfair."

Sean walked got up to walk out of the room when he saw Sheena walking out with a deliberate step, clicking her high heels and turned at the door to look at Sean. There was a brief wave of right hand with a silk handkerchief and a smile. Just as she stepped out, she winked at Sean and disappeared among the throng of waiting reporters and crowd with flashing cameras. It was as if to tell him that she has won.

Stoker joined him at the door of the courthouse looking down at the crowd on the stone steps. Sean saw the reporter, Derek Jacobs pull his hat down and walk away from the courthouse with his hands in his pockets.

"She has won, Sean."

"Yes. Justice definitely did not."

THE RETRIBUTION

Sean saw her fielding the questions of the reporters and the TV crew with style. She could have been a professional all her life with the ease with which she was handling the press. He waited around the corner of the building out of sight of the press and still within earshot of what was being said. Most of them were inane questions about her reaction to the verdict. Stoker made a bland statement about how wonderful the support the police force had from the Asian community as well as the gay community in their enquiries leading up to the arrest. Dev's brother, Kishen made an emotional statement and thanked the Leicestershire police force for the "hard and relentless work" they had done. One of the police officers herded the family into a waiting police car to whisk them away. Sean jumped out of the shadows just as Sheena was getting into the car. She had the door still open when Sean put his hand on the door to stop it from closing.

"You must be pleased, Mrs Sharma?"

She looked at him with a question mark.

"Of course I am. Why do you ask?" A tone of hesitancy in her voice. "But that still does not bring my husband back does it?"

She knew Sean's eyes were not on her face but on her top which had swung open slightly. She appeared to have suddenly regained her composure very quickly. She knew how to play the game.

"Can I have a few minutes of your time in the next few days?" Sean stuttered.

"Why Inspector O'Connor?" Kishen interjected from inside the car. "The case is finished and the murderer has been sent to jail. What is there to discuss? It will just cause more pain."

"I am sorry sir. I do understand. But there are a few loose ends still to be tidied up. I will be as brief as possible."

"That is OK *Bhaiya*." Sheena replied to Kishen and turning back to Sean, "Give me a call and we will meet up. You still have my number?"

Sean smiled. "Yes, I have your number."

The car pulled away as soon as he let go of the door. He turned around and nearly bumped into the reporter, Derek Jacobs.

"I thought I had seen the last of you. Don't you have to file your report to the newspaper or something?"

Derek rubbed his forehead and pulled the collar of his jacket up against the cold wind. Early June was still cold with incessant rains the previous few days. Spring was yet to arrive in Leicester that year.

"Yes, I do. But I don't think the story is over yet."

"What do you mean? Did you not hear the judge? Lenny has been convicted and is on his way to jail as we speak."

"And do you believe that Inspector?" Derek's voice was sarcastic.

"It does not matter what I believe. Does it?"

"Maybe not. But I have a feeling that you are not going to let that come in the way of your thinking." Derek said as he pulled away from Sean.

"What did that creep want?" Stoker's voice made hi turn sharply.

"Newspaper reporters chief. You know what they are like?

"I'm starving. Fancy a bite to eat Sean? There is a nice little pub around the corner from here where all the lawyers hang out."

"Sure chief. I am starving too. Haven't had any breakfast this morning. If we hurry, we might be able to catch a bit of lunch:"

Sean pulled up his collar against the cold wind and the two of them walked across the wet and dark car park to the pub. Inside the pub was even darker with murky lighting. It appeared to be completely empty apart from a drunk who was dozing in the corner and a table at the far end with three people sat around it. They appeared to arguing quietly with a lot of gesticulations. It was difficult to make out who they were or what they were saying. Sean glanced in their direction and passed over to the bar where the Bartender was clearing up.

"Do you think we can still get a bite to eat?" Sean said as he perched on the nearest bar stool.

The barman stopped cleaning the glass he was holding and said, "I wouldn't know. I will go ask in the kitchen. In the meantime, do you want a drink?"

"Couple of beers please." Stoker replied.

Sean sat up on the bar stool and was drumming on the bar top while looking around the back of the bar when Stoker said,

"Isn't that the creepy reporter in the corner?"

Sean turned around to have a closer look.

"Yes it is. I wonder what he is up to now. Those two guys look familiar too."

It was almost as if they sensed being scrutinised and stopped talking and looked furtively around. Suddenly one of them got up and dragged the other guy off the chair. As the other guy appeared to be protesting, he whispered something bending down. The two of them made for the door going along the back wall. It was not until they were silhouetted against the door when Sean recognised them.

"I know them. They have been hovering around the court room almost every day since the trial began."

Both were obviously of Asian descent. One of them was a large burly figure with thick beard and the other a weedy guy in his thirties. They appeared to be in a hurry as they hustled out of the pub. Neither of them looked at the two policemen sitting at the bar and had their heads down almost on their chest. As the-two of them kept staring at the door, they could hear a car start and scream out of the car park.

"Now, now. I wonder what did they have to hide from us?" Stoker said to no one in particular.

"Wouldn't you like to know?" It was Derek Jacobs again at his elbow now. He had sidled over while they were concentrating on the two men.

"We can't seem to get rid of you somehow." Sean said with a barely disguised irritation in his voice. "What do you want now? And who were those guys?"

"It may be worthwhile you spending a little time on those two guys Inspector." Derek said completely ignoring the sarcasm in Sean's voice. "You might learn something."

"Now, listen here. I have been very patient with you all this time. If you know something, I want to you to tell me now."

"I did tell you a long time ago Sean. You ignored me then."

"The case is closed now and the murderer has been convicted. He is well on his way to prison right now. Or did you miss the big black van pulling out with all of your fries snapping way their flashbulbs at its windows?" Sean would not hide his sarcasm.

"You know very well as well I do that the wrong guy is behind bars."

"Mr Jacobs, you better tell us what you know and let the police do their job."

"I have heard a lot about you Mr Stoker. I am sure you would want the right guy in prison. All I am saying is this: you should talk to the widow."

"We have already spoken to her and I don't think there is anything we have missed."

"I am not saying you have missed anything Mr Stoker." Jacobs said as he pulled away from the two policemen. He took his little notebook out of his jacket and scribbled something. Tearing off the page and handing it to Sean he continued, "At least talk to these two guys."

He walked over to the door and turning back, "You might want to ask them if they know anything about the beating up of priests."

He had shut the door behind him before Sean had a chance to reply. The two of them were still staring at the door when the barman said,

"Yes, the cook says he can rustle something up for you. Have a seat. The waiter will be with you in a minute."

Sean recovered first and said, "Thank you."

The two of them moved to the table vacated by the three men.

"Now, what do you think of that?" Stoker asked.

"I am not sure chief. There is certainly something not right here. He obviously has an axe to grind, but what and why?

"Or maybe he really has a story to tell. What has written in that piece of paper?"

Sean opened the crumpled piece of paper and squinted at it in the dull light of the pub.

"There are two names here chief, Asian names with phone numbers." Sean looked up. "That must be those two characters he was with just now."

"It won't do any harm to have a quite chat with these two men."

"Will do chief, once I have something to eat." Sean said looking around and rising his right hand at the Barman. "Where is this waiter he promised?"

An young boy could be seen coming out of the kitchen door

in the corner just as he spoke. He came straight to their table and said,

"The cook can rustle up some fries and cod."

The two men looked at each other and nodded at the young boy in unison, "That will be fine, Thank you." Stoker said to the boy. As they were waiting for their fish to arrive sipping their beers, Sean said.

"Now the little red book has become even more crucial. I want to have another look at it. I bet the missing pages have a story to tell."

"You are right. Pity you did not get a chance to copy it."

"I didn't have a chance. I only had it for a few hours. I am going to have chat with the widow and see if I can have another go at it."

"Best of luck with that. I have a suspicion she won't part with it."

They stopped talking when the food arrived. There was very little talk as they`wolfed the delicious fish down and the last piece of fried chips was picked up. They finished the beers an as they walked down to their cars in the court house car park, Stoker said,

"I don't think you should say anything to anyone in the force till we have something more."

Sean nodded his head, "Sure chief. I will get on to it right away and keep you posted."

Sean was deep in thought as he drove his battered car down the motorway back to Leicester. His head was full of voices of Sheena and Jacobs and pictures of the two Asian men getting out of the pub in a hurry. Finally he could not take it anymore and stopped at the motorway services. He switched the engine off and dialled the first number in the sheet of paper Jacobs had given him.

"Hello, who is this?" a gruff voice said over the mobile.

"Is that Mr Prem Chandani?" Sean asked.

"Who wants to know?"

"This is Detective Inspector Sean O'Connor." He had heard the voice somewhere before. He was scratching his brain to think where.

"What can I do for you Inspector? I have already answered all your questions weeks ago." The Brummy accent was unmistakable. It suddenly clicked. Prem was one of the men questioned while they were looking into the Asian connection of the murder. The burly guy they had seen in the pub a couple of hours ago.

"I know Mr Chandani. I am just tying off some loose ends."

"What do you mean? The case is over and the culprit has gone to jail." There was a note of irritation in his voice. "This is just police harassment."

"You are right sir. We are investigating the assault of Mr Sharma a few years ago" Sean was thinking fast. He thought he heard a sharp intake of breath over the phone. "His family have asked for answers."

There was silence at the other end for a minute. Sean thought he had been disconnected. "Mr Chandani, are you still there?"

"Yes, I am Inspector. What is that got to do with me? I know nothing about any assault," and the phone died.

Sean sat there digesting what he had heard. *Has this man has something to hide? Or was he just an innocent guy irritated by repeated questioning?* He called the number couple of more times with no response. He picked up the piece of paper again and rang the next number several times with no response. On an impulse he called Seena's number. She answered at the first ring.

"Yes, Inspector." The voice sounded a bit strained. Not the confident woman of that afternoon. "I was not expecting your call for a few days at least."

"I am so sorry to call you so soon after the verdict." Sean

wanted to sound remorseful. "If you want, I can call you another day."

"No, that is OK. Tell me what can I do for you?"

"I need to ask you few more things to tie up some loose ends of the case. It is better done when it is still fresh in your mind."

"I am not sure it is such a good idea Inspector. I am tired now. The hearing has been very draining."

"I fully understand Mrs Sharma. I will not take up too much of your time. You tell me when we can meet up and I will come."

She said bye and disconnected before he could say anything else. Sean's head was heavy as he drove the rest of the way back home to Leicester and had a splitting headache by the end. Time for one of the brown paper packets tonight he thought as he walked into his dark apartment. He was in a muddled stupor when his telephone rang.

"Are you awake?" It was Stoker.

"Yeah. Just about. What's the matter?" Sean could barely get his words out of his dry mouth. He still had a splitting headache and he could see bright coloured spots floating in front of him. '*Why is the light so bright?*' He thought rubbing his eyes.

"The big chief wants a debriefing session like yesterday. Did you call any of those numbers last night?"

"No joy with either of them. I'll be over as soon as I can get the floor spinning round."

"It will be the death of you one of these days. Are you fit to drive?"

"Don't worry about me chief. I'll be fine."

Strong black coffee and a hot shower got him to be nearly human and was in his car again within the hour. The debriefing session was a bore. Mick Mills tried to hog the glory as usual and was nearly patting his own back for 'putting away the murderer behind bars'. After about an hour of this, Sean's headache was coming back. 'I should get some of Johnny's specials', he thought. The debriefing took most of the morning with copious amount of writing. When he thought about the report he had to file, his headache got worse. He spent the afternoon trying to concentrate on writing his report and could not wait to get out of the office. He was on his second black coffee when the phone rang. He did not really want to pick the phone up when Stoker walked in and said,

"Are you picking up the phone?"

Sean picked up the phone reluctantly.

"Hi Sean, it is Brennan here at the hospital. I got a guy here who wants to talk to you." There was an undisguised smirk in his voice.

"Who is it?"

"They are not sure yet. There was no ID on him. He has been given a good going over. He is barely conscious. You better hurry. The docs are not sure if he will last the night."

"How do you know he wants to see me then?" Sean was more than a bit irritated.

Brennan laughed at the other end. "The only thing he has said since waking up is your name."

"OK. I will be there as soon as I can."

Sean did not really hurry to the hospital. It was late by the time he reached the hospital. Brennan was sitting in the car park outside the accident department smoking furiously. He got out of the car as soon as he saw Sean's car pull up.

As Sean got out of the car he hissed loudly, "Where the hell have you been? I have been waiting here for hours."

"Don't exaggerate. It has only been an hour. I was finishing off the bloody report for Warraker."

At the mention of Warraker's name, Brennan appear to simmer down and said, "Come on. We better go and find out what this guy has to say before he pops his clogs."

Sean followed him into the hospital through several corridors to reach the Intensive Care Unit. They had to wait at the locked security door for one of the nurses inside to answer the intercom.

"Yes, who is it?" The voice of authority mixed with tiredness. A recognised tone in hospitals everywhere.

"It is Brennan sister. From the constabulary."

There was a loud click in the quite corridor and Brennan pushed the door open. One of the nurses saw them and came over.

"You got to wear this." She said handing some plastic gowns and gloves to them.

"Have you brought Sean O'Connor? He has been asking again."

"Yes, I have sister." And turning to Sean, "this is him."

Sean put his hand out and said, "I am Inspector Sean O'Connor, sister. It is nice to meet you."

She smiled but did not take his proffered hand. "Follow me." She said with a smile.

They followed her through the open ward with several seriously ill patients on either side with drips and tubes attached to them. An aura of death seemed to suffocate the bright lights of the large hall. The entire place was eerily quiet with just the sound of the ventilator and an occasional silent alarm from one of the monitors which saw a flurry of activity. The activity was hurried and at the same time controlled. The large area had a central island with banks of monitors watched by nurses and doctors who barely noticed their arrival. The two of them too scared even to breath loudly for the fear of upsetting something or someone. They literally tiptoed down behind the nurse to the far corner bed which was screened off. She stopped at the curtain and whispered to Sean,

"I am not sure how much your friend has told you, but this patient is not very well at all. " She stopped and looked quizzically at Sean. "I don't know why he wants to see you. But that is the only thing he has said after he was extubated."

Sean and Brennan looked at her with a question on their faces. She sighed and continued,

"He has been on the ventilator since he was brought in this morning. You have to be quick." Turning to Sean, "I hope you can tell us who he is."

"Do you know what happened to him Sister?"

Sean asked.

"He has multiple injuries including some fractures. They have fixed him as best as they could. If he improves he might need some more surgery. It depends on how he does over the next day or two."

She pulled the curtain to show a man lying on the bed with drips coming out of everywhere. His face was badly bruised and face appeared twisted. Sean could not recognise him at first. The sister bent over the man and touched his shoulder.

"I have brought Sean for you to see." After the second attempt, he opened his eyes to look at the sister and turned his head towards Sean. Recognition hit both of them at the same time.

"Mr O'Connor!" he said feebly at the same time as a sharp intake of breath from Sean.

"Derek Jacobs!" Sean exclaimed. "What happened to you?"

He tried to speak, but words were not coming out. He tried to mouth some words with some difficulty. They could see the effort and pain in his eyes half closed by the large bruise. He was getting increasingly agitated at his inability to speak and started to breathe faster heaving his chest at the effort. The sister bent forward and took out the oxygen mask from his face and whispered to him.

"Would you like a drop of water to sip? That might help you speak."

She picked out a cube of ice from a box on the trolley and touched his lips. He stuck his tongue out to lick the ice cube. He tried to speak again.

"She is in trouble."

"Who is in trouble Derek?" Sean knew exactly who he was talking about. Derek had closed his eyes again. His breathing had become shallow and appeared to be sleeping. They tried to speak to him for again with no luck. As Sean turned around to leave as the sister was getting a bit agitated he opened his eyes again a whispered something. Sean turned back quickly and said,

"Did you say something Derek?"

"They will … They'll kill her." And closed his eyes. The monitors at the head end started to go haywire.

The Nurse shoved he two of them out and closed the curtain. Sean could see one of the Doctors from the central console spring to his feet and rush across. There was intense activity and the two of them were completely forgotten. They knew they were an intrusion and made their way out as quietly as possible.

"I think he has had more than a good thrashing." Brennan said as he walked into the dark car park.

"What do you mean? Sea asked.

"The sister said there were puncture marks on his arms. He had been drugged as well, I think."

"I am sure we will find out once he recovers well enough to talk to us." Sean replied.

"If he recovers." Brennan said.

Derek Jacobs' face was stuck on his mind as he drove back home in his battered old car. It had started to rain quite heavily and the visibility was poor. The worn our wipers were struggling to keep the water out of windscreen and it was a losing battle. He had to slow down to a crawl to see where he was going and it was quite late by the time he got home. He kept thinking about what Jacobs said, '*They will kill her.*' He obviously meant the widow, Sheena. He could not understand who would want to kill her and why?

"I don't understand either Sean." Phillip Stoker said when he told him the following morning. "Maybe, it is time you met this widow and had another chat. Have you called her yet?"

"No. I have not done. I will do that today. I wonder if she is still in Leicester or gone back to Leeds." Sean replied.

"Don't you think it is better if you can chat with her before she leaves Leicester? I bet there is something in that little red book which could solve some of these mysteries."

"I don't know if the answers are in those missing pages."

Sean did not get a chance to call her through the day. Derek Jacobs had lapsed into a coma and was back on the ventilator. Sean sat in his car late that evening outside and called Sheena's number. There was no reply. He gave up after several attempts. He left a message asking her to return his call. It was quite late at night as he was drifting off to sleep when the phone finally rang.

"Hello Inspector O'Connor. I am sorry I missed your call earlier. I was a in a meeting." The dulcet tone of Sheena was rather mooted.

"That is OK Mrs Sharma. I would like to meet up soon. There are a few loose ends I need to tie up."

"Sure. No problem. We can meet up at the restaurant we met in before."

He knew exactly where she meant. That was the first time he had met her and where he had seen the little red book for the first time.

"When shall we meet?"

"Tomorrow, around eight in the evening."

"Thank you. I will be there."

She had hung up before he could say anything else. His head was spinning with the thoughts of Lenny going to prison and

Derek Jacobs words and the little red book. He could not sleep for a long time. He was tossing and turning in the bed when his mobile phone rang. He looked at his watch. It was nearly one in the morning. He scrambled out of the bed and nearly fell down trying to find the phone. It was Sheena's number.

"Yes Mrs Sharma." He said trying to sound fully awake. But there was no reply from the other side. He could hear someone breathing on the other end. "Are you there Mrs Sharma? Are you OK?"

Still no reply. He could hear some shuffling on the other side. Then there was a whisper. "They are here. They are trying to get into the house."

"Who Mrs Sharma? Who is trying to get into the house?" Sean was fully awake now. "Have you called 999?"

There was no reply. He looked down at the phone. It was still connected.

"Mrs Sharma, I am coming over. Please stay on the phone. I will get the police to you."

He dressed quickly and literally ran out of the apartment and into the car. It would not start. The engine kept revving and coughing. He cursed the old car a few times and just as he was about to give up it started up. He put the car in gear and sped off the parking lot with tyres screeching loudly in the stillness of the dark night. He took the phone out of his pocket to check. It was still connected.

"Mrs Sharma. Are you still there?" There was no answer. He could hear the breathing sound on the other side. He picked up the radio in his car and called the controller.

"This is Inspector Sean O'Connor. I need you to despatch units to George Street. There is a crime in progress."

"Copy that Inspector. Two units on their way." The operator replied.

He picked up the mobile phone. "Mrs Sharma. Police are on their way. They should be with you in a few minutes. Hang on."

"You better hurry. They are inside the house now." She whispered. There was shuffling noises.

"Where are you now? Lock yourself in your bedroom. The police will be there in minutes."

He could hear loud noises coming from the phone and a loud crash and splintering of wood. The phone became very quiet.

"Mrs Sharma. Hang in there. The police must be nearly there now."

There was no reply. He looked down on the phone. It was dead. Sean pressed the pedal down to the floor and could see the lights flash past him. The roads were nearly empty at that time of the night. As he turned the car into George Street, there were two squad cars with blue lights flashing and officers running. The front door of the house was open but none of the lights were on. He jumped out of the car and rushed into the house, past the police officers. There was no one in the house. The bedroom door had been smashed open. Sean ran from one room to another shouting her name out. Nothing. The officers now had all the lights switched on and the police wagon with more officers had turned up by then. Sean spent the next few hours searching for clues in the house. The forensic crew went through the house. Whoever was there were obviously professional. There were no clues. No finger prints apart from Sheena's and the family.

He finally came out of the house dejected and tired into a sunrise which was lifting the fog slowly. There were numerous police officers searching the neighbourhood. Somehow he knew they would not find anything. As he slumped into his car, he realised. Still no sign of the little red note book. The car started at first turn of the key and as he drove slowly out of the street, he knew he would not see Sheena again.

OTHER TITLES BY SHANKAR KASHYAP

The Lure of Soma

It is in this context that the lives and trials and tribulations of people living in the Indus valley during the middle of third millennium BCE are tackled in this book. I have used existing archaeological evidence along with known historical evidence in writing this book. Rigveda talks about several conflicts among the descendants of the emperor Bharata and the Avestan scriptures talk about the conflicts between the Aryans and the Dasyus. There have always been fierce debates about who exactly these Aryans were and the Daevas mentioned in the Avestan scriptures. I have used some poetic license to accommodate the dates and times of various individuals and events to suit the story telling. The book tries to portray the life of ordinary people during the period of Harappans, while trying to tell the tale of the priestly kings, Magi, Rishis and Sages of the great Indus Valley Civilisation during the middle of third millennium BCE. This is the story of our hero, Upaas, a trainee physician from Harappa. It is a story of a young man growing up, falling in love, getting involved in adventures and finally fighting for the city he loves most – Harappa. The story shows the human elements of people around him. He faces friendship, love, hate, jealousy, treachery and deceit in day to day life. There is generous sprinkling of magic and sorcery. As the country of Ariana, west of Hindu Kush dries up, the Avestansfacing with near extinction take up arms against their neighbours to obtain the precious Soma. The tactics used include deceit, sorcery and finally a war between the Meluhhans and Avestans

The Soma plant has been the centrepiece of several hymns in the Vedic scriptures. It is a plant still not accuratelyrecognized. The Vedic people revered it as a God, drank the extract from the stalk of the plant, used the plant for medicinal purposes and it is supposed to have magical properties. There are hymns composed to the Soma within the Vedas. The Avestan had a similar plant and called it Haoma and their scriptures also revered the plant for its spiritual properties. Vedas describe it as growing in a sacred mountain around a sacred lake (Mount Mujavant and lakeSharynavat). Avestan scriptures describe a similar sacred mountain and a sacred lakein Sistan where the Haoma plant grew. Similar to the Soma of Indus valley, we still do not know exactly what this plant was as it disappeared at the same time as the Harappans. It was considered the mushroom, Amanita Muscaria for a long time because of the "hallucinogenic" effects the Soma was said to produce when consumed. This may be a misconception by the writers who tried to explain the events described in Vedic scriptures and the powers of ancient sages.

The Fall of Shuruppak

Harappans appear to have ventured far and wide with their trade, both on land and sea. Harappan settlements spread as far west as Shortugai in Afghanistan at the head of river Oxus, which was the centre of raw materials such as Lapis Lazuli, Gold and Silver for the Harappan artisans. Harappan seals, jewellery and pottery have been found in Elam (present day Iran), Egypt, and Sumer. Jewellery found in Queen Puabi's tomb had all the hallmarks of Harappan artisans. The cylindrical Carnelian beads with central core drilled after hours of careful work is typical of the Harappans.

Cylindrical seal of Shu-ilishu, the translator has the typical humped bull on one side and cuneiform text on the other side. Archaeologists agree that he must have been a translator of Sumerian and Akkadian into Meluhhan language. He is placed to have lived in Lagash around the middle of third millennium BCE. There is archaeological evidence of Meluhhan enclaves around Lagash.

Sargon the great who ruled most of Mesopotamia from around 2300 BCE, boasts of ships from Meluhha, Dilmun and Magan docking in the port of his capital city, Akkad. The Meluhhans obviously had marine trading links with Akkad for a long time with some of them settling down in Sumer. Despite elaborate description of the city of Akkad in several tablets in cuneiform texts, the city eludes detection.

Epic of Gilgamesh is a well-known story with an almost entire story written and transcribed from cuneiform texts. Emperor Gilgamesh befriends an uncouth Enkidu from the deep forests and a deep friendship ensues. The epic is that of undying love, sacrifice and heroism. Enkidu is mortally injured fighting a -mythical demon and only a meluhhan sage can save him.

The Battle of Ten Kings (Dasharajna)

Book six of Rigveda describes a battle between King Sudas and "ten kings." It is a confederacy of ten to twelve kings compiled by disgruntled descendants of King Yayathi's sons who felt hard done by when the ageing king gives the central part of the great Bharatha kingdom to the youngest son, Puru over the elder four brothers – Yadu, Turvasu, Druhyu and Anu. King Sudas is brought up and trained by sage Vishwamitra and Vasishta. Vishwaimtra falls out with the king and the senior sage Vasishta and joins the confederacy of ten kings. A bitter battle ensues on the banks of River Parushni (present day Ravi) between the forces of King Sudas, highly outnumbered by the huge army of "sixty six thousand" of the confederacy. God Indra intervenes and takes the side of "righteous Sudas," and a flash flood destroys most of the army of the confederacy.

While there is no archaeological evidence of the battle or the actors within it, there is enough evidence within the Rigveda itself to place the event around the third millennium BCE. River Parushni is easily identifiable as the present day Ravi and the kingdom to be the present day Punjab, Haryana and parts of northeast Pakistan with seven rivers. This epic is considered by many to be the third epic of India, after the great epics of Mahabharata and Ramayana. Descendants of king Puru for the famous Kuru dynasty who are the actors within the great battle of Mahabharata. This battle has often been used by the proponents of the Aryan Invasion theory as proof of mighty Aryans invading India and destroying the Harappan civilisation. It is claimed that they brought the horses and Iron weapons to destroy the great Harappan empire.

A Kangaroo Court: A Triumph of Mediocrity

When Upaashantha was appointed as an orthopaedic Surgeon, he thought his life was made. He did not realise he would come across unscrupulous people like Serpe and Pakshar. He ends up fighting incompetence and corruption among the bureaucrats to save his career and life. This book is a damning indictment on greed and treachery among the "noble" medical profession. As the story unfolds, the question of the age renowned adage of "innocent until proven guilty" is thrown to the winds and under the pretext of "patient safety," the physician is "guilty until proven innocent." There are further doubts about the ability of the regulatory body to conduct a fair and unbiased enquiry as stipulated in their manifesto. A simple complaint that should possibly have dealt with at a local level develops momentum that spins out control. 'The title of the book is apt and the concerned organisation is a pack of circus clowns. A must read for the doctors of this land.' - The Doctor

BOOKS REVIEWS

"I loved Shankar Kashyap's novel, Harappa: The Lure of Soma. An epic tale of mystery, black magic, love, and adventure set in the most intriguing period of India's ancient history, it wraps you up in the predicament of its central characters and stands as a magnificent and compelling parable of the age-old battle of good against evil."

Graham Hancock,
Author of the international bestseller
"**Fingerprints of the Gods**"

"Shankar N Kashyap has created a brilliant and fascinating story about one of the most mysterious eras in human history, yet one that has implications for all humanity even today. His narrative draws us back to the ancient era of India of the Sarasvati River, long before most of what we call civilization, and sheds light upon the profound culture that existed then and its relevance for the entire world."

David Frawley

Director of American Institute of Vedic Studies
(www.vedanet.com)

Author of "**Soma in Yoga and Ayurveda**",
and thirty other books

SHANKAR KASHYAP is a natural story teller with a great sense of imagination which is not only vivid but also realistic in all aspects. Like a master creator, he has created a world in the ruins of Harrapa and Mohenjo daro. Once he establishes his characters – and their culture, tradition, and beliefs – they almost become alive and start behaving the way they should have done so in their lives. It is but natural to have all known human emotions and experiences in the lives of his characters, and one finds love, romance, politics, conspiracies, wars and natural disasters in his world.

The plot has an element of suspense from the very beginning. The story opens up and tells us about the lost civilization's culture, tradition and believe system. He goes into the geographical details of 5,000 years old territory and stays within the borders of countries with their political issues, personal jealousies, and powerful individuals who desire to change the world for better or worse. This is what exactly is happening in human societies since the age unknown and will continue to happen till the doomsday. Shankar has highlighted all these issues with great sense of imagination and background knowledge of history. More than a master creator, he acted like a god as left the world that he created in these pages on its own after creating it. He has become a historian and record keeper of that world. He writes in detail about the courts and its proceedings. He tells us about the way medicine was practiced in those days. He gives us a detailed account of war, warriors and their weapons. He also carefully describes the rituals playing important role in the lives of people living in that era.

It is a story of love, the beauty of nature, and man's struggle against those evil forces who are present in our lives from the first day of our self-determination.

Dr. Shershah Syed

Pakistan

Author of "**Vision, not just a dream**" and winner of Clinton Global Initiative Award

A story written after historical research into the ancient civilisation. Though it is fiction, the author leads you to visualise life as it would have realistically been in the time frame of Harappa. This has obviously been possible after extensive analysis of the evidence available from Indus Civilisation.

One is led to believe the saga of Soma, which currently is the flavour of fiction and documentaries. I look forward to reading forthcoming sequel of this novel.

A easily readable book though the cover does not do justice to the book-though this a personal preference.

Dr. S. Balupuri

Shankar is a great storyteller. He has made me live an ancient in recorded past and kept me yearning for more. An absolute Must Read. Hope there are more to come.

Hemant Misra

Excellent book - eagerly awaiting next instalment by this author. A must must read for anyone interested in other cultures.

Kindle Edition Verified Purchase

Printed in Poland
by Amazon Fulfillment
Poland Sp. z o.o., Wrocław

54347363R00167